THE TORMENT OF TWO

USA TODAY BESTSELLING AUTHOR

K WEBSTER

DEDICATION

To Blue—
You're the ultimate writing buddy.

The stalker is the least of my problems, though. When Two reveals the true reason for hating me—the crushing secret that has tormented him his entire life—my own world is suddenly turned upside down. I feel inadvertently responsible and want to somehow make it all better.

A budding romance burns hot between us as our walls come down, but we have to keep it a secret. My parents will vehemently disapprove of our coupling, and his will be utterly destroyed. Under the guise of our project, we're able to spend stolen moments together, stoking the flames of our growing feelings for one another, keeping the bitter truth from our families.

But my stalker has other nefarious plans that keep escalating in nature.

In order to get help from my father and my brother's cop fiancée, I will have to come clean. My life may depend on it. Ugly truths will be brought to light and Two's family will no doubt suffer the consequences. I dread the day I'll be forced to spill the truth. Is this thing between me and Two worth all the heartache and pain destined for our future? Only time will tell…

*** *This is a complete M/F standalone novel with a happily ever after. Tropes for this book include: enemies-to-lovers, grumpy/sunshine, college, new-age romance, opposites attract, historical preservation nerds, hidden rooms and treasure hunts, romantic suspense, mental health rep, and secret romance.* ***

Shameful Secrets Series

1 – The Teacher of Nothing (Callum's Book)
2 – The Tangle of Awful (Hugo's Book)
3 – The Heart of Smoke (Jude's Book)
4 – The Law of Deceit (Dempsey's Book)
5 – The Torment of Two (Gemma's Book)

Trigger Warning

This book has triggering scenes for some readers including physical and mild sexual assault (not by main character), past family traumas, kidnapping, stalking, drugging, and other potentially upsetting subject matter. Please read with caution.

THE
TORMENT
OF
TWO

PROLOGUE

Tristan "Two" Sheridan
(Nine Years Old)

SANTA *IS REAL.*

I hate Dax for lying and saying he isn't. Dad always tells me you have to believe to get presents. Does Dax not want presents?

Stupid Dax said he could prove it. That if I went and dug around in my parents' closet, I'd find them and all the candy that goes in the stocking.

I should have just ignored him, but I have to show him he's wrong. My dads have never lied to me. They wouldn't lie about Santa.

The garage door rumbles and then silence falls on our house. Dad said he had to run to the office to help Pops with something and that he'd be right back.

Usually that takes about fifteen minutes.

I'm going to have to hurry.

As soon as I'm sure Dad has left, I rush over to the front windows and peek out just in case. Dad's SUV speeds away, leaving me to my mission.

Dax is going to feel so dumb when I tell him off when we play Xbox later. I can't wait to laugh at him until my belly hurts.

Backing away from the window, I peek over at the

decorated Christmas tree. There are so many gifts from my dads underneath, all of them wrapped perfectly with matching bows. There's no way they'd also get me all the stuff Santa buys too. I'd be spoiled and Dad is always worried they're spoiling me.

I'm telling you.

No freaking way.

I race out of the living room and go straight for my parents' closet in their bedroom. Dad loves clothes. A lot. Pops built him a humongous closet for all his outfits a couple of years ago. Dax's mom doesn't have nearly as many outfits as Dad and she certainly doesn't have a closet as big as my bedroom.

Dad really, really likes clothes.

I haven't ever had a need to go into their closet much before. When Dad makes me help with laundry, it's usually just to fold towels or put my own clothes away. Their closet is boring and filled with dad stuff like boots and ties.

Toys and candy too if Dax is right.

Which he's totally not.

I flick on the light switch and take in all the clothes. Dad's clothes take up most of the closet. Pops has a small section with the same ol' blue jeans he always wears and his company T-shirts.

Ha!

No candy and toys!

Just as I'm about to leave, a small bulge behind Dad's coats gets my attention. Slowly, I walk over to it, readying myself for toys to fall on top of my head. There's not going to be toys behind these coats. There's not.

I push one of the big leather coats aside and see a wooden

trunk sitting on the floor up against the wall. It reminds me of one you'd find treasure in.

What if the treasure is Santa's gifts?

My stomach twists at that thought. I'm going to be upset if Dax is right. He's always right about everything and it's so annoying.

Kneeling down in front of the chest, I notice my heartbeat is pounding so hard I can feel it echoing in my ears.

I have to know.

Is Santa real?

I hold my breath and force myself to open the trunk. Squinting, I try to shield my eyes from the truth.

Toys and candy galore.

Except…there's neither.

It's filled with papers and pictures.

A laugh bubbles out of me. I knew it! Stupid Dax is wrong! I'm about to close it when a picture catches my eye. It's the window from my room. I love that window. Dad says it's original to the house and really, really old. The stained glass is pretty to look at.

I pull the picture out from beneath some papers to inspect it closer. It's not my room, though. Well, it is, but it's missing the Legos on the shelves. And where are the model airplanes Pops helped me build? They're usually hanging by dental floss from the ceiling.

My eyes leave the shelves in the picture and land on the color of the wall. Pink. Ew. Why is the wall pink? It's supposed to be navy blue like it is now.

In the center of the room, my bed isn't there like it is now. There's a baby's crib with frilly pink blankets instead.

Above the bed, it says, "Gemma."

My stomach starts to ache. I don't like the gross feeling I'm having. Something doesn't feel right.

Maybe this picture belonged to the family before us who lived here.

Or maybe I had a sister and she died.

I don't like that thought. There could be more pictures to give me clues. I set the picture down to dig in the trunk some more. I find the adoption papers from when my dads took me home when I was just two years old. Since I don't care to learn anything about my birth mother, who clearly didn't love me enough to keep me, I'm not interested in reading all those boring papers.

An envelope under the pile of papers sticks out. It's pink and written in girly handwriting, addressed to Dad and Pops.

Dearest Leo and Grant,

I'm so sorry, but I've decided to keep the baby. I know you were so excited to start your family and this will ruin everything. I'm gutted for you. Believe me, I've cried a lot over this because I know how badly the two of you want to be parents.

When we started this whole process, I didn't think Nathan would choose to stay with me if he knew I was pregnant. But he did, and we're planning to get married. I'm going to be the best mom, I promise. I believe you'll find a different baby to love and care for that was meant to be.

Please find it in your heart to forgive me. I never meant to hurt you. If it will make you feel any better, I decided to keep the name you chose for her to honor you both if it turns out to be a girl like Leo's psychic said it would be.

As sad as this is, I think it's best if we don't contact each other again. It's too painful for everyone involved.

Sincerely,
Jamie Booker

◎

They were going to adopt a baby girl before me? I was their second choice. Dad and Pops always tell me I'm their entire world. But I almost didn't get to be a part of it.

When they adopted me, I was no longer a baby. I was young, though. So young, I didn't even know my own name. The only word I'd say was "two" at the time of my adoption, which is how I came to get the nickname Two.

Did all the families before my dads want a baby? Why else would I be fixated on that word? Was I asked my age a lot? Did my dads feel sorry for me and adopt me even though I wasn't the baby they wanted?

This is much worse than discovering Santa isn't real. All the loving, happy stories my dads told me about the magical creation of our family was more of a fairy tale than Santa.

They lied to me.

They didn't tell me there was a girl before me who they wanted badly enough to decorate an entire room for her.

I'm going to be sick.

My cheeks grow wet with tears and I shrivel inside. Dax never cries, but I cry over the stupidest stuff. This certainly feels stupid.

I'm second best.

Two seems fitting of a name for a kid no one ever wanted.

The sound of the garage door opening has me jolting. I quickly shove everything back into the trunk, close the lid, and move the coats to hide it once more. By the time I exit their bedroom, Dad is coming through the garage door into the house. I swipe all the tears off my face and force a neutral expression.

"Two, buddy, grab your coat and hat. Pops is taking us for pizza and then we're going to look at a house we're going to restore. Maybe you'll find some cool treasures. The owner said we can take whatever we want."

I stare at my smiling dad, feeling a stabbing, burning pain deep inside my chest. It's so easy for him to pretend that I almost wasn't their son. They almost had Gemma. Their perfect, precious baby girl.

"Everything okay?" Dad asks, coming to stand in front of me. He cradles my cheeks with his cold palms and studies my face. "You look sad."

Not sad.

Destroyed.

There's a difference, Dad.

"I'm good. Can I get Pepsi?"

Dad purses his lips, clearly biting back what he's really thinking before he nods once. "Just one and you can have it with dinner, not before." He drops his forehead to mine and grins at me. "Love you, Two."

"Yeah, Dad, I know."

He's not the only liar in this family.

CHAPTER ONE

Gemma (Present Day)

KNOW I'M A JOKE TO MY FAMILY.

They think my job as an influencer is made up and silly. Dad is convinced it's dangerous and not something I should do long-term, often lecturing me on putting my focus on school rather than my platform.

For me, though, it's something I'm proud of. I built it from nothing and shaped it into something that not only awards me a viable income but also gives me a voice to help other people.

Sure, sometimes that help is showing my followers what moisturizer I use or my favorite lip gloss, but it feels bigger than that. One day, I hope to use it in a way that's more impactful.

One day.

I'm not really sure how I'll turn my content around without some blowback, but I'll figure it out. It's why I'm majoring in marketing at PMU.

What my family and followers don't see is all that goes into maintaining and growing my audience. Each day, I spend hours strategizing content, researching what others are doing, and replying to my followers to cultivate and build solid relationships. So many girls my age and younger have reached out to me to let me know they aspire to be like me. It makes me feel good that I'm inspiring them, even if it's just to feel better about their outward appearance.

I'm making my way through my messages when I come to a strange one.

@TwoCanPlayThisGame.

The username sends a chill down my spine.

I read the message, trying to make sense of it.

I see you. The real you. The you no one else but me sees.

I click on their profile to see what sort of person is sending me this message. From another girl like myself, it could mean something totally different than some random weird man. The profile, though, has nothing to offer. It's a new account. They're not following anyone but me and they have no posts. The picture is a screenshot of my profile page.

This is the kind of stuff Dad is worried about, but thankfully, I know how to handle it. It's not the first weirdo to message me and it certainly won't be the last. I quickly block the person and delete the message without giving it another thought.

I move on to more sweet messages about how my recommendation for an acne treatment helped one girl's skin clear up and now she's feeling more confident. As I read through them all—each one kind and uplifting—I can't help but keep thinking back to the creepy message.

I see you. The real you. The you no one else but me sees.

It's a scary thought. The real me, the girl buried deep beneath the perfect makeup, style, and smile, is insecure, feels smothered by her father wanting to keep her safe, and wants to be seen for more than a trophy. That girl isn't as confident as the one she outwardly portrays for the internet. Knowing someone else might see her leaves me feeling exposed and raw.

I suck in a deep breath and exhale heavily. My nerves are brittle, making me feel slightly nauseous. Imposter syndrome claws its way up inside me, mocking me.

Who do I think I am?

Maybe I'm just a joke.

I give my head a sharp shake and look at my follower count that's recently surpassed a million. I'm doing something right or these people wouldn't be here.

With a quick check of my makeup, I turn the camera on me and push the live button. My smile is wide and bright—you can't even tell it's fake.

"Hey, Gems," I say, waving at the camera. "If you're new here, I'm @GemmaLovesUx2 and I'm dying to tell you about this new primer I just got. Your makeup will look as flawless when you go to bed as when you applied it in the morning. I'm telling you guys you're going to freak out at how amazing this product is."

The hearts and comments start flooding in, reminding me I *am* good at this.

I won't let some creep torment me and throw me off my game.

I'm Gemma freaking Park.

I *invented* the game.

○

Family dinners each Sunday with all my siblings and their significant others are becoming quite a circus. Now that Jude got his porch fixed, even Grandpa and Violet come over. There are spouses, fiancés, fiancées, babies, dogs, and now old people. Everyone has someone.

Everyone but me.

I'm young, so it's not like I'm looking to date anyone, but I can't help but feel slightly jealous of my friend Willa, who's happily married to my brother Callum. They have baby Bane, who is so cute and perfect. Willa's not much older than me either.

And then, there's my twin, Dempsey. At eighteen, he's engaged to Mom's best friend and local detective, Sloane Thurman. They don't want kids from what my brother tells me, but they recently adopted an adorable puppy named Beauty.

Dad always said no pets.

The second Dempsey moves out, he gets one.

I'd stupidly assumed this past summer that starting at Park Mountain University, I could stay on campus and finally have my freedom. Dempsey got his freedom. Unfortunately, Dad made it very clear I'd live at home through college.

So unfair.

Luckily, he budged on his rules for the Tahoe he got me and Dempsey. At one time, we were only allowed to drive it if the other was in the car. But since Dempsey moved out and got his own car, the Tahoe would sit in the driveway, never getting driven unless Dad gave in.

The highlight of my day is when I get up and go to school. I've completed a whole semester already. It's been so much fun meeting new people. Getting out from beneath my dad's overprotective blanket is a plus as well.

"Gemma, sweetie, you've barely touched your lasagna,"

Mom says from beside me. "You feeling okay? I can make an appointment with Dr. Thacker in the morning."

Dad's not the only overprotective one. Sometimes, even though it's always filled with love, I feel smothered by my parents. It was worse for Dempsey. He could barely stand it and took off the second he was able to.

I'm stuck until I graduate.

Not because I don't have the money or whatever. I have a trust fund, allowance money, fun money Dad gives me, and all my considerable earnings from my sponsorships. It's just, I'm afraid of being lonely.

"I'm fine," I assure my mother, giving her my most perfect smile that fools everyone, including myself sometimes. "Just nervous about starting a new semester tomorrow. One of the teachers I got is supposed to be really hard. He comes up with crazy projects that totally suck."

"You'll do great." Mom reaches over and clutches my hand. "Get through this week and we'll go get massages on Saturday."

I do love a good massage.

"You're a lifesaver, Mom."

Dinner continues, every single person absorbed in their own personal happiness. I'm so used to deflecting my own emotions just to please my parents that sometimes I feel slighted.

Why can't I just blow up at dinner and tell everyone off like Dempsey has before?

The thought of doing that, though, makes my skin crawl. I need to just get over my weird feelings lately. My parents have always been this way, but it's not because they're cruel. They just love us so much and want to protect us.

"Want to get up early and meet for coffee before your first class?" Tate, my brother Jude's fiancé, asks from my other side. "I feel like we need to catch up."

I love Tate. He's perfect for my brother and really brought him out of his reclusive state. Tate fit right in with our family. It also helps he's a therapist. This family needs lots of therapy.

Except me.

Dad says I'm perfect. I never do anything wrong and am always succeeding in whatever I do. What do I need therapy for?

Maybe he's right.

Sometimes, when I'm about to get my period, I feel sorry for myself. I must be getting ready to start soon.

"Sounds fun," I say, flashing him another perfect grin. "Maybe Dempsey will join us."

My twin brother is now a coffee lover like me, Tate, and Willa. Tate likes to take credit for that win, but I'm pretty sure it has something to do with the fact Sloane is obsessed. Since Dempsey is obsessed with her, it makes sense.

"Oh," Tate exclaims, "I forgot to tell you I hired Vada to plan the wedding. She's hella expensive, but Jude says I'm worth it." He sighs heavily. "The sad part is, we have to move the wedding to the fall in order to get everything I want. Jude says he'll wait forever for me because I'm his everything."

This time, my giggle is absolutely real. I love it when Tate preens about how much Jude loves him. It's the truth, too. Tate's ex was a monster, but my brother treats him like the prince he is.

"Do I still get to help pick out the tuxes you two will wear?"

Tate smirks. "Duh. You're a bridesmaid. Part of the job."

As he babbles about colors that would be so hot for fall, I can't help but feel sad that he didn't choose me for his maid of honor. I'm Jude's sister after all. He asked Willa, and while I'm happy for her to be included, it still hurt. Even Tate, my adorable brother-in-law-to-be, has a better friend than me.

I hate that I can't shake this icky feeling that's coated over me lately. Since starting college, I always feel weighed down by a shroud of…something.

Unhappiness? Depression? Inadequacy?

Whatever it is, I don't like it. No matter how hard I pretend that everything is fine or force myself to keep trudging through it with a smile affixed, it never really goes away.

I kind of wish I could schedule a meeting with Tate. An official meeting where I brain dump everything that's bothering me so he can quickly tell me how to fix it. Once it's fixed, I can move along business as usual.

Tate stops talking mid-sentence and frowns. "Something's up, Gem."

"Nothing's up," I say with another fake grin. "I just had this horrible thought of you choosing yellow."

Tate's lip curls up. "Ew. No. Don't worry. I'm leaning toward lavender. Wouldn't Jude look so hot in lavender?"

It's my turn to balk. "Ew. Wrong bridesmaid to talk about that stuff with. I'm sure Aubrey or Willa would love to agree, but I think Jude and hot don't belong in the same sentence. Don't be disgusting."

We both laugh and then Tate is being pulled away to a conversation with his hubby-to-be. I stifle a sigh and take a moment to appreciate this wild, crazy family I have. Most people would love to be me. I literally have it all: loving parents, tight-knit family, great hair, awesome car, financial means, and paid-for college.

I mean, a million people follow me because I'm a picture of perfection.

Except *@TwoCanPlayThisGame*.

That person claimed they could see the real me. The one beneath the polished exterior. The sad, confused, lonely girl.

Pulling out my phone, I quickly do a search for content creators who are known for positive self-talk. Once I've followed a few, I decide I'll do a deep dive into their pages for answers on how to get myself out of this funk.

I can totally do it.

I achieve things all the time that seem impossible to others.

Tomorrow, school will start back up and things will get easier. I'll be around new people, busy with homework, and free to just be me. All I need to do is get through tonight.

In the morning, I'll be back to the Gemma everyone loves and adores both on the outside and the inside.

I'm allowed one bad day.

Only one.

CHAPTER TWO

Two

Dax: Dude, stop ignoring me.

I groan and quickly read through the onslaught of messages my best friend sent over the past two hours. He knows if I don't answer, I'm busy with a project. I swear I chose the most high-maintenance guy in the world to be friends with.

Me: I'm not ignoring you. Cedarwood Mansion has my immediate focus.

Dax: The real one or the replica?

Me: The replica IS real.

He sends me a fuckton of eye roll emojis. Sometimes I wonder how two completely different guys like me and Dax Summers could ever become and stay friends. We're so different it's almost hilarious. Dax drives a tricked-out matte-black Beamer, plays football for PMU, and has a jock style that makes every girl in the vicinity drool over him.

Meanwhile, I drive Pops's old 1988 Land Rover Defender 90, which is the complete opposite of Dax's chick magnet. I certainly don't play sports like him. And my style? While I think it's cool, Dax has told me numerous times that it's not.

What's not to love about an olive-colored M-65 field

jacket from the Vietnam War? It's vintage and was a badass find. No one, and I mean no one, is wearing this jacket.

Dax: Do you want help?

Me: No.

I tear open a brand-new bag of butterscotch hard candies. They've been my favorites for as long as I can remember. Once I'm armed with a candy on the inside of each cheek, I turn on the dust-covered Magnavox CD player boombox and toss in one of The Rolling Stones albums I own. Classic rock isn't my favorite, but it's Pops's and he's the one I inherited this thing from.

Dax: You need an intervention.

Me: I just need to finish this piece.

Dax: Dude, this is why you don't have a girlfriend.

Now it's my turn to blast him with middle finger emojis.

Me: Remind me again, what's your girlfriend's name?

I chuckle before tossing my phone back down on my shop table. Dax dates girls here and there, but he hasn't ever kept one long enough to call her his girlfriend. And he wants to give me shit.

Pushing away all thoughts of Dax, I lose myself once more to the intricacies of my small-scale replica of Cedarwood Mansion. It's created completely with salvaged materials from one of the historical sites Pops recently did a job at. The real Cedarwood Mansion sits on the outskirts of town, neglected and forgotten. Pops and Dad complain weekly about what a waste the historical site is. They've approached the owners many times about a restoration or even purchasing the property from them, but are always met with a simple, "no."

At least my replica will look like the original. I spent months researching photos on the internet and in the Park Mountain Library to get a sense of what it should look like in its pristine condition. My replica is a twelve-by-twelve-inch version that opens the mansion up like a book so you can view all the intricacies of each room. I'm about seventy percent done, which means Dax will have to stop bugging me because I won't stop when I'm this close to completion.

I quickly become engrossed in my project, ignoring time and all thoughts that don't pertain to Cedarwood. My neck starts to ache and my stomach growls violently, but I'm not ready to quit for the evening.

"Two, kiddo, time to eat."

Groaning, I sit up and blink several times to clear my daze. Swiveling around in my ancient, rusty barstool, I find Dad standing in the doorway, arms crossed over his chest.

Great.

He's giving me the "you're in trouble, buddy," look that I always hated as a kid. But, to my dads, despite being in my third year of college, I'm still that strange child they brought home with them one day and decided to let stay.

"What?"

He purses his lips and slowly walks into my workshop, gaze scanning the chaos that is my happy place. Once, a couple of years ago, he and Pops cleaned it out and organized it to surprise me. I freaked the fuck out because all the things that had a place were now gone and in some other place. It took forever to find everything again.

"You're awfully hyper focused on this project lately," Dad

says, coming to stand near me. His neatly manicured eyebrows pinch together. "Everything okay with you?"

I cringe at the thought of him worrying about me. Last time he and Pops worried about me, I ended up with a prescription for Prozac and a higher dosage of anxiety meds.

"I'm fine," I assure him with a huff. "You sound like Dax now."

"Dax, God bless his birdbrained soul, knows you better than anyone. If he's worried, then there's a need to be worried."

Dad takes one of my hands that's crusted in plaster and warms it between his hot ones. "Did you even realize your space heater isn't on? It's well below freezing out there."

My head jerks to the left, and sure enough, the thing isn't on. Probably explains why I have the sniffles and my fingers are numb.

"I got hot," I lie, meeting my dad's stare with a defiant one of my own.

Worry softens his expression and he nods. "Well, I'm pulling rank now. Time to get your crazy butt back inside. Pops made ribs in the crockpot."

My stomach grumbles again and Dad laughs. I'm not laughing, though. Sometimes I still feel like a small child with massively big emotions that no one else understands. At least when I'm focused on my projects, I can just be for a little while without overanalyzing everything and everyone.

I slide off my stool onto weak legs. A quick look at my watch—a vintage Timex piece from Pops' dad, my gramps—to learn I've spent the better part of eight hours in my shop at the back of our property without food or even a restroom break.

Okay, so sometimes, my dads and Dax have a point.

I obsess a little.

Dad leads the way out of my shop, waiting for me to close it up and lock it. I'm closer to Pops's height at six-foot-two. Dad, despite being closer to five-foot-six, is definitely the boss in our family. What he lacks in height, he makes up for it in attitude.

"Your hair is getting long, Two," Dad says as we walk briskly, hurrying to get out of the harsh cold. "Want to go see Aunt T and get a cut?"

I fling my head back, which makes the hair that was drooping into my eyes bounce away for a second before it lands right in the spot where it was.

"Maybe," I say with a noncommittal grunt. "I'm busy with class all next week and I have to get Cedarwood Mansion done."

Dad stops right before we reach the back door. He places his warm hands on my cold cheeks, bringing me down so we're at eye level. "The second it's done, you're marching yourself over to her house for a cut. And you're taking a much-needed break. Your classes will demand a lot of your time and winter break is over."

I roll my eyes, which makes him smirk.

"I'm serious, Tristan." He kisses my nose like he used to when I was little. "Love you, kiddo."

He turns and heads inside while I examine his words. I do believe my dads love me. I feel it down to my soul. Sometimes, though, I can't help but pick apart the reasons why and how they love me. When did it happen? Was it days, months, or years after they had to take literal option number two over their precious little girl?

My therapist doesn't know about my feelings.

No one does.

It feels selfish and ungrateful to bring to light my emotions regarding the love of my parents. They did take care of me even if I wasn't their first choice. I've never hurt for a thing and know I fared better than those other kids who started in the same predicament I was in.

Plus, my therapist makes me feel like a child. Technically, she's a pediatric therapist and I've just been grandfathered in, so it's not her fault. But I don't have to open up to her. She'd probably just tell my dads and it would hurt them.

I'm not in the business of hurting the two people I love most.

It's easier if I'm the one doing all the hurting. At least I can handle it. Dad would cry. Pops would do that thing where his jaw works and he swallows hard but otherwise looks like a stone statue. I don't want that shit.

Inside the house, it smells of barbecue and steamed corn. Pops is pouring glasses of sweet tea, his muscular back turned to us. When I was little, I thought Pops was an actual giant or a lumberjack. He'd pick me up and fly me around the living room while I squealed with delight. Sometimes he'd even let me touch the ceiling. Dad would freak out the whole time, panicking that he'd drop me.

"Hey, Pops," I say, coming up behind him and resting my head on his shoulder. "Smells good in here."

He reaches up one of his calloused hands and pats my head. "You know I love an easy dinner that tastes better than anything you can grab in town. How's Cedarwood?"

I light up at his question. "I worked on all the crown moulding today." I hold up my plaster-covered fingers for him to inspect. "It's taken the longest because it's so intricate, but I'm loving how it's looking."

Pops chuckles. "Can't wait to see when it's finished. Wash up, Son. You're not licking sauce off those crusty fingers."

My sullen mood improves as I get cleaned up and take a seat at the table. Dad regales us with a tale of this woman who asked for a bid to redecorate the front room of her house. Apparently, she's a hoarder and didn't mention the piles of bullshit everywhere. Dad said he nearly croaked from horror at the mess, gave her an outlandish bid, and then ran so fast out of there you'd think his ass was on fire.

"Maybe me and Dax can start a hoarder clean-out business," I say with a grin. "Think of all the treasures I could find."

Both dads shout, "No!" at once.

I've been teased a time or two about my hoarding tendencies. I just like cool shit and there's lots of it out in the world. Who needs to go to the mall or big box stores when you can find everything you need in someone else's trash pile?

"Good luck getting Dax to do that," Dad says, shaking his head. "I thought he was going to medical school after PMU."

I snort. "Dad. His grades are just good enough to keep him eligible for football. He's going to have to take what he can get."

"There's always positions open at LGS," Pops says. "We could use a couple of big guys like you two to carry lumber around."

"School comes first," Dad reminds us. "If Two wants to work this summer for you, that's fine, but I don't want him getting distracted."

My grades are fine. Not perfect but not below average like Dax's. School is just something for me to do and not something I love. Because of my love for architectural salvage and exposure to my dads' restoration and redecorating firm, I could easily work for them full time one day and be happy.

"Oh," Dad says, absently picking at his ribs. "I forgot to tell you. Dr. Wynn is retiring. She emailed me a few names of therapists, but I actually met a pretty nice guy who recently opened a new clinic. He's not a dinosaur like Dr. Wynn, either. I'd say he's in his late twenties and someone you could connect with easier. Felt like divine timing."

A new therapist?

Dr. Wynn is a dinosaur, but she's the dinosaur I know.

"Do I have to?" I ask, voice small, reminding me of when I was little and learning my place in my new family.

"It would make us happy if you'd try," Pops adds, giving me a sympathetic smile. "If you don't like him, we'll try someone else."

"Maybe I don't need therapy anymore," I suggest, voice rough and resigned.

Dad shakes his head. "Sorry, kiddo, that part's not up for debate."

Kiddo.

"And if I say no?" I challenge, a flare of anger sparking inside. "Are you going to kick me out?"

Pops grunts and Dad rolls his eyes.

"You'll go because it's what's best for you," Dad says in his bossy tone that leaves no room for argument. Then he flashes his winning smile that charms everyone in his vicinity. "Who wants baklava for dessert? I picked some up at the coffee shop earlier."

As my parents happily move on to other subjects, my

mind is still turning over this new revelation over and over again.

New therapist.

I'm going whether I want to or not.

I hope my new therapist enjoys hearing about my historical replicas and my love for architectural salvage because one thing's for sure, if I didn't open up to Dr. Wynn, I'm not opening up to some random stranger.

CHAPTER THREE

Gemma

CHECK MY TEETH IN THE REARVIEW MIRROR FOR A THIRD unnecessary time as I listen to Willa tell me all about Bane's sleep schedule. While I love my sister-in-law, sometimes the baby tales are too much. We're in such different places in our lives right now.

I'm about to start my second semester in college and she's about to change yet another diaper. I certainly don't envy her at times like these.

"I'm sorry," Willa says with a tired sigh. "I know you don't care about all this stuff."

Jolting at her words, I shake my head, though she can't see it. "What? I do care. I love my Bane-bae. I'm just nervous about one of my classes. I randomly chose it because all the ones I wanted were full, thinking it was a blow-off class, but I heard since then it's not exactly an easy one."

"You'll do fine. You kill it with everything you do. What's the class?"

"Historical Preservation and Urban Design. Womp, womp."

She chuckles. "That does seem like the least Gemma Park class to ever exist, but I'm sure it won't be so bad."

"Says the nerd who married her teacher."

We continue chatting until Bane starts wailing. Once

we're off the phone, I check my appearance one last time before grabbing my backpack and the giant Michael Kors handbag my parents got me for Christmas. The familiar nerves are in place as I attempt to gracefully climb out of my Tahoe.

Breathe, girl.

You've totally got this.

I affix my signature smile and start through the parking lot toward the building where my class is located. An old hunk of junk nearly plows over me, forcing me to jump back with a squeal. Several other students in the parking lot briefly look my way. The careless driver whips into an open spot nearby and parks partly on one of the lines.

The idiot drives like Dempsey does.

With a huff, I make sure no other runaway clunkers are about to take me out before making my way safely to the walking path. I can't help but glance over my shoulder at the perpetrator. Some tall guy in a military jacket and messy dark hair flings himself out of the vehicle. His bag is half open and several papers fly out of it. Of course he doesn't seem to even notice, kind of how he didn't even see me crossing the lot.

What a dick.

Turning my attention back to the building, I lift my chin and walk with all the confidence I can muster. A couple of girls whisper and point at me before they both giggle. I give them a small wave that they don't return.

Being a Park and now a pretty successful influencer, I've earned my fair share of notoriety. Sometimes it makes me friends and other times it makes me the butt of a joke. Most often, when people take the time to get to know me, they end up liking me. It's just getting there that's the problem.

"Weirdo," one of the girls mutters as she passes.

I turn just in time to see the reckless driver hot on my heels. It's then I realize they were laughing at him, not me. He's absently unwrapping a piece of candy, not paying a bit of attention to the fact he's about to slam right into me. Right before I start to move out of his way, another big guy pounces on him.

"There's my boy!"

The weirdo grunts as he attempts to swat away the other guy, who's now trying to put him in a bear hug. I step aside to watch them. They're both older than me and one of them wears a PMU letterman jacket with a football patch and the number fourteen below it.

"You're not in this building today," Weirdo says, voice low and quiet. "Why are you here?"

"To see you, dipshit. You've been avoiding me and I'm over it." The football guy finally pulls away to grin at his friend.

"Dax," Weirdo huffs, "I told you—"

"I know," Dax says with a groan. "Cedarwood comes first. Dude, sometimes you make it difficult as fuck to be your bestie."

What is Cedarwood?

As though I've asked the question aloud, Dax turns his head my way. His green eyes rove appreciatively over my carefully selected outfit before landing back on my face.

"Hey," Dax says, lips curling into a grin. "What's up, beautiful?"

"Tell your friend to watch where he's going," I blurt out, ignoring his attempt at flirting. "He nearly ran me over with his hunk of junk."

The weirdo snaps his head up, finally giving me his attention, and pins his light gray eyes on me. His almost creepily pale eyes slice right through me, penetrating me in a way that makes me shiver, and not from the chilly January wind.

"It's a 1988 Land Rover Defender 90," the weirdo clips out, scowling, the scent of butterscotch enveloping me with his nearness. "It's called a classic, not junk." His eyes dart over me quickly, instant dislike twisting his features. "And the parking lot is for cars. You should have been paying attention to where you were going."

I gape at him. What a dick.

"Two, bro, chill," Dax says, moving to stand in front of his friend. "Sorry about that. His dads dropped him on his head a lot when he was a baby."

My alarm on my watch beeps, reminding me I need to be in class now. I wave off Dax before pivoting and storming away from the two men. What kind of name is Two anyway? And did he seriously just chastise me for nearly getting run over by him?

Rude.

Whatever.

I'm not going to let that guy ruin my day. Forcing another smile, I make my way into the building and down the hall to my classroom. Since I'm late, there's only one available table right up front. The professor, a man with a long, graying beard, arches a brow at me but doesn't mention my tardiness. I'm just settling into my seat and unzipping my bag when another person enters the classroom.

"Mr. Sheridan," the professor says, a smile tugging at his lips. "I was wondering if you were going to show up."

Two Sheridan gives the man a slight nod before he scans the room for a seat. His eyes land on mine and then dart to the chair beside me. He flares his nostrils as though the thought of sitting beside me is annoying.

Join the club, buddy. You're no prize peach yourself.

Ignoring him, I face the professor, eager to get class started. My morning has been off and I'm ready to get it back on track again.

"I'm Jack Pederson," our professor says, hands on his hips, "and this is not a blow-off class. If you signed up thinking you were going to sleep through this one, you may as well take yourself down to Administration and drop this course."

One guy playfully pretends to stand up, but Mr. Pederson waves a dismissive hand at him. "Charlie, don't be cute."

Charlie sniggers but settles back in his seat. I'd been hoping it would be easy, but as Mr. Pederson passes out the syllabus, I'm beginning to question that initial line of thinking.

"As you can see," Mr. Pederson says as he makes his way back to the front, "this class will be comprised of lectures on architectural history, seminars on preservation techniques, case studies that analyze successful examples of historical preservation and urban renewal projects, and of course various class trips to local historical sites." He waggles a finger at Charlie. "Yes, the field trips are for a grade. You skip them and you get a zero."

Charlie groans. "Hard-ass."

"You're still here." Mr. Pederson shrugs. "That makes you a masochist."

The class, everyone aside from me and Two, sniggers. There's clearly history—no pun intended—between Mr. Pederson and some of the students in this class, including Two. Once again, I feel like an outsider.

"What about the semester project?" a girl with fiery red

hair asks. "This says it's worth seventy-five percent of our grade. When do we choose partners? When is it due? When do we start?"

Mr. Pederson waves her off. "We'll get to that. First, I want you to look at your table partner. This will be your seat for the entire semester and your partner for the semester project. I want you to take the next five minutes to get to know the other person."

My heart sinks. I have to partner up with the guy who almost ran me over? As if this day couldn't get any worse. Ugh.

The classroom breaks out into a hum of chatter. Reluctantly, I turn to look over at Two. He's swiping rapidly through his phone. I try to peek at what he's doing, but it looks like he's just scrolling through his camera roll.

I know his type.

I'm going to be stuck doing this whole stupid project alone and he'll pop in at the end to get half the credit. Maybe I should go down to Administration and drop this class.

Dad would be disappointed.

"You got lucky, miss," Mr. Pederson says as he walks by our table, rapping his knuckles on the wood surface. "Mr. Sheridan, for the love of God, let her do some of the work."

Two grunts but continues his rapid-fire scrolling. He pauses long enough to dig around in his bag. Once he pulls out a butterscotch candy, he unwraps it, pops it into his mouth, repeats the process with another, and then continues his scrolling.

Right.

So lucky.

I suck in a deep breath and slowly exhale to settle the

irritation burning in my gut. While I wait for him to finish whatever the hell he's doing, I skim through the syllabus again.

Seventy-five percent of my grade depends on this whack job.

"So," I utter, forcing myself to look over at Two. "Tell me about yourself."

He runs the candies along his teeth, making a clanking sound that has my eye twitching. I arch an eyebrow, waiting for his answer.

Nothing.

When he finally finds whatever he's looking for, he lets out a sharp whistle that has everyone looking his way. Mr. Pederson chuckles and saunters over to us.

"Cedarwood," Two says, thrusting his phone at the professor.

Again with this Cedarwood.

Mr. Pederson's eyes widen. "Wow, Mr. Sheridan. You've got quite the gift for this."

"Yeah, I know."

Arrogant much?

"Thanks for sharing," Mr. Pederson says as he returns the phone. "Now get to know your partner, please."

Finally, Two pockets his electronic distraction and turns his critical stare my way. "Why do girls wear fake eyelashes?"

I blink at him in confusion. "What?"

He points a long arm my way, his bony finger inches from my eyeball. "Fake."

Though he's talking about my eyelashes, I can't help but flinch at the word. Some of my harshest critics in the social media world accuse me of being fake. I'm not fake. I just don't share all the imperfect parts of me.

"Why are you so dismissive and rude?" I snap back, cheeks growing hot.

His brows knit together. "It was just a question. Why are you so sensitive?"

The gall of this guy.

It takes a lot to get me riled up, but Two has managed to boil my blood since the second he nearly took me out with his car. And I'm supposed to deal with this all semester? Yeah, right.

"Tell me about yourself," I grit out. "What's Cedarwood?"

His pale eyes glimmer with excitement and he flashes a shockingly handsome smile my way complete with dimples and all. "Cedarwood Mansion. I'm working on a miniature restored replica. It's all hypothetical and based off historical photographs since those bastards won't fix her up to her original beauty."

Okaaaaay.

Not at all what I was expecting.

It makes sense now why he's apparently besties with our professor.

Two is still grinning at me, and it's a bit disarming. Maybe this terrible day is because of my mood, not his. He's an oddball but an attractive one.

"Can we start over?" I ask with a tentative smile as I thrust my hand at him. "I'm Gemma Park. Nice to meet you."

The dimples fade and his full lips tug into a frown. "Are you fucking for real?"

Oh great. What did my family do now?

"Excuse me?" I ask, the heat once again burning at my cheeks.

"Is your mom named Jamie?"

I stiffen and gape at him in confusion. Usually, it's my dad or one of my brothers or Spencer who earns the shocked gasps or pissed-off snarls. Never Mom.

"Yeah. Do you know her?"

He sneers at me, "Nah, Golden, and I hope I never have to."

What the actual hell?

CHAPTER FOUR

Two

I T'S HER.

Numero Uno.

Prime choice for a prime couple.

The golden child.

Of all the luck.

Gemma, perfection personified, continues to gape at me like a goldfish gasping for air. Her long, dark hair is sleek and silky, not a strand out of place. The lips that remain parted are glossed in a pinky hue that reminds me of strawberry Starburst. Freakishly long and thick eyelashes continue to blink at me.

I think I broke Homewrecker Barbie.

Turning my gaze away from her, I spear my hand into the air to get Mr. Pederson's attention. He frowns before ambling our way.

"What's up?"

I jut my thumb in her direction. "Can't."

Gemma scoffs. "Unbelievable."

"Can't what, Mr. Sheridan?"

"I can't do this with her."

The older man tugs at his scraggly beard, eyes narrowed as he studies me. "Too bad."

Too bad?

Is he for real?

"Unless you can give me a perfectly logical reason for not partnering with this nice young lady, I don't want to hear another word on the subject."

Oh, yeah. He's fucking serious.

It's not like I can tell him the real reason I don't like her besides her brattiness over our parking lot debacle that was clearly her fault. I can't tell anyone. Not Dr. Wynn, not Dad or Pops, hell, not even Dax.

I'm alone in my misery.

Fucking wonderful.

"Whatever," I grunt, waving off our professor. "I'll deal."

"Please do." Mr. Pederson walks off, shaking his head in frustration.

Makes two of us, man.

Gemma pushes her syllabus across the desk until the paper is in my line of sight. Her fingernails are long, pointy, and matte black with shimmery rhinestones on the middle nails. How can anyone function with nails that long? How does she wipe her ass?

She probably has people for that.

Gemma looks rich as fuck.

"This," Gemma says icily, tapping on the semester project, "is a huge part of our grade. I don't exactly understand what your problem is with me, but I wish you could squash it for five seconds and focus on this."

I snatch her paper up and glower at the ink. Seventy-five percent is a lot.

"Fine," I grunt. "I'll do the project. You can sign your name at the top. We can avoid each other until then. Problem solved."

She scoffs again. "Problem solved? You're an arrogant piece of work, Two."

My shoulders tense at her addressing me by name. It's like a lash of a whip with thousands of micro whips all attached to blades. Cut after cut digs into my flesh, making me shudder.

Two.

Second best.

"Tristan," I grit out, "is my name."

"Then why do they call you Two?"

"None of your business, Golden."

"Stop calling me that. It's Gemma."

Someone sniggers nearby. Charlie makes a crude motion of sucking dick. Does he think this is some fucked-up version of foreplay?

I flip him the bird before tossing her paper back at her. It flutters to the ground. Her face grows redder and redder with each passing second. If she gets any more pissed, her head is going to burst like an overfed tick and her eyelashes are going to shoot out like darts, sticking to everyone in this room.

"Chill, Golden."

"I said." She lets out a slow, measured breath. "You're messing with me, right? To get a rise out of me? Unfortunately for you, I have four brothers and I'm the baby sister. Believe me, I know all about getting razzed for the sake of someone else's enjoyment."

And to think, she was almost an only child like me.

Would she be even more spoiled than she is now?

"Trust me," I spit out. "Nothing about this interaction brings me joy."

She flinches at my words and grows eerily quiet. I glance

over to find her chewing on her bottom, heavily glossed lip. Her eyes are slightly glassy. Is she going to cry?

It's satisfying to know that she might. I've cried hundreds of times over this shit. Maybe even thousands. I'm all cried out lately, though. I feel empty and bitter. It's someone else's turn to be fucking gutted for a change.

And who not better than enemy number one?

Gemma clears her throat and then turns to face the front. She lifts her chin, staring at the board in front of her. I'm guessing she's moving on to ignoring me. Good. That's definitely for the best. Otherwise, I'm going to continue to say mean things because they don't seem to want to stay trapped deep inside where they've been living since I was nine years old.

My phone buzzes, distracting me for a moment.

Dax: I'm going to get that chick's number. She's hot AF.

What chick? *My* chick?

Me: The crybaby from this morning? That girl?

Dax: Yeah, dumbass. The only hot girl we encountered this morning.

Me: No.

Dax: What do you mean no?

Dax: Wait… You like her?

Dax: Dude, this is awesome. I don't think you've ever been interested in a girl like ever.

Me: Hazel. I was interested in her.

Dax: She used you to lose her virginity the summer

after we turned sixteen. I'm surprised you even remember her name.

Me: I said no, Dax.

Dax: You DO like her! Fucking hell! Get her number, 2!

Me: No.

Dax: We're not done discussing this. Either you get her number or I will.

I continue to text him no, but he stops responding. Irritation sours my gut. Of all the women who could interest my playboy best friend, why is he putting his sights on my enemy?

You could tell him.

Dax is loyal. If he knew why you hated her, he'd back off and be supportive.

That's not happening.

"Okay, everyone," Mr. Pederson says after the longest five minutes of my entire goddamn life. "Now that you're acquainted with your partner, I'll get into the specifics of the project. Then I'll lecture a bit before you all are free to get going for the day. Don't get used to it, though."

When I glance back over at Gemma, she's sitting ramrod straight with her notebook opened in front of her and a purple pen in her raven-claw grip. With swooping, graceful strokes, she begins to take notes. I watch her make sense of Mr. Pederson's words and convert them to girly art in her notebook.

Everything Mr. Pederson yaps about is common knowledge in my opinion. Considering I grew up exposed to the subject of Historical Preservation and Urban Design, it's not necessary for me to pay attention.

Right now, I'm more focused on learning about her.

Gemma *Golden* Park.

Her last name was always irrelevant to me until now because I had no desire to ever track her down. There's a reason why I never went out looking for the mysterious Gemma—the little girl who claimed my bedroom before I did, before she was even born. Hating a name is easier than hating a person. Seeing her in the flesh and experiencing her utter perfection firsthand is a sucker punch to my gut. I'd wanted to avoid this feeling at all cost. I'm dizzied and nauseous. Painful memories assault me from every direction.

I hated who I became after I found that picture and read that letter.

I became exactly as my nickname suggested. Second best. An afterthought. Leftovers.

I've been struggling ever since to shed that cloak of shame and hurt, but no matter how hard I try—no matter how much medication and therapy I'm on—I'm never able to shake it off.

It clings to me like a second skin.

The only time I'm not obsessing over it is when I'm lost in my projects—my only real time to be happy.

I'm a grown-ass adult now. Maybe I should move out. Living in the same room I discovered belonged to someone else for over a decade can't be good for my mind. It's a constant reminder.

But where would I live?

Alone?

The thought of being by myself, away from my dads,

makes my gut clench. Despite being their second, they were always my first. I loved—still love them—with my entire soul.

Who knew I'd be eating depression with a side of despair for breakfast this morning?

My mind reels as Mr. Pederson drones on. Maybe talking to a new therapist will be good for me. Maybe this new guy can teach me how to shove all the pain back into that wretched trunk in Dad's closet.

How freeing would that be?

Time flies by and the next thing I know, everyone around me is getting up to leave. Gemma doesn't move. I jerk my head her way to find her staring at me, a slight frown on her pink lips.

"What?"

"You didn't take one single note. I don't think you were paying attention at all." She sighs, resignation in her voice. "What's your number? I'll text you a picture of my notes. We're going to need to be able to contact each other for this project anyway."

She wants my number?

Would Dax leave her alone if he knew we exchanged numbers?

That certainly would help me avoid telling him why I despise her.

I pluck her sleek phone from her grip and find the contacts. I enter in "Tristan" because giving her the satisfaction of seeing Two on there boils my blood. Once I shoot a test text, I drop her phone onto her desk with a loud clank.

"You're welcome," she grumbles, snatching her phone from the desk. "I'll send it later."

She gathers the rest of her things and then bolts from

the classroom. As other students begin entering for the next class, I open my phone and look at the text I sent from her phone. Once I save her as "Golden," I shove my phone into my pocket and grab my bag.

"Your syllabus is on the floor, Mr. Sheridan," Mr. Pederson remarks with a heavy sigh. "We're barely one day in and you're already scattered. Looks like I paired you up with someone who might keep you in line."

I curl my lip up in disgust as I bend to grab the paper that now has someone's dirty shoe print on it and cram it into my bag. "It's a mistake, Mr. P."

"You say mistake. I say serendipity."

Giving him a curt wave, I stalk out of his room and out of the building. As I near the parking lot, I receive another text.

Dad: Can you do 11 since you have a break between classes? I'll send you a pin of the location.

Dad's questions aren't suggestions, they're law. So much for going home and spending a couple of hours with Cedarwood Mansion.

Me: K.

It's the response he always gets from me when I'm angry. I don't know why it pisses him off so much, but it always has. He responds with an emoji that's cursing, which makes me bark out a laugh.

I'm nearly at the parking lot when I see a couple standing near a badass sports car. It's one of the newer muscle cars—a remake of the classics—but still looks pretty damn cool. The owner of the sweet ride has a girl pulled against his chest and he hugs her tight. It's then I recognize the shiny brown hair.

Gemma has a boyfriend?

The dude in question has tats on his neck, arms, and hands. His dark hair is a chaotic mess. Our eyes meet and he narrows his at me.

Don't want your girlfriend, bro.

In fact, I want nothing to do with your girlfriend.

His eyes follow me as I make it to my car. I fling my bag into the passenger seat, inhale the natural musty age of the vehicle, and then fire it up.

Well, not on the first time.

My car never fires up on the first time.

Third time's a charm, though, and within seconds, I'm peeling out of my spot. Golden's imperfect boyfriend glowers at me and then flips me off.

Fucking prick.

I use both hands to flip him off for extra impact, but then my steering wheel starts veering toward a row of cars, and I'm forced to grab back on to straighten it. Normally, I don't mind dealing with wonky steering, but today it's just a reminder of what I am.

Two.

Broken little boy driving a broken old car.

What a great day for therapy.

CHAPTER FIVE

Gemma

CALL IT TWIN MAGIC.

For as long as I can remember, Dempsey, my brother, twin, and built-in best friend has always been there to comfort me or cheer me up whenever I've had a bad day.

Today has been awful and Dempsey's timing is impeccable.

"Want me to have Sloane arrest him?"

I chuckle as we cruise out of the parking lot in his beast of a car. I'm low-key jealous he got himself this bad boy when I'm stuck driving the practical Tahoe.

"You can't arrest him for being an asshole," I say, shaking my head. "But if it were possible, he'd totally be in cuffs right now."

"I'm sure my woman can dig up some dirt on him. She's pretty good at that shit."

I reach over and pat Dempsey's hand that's on the stick shift. It's a reminder of why I can't drive a car like this. I'd have no idea how to even make it go.

"I love you," I tell him. "Just knowing you hate him on principle because I do makes my day."

He groans when I disconnect his Bluetooth and hook mine in. It's our deal. If he's going to drive, I get to choose the music. I settle on something new I heard while scrolling through social media the other day. The smooth voice of the singer calms my erratically beating heart.

"I found a new place the other day," Dempsey says as he dutifully uses his blinker. Sloane must be rubbing off on him. He's marrying a cop who doesn't put up with his bullshit. "It's small and cozy. They probably don't even have a Facebook, so you can't post it to the 'Gram or whatever."

My brother seriously has no clue what I do. I think he thinks I make posts and people pay me for it. Technically, when you boil it down, I suppose they do. Well, the sponsors at least. But I hate when he minimizes it.

However, the thought of going someplace hidden and private sounds enticing. I'm in need of Dempsey time without an audience.

"Sloane meeting us there?" I ask, glancing at the clock on the dash.

"Nah," he grunts. "She and Montgomery are working a case. There was a body found on Park Mountain Lake this weekend."

"It's too cold to swim," I say, shivering. "Do you think they drowned or…"

"Or. Definitely or. But Sloane doesn't need my help."

Dempsey drives us down Main Street and whips into a parking spot. The building in front of us is weathered and the windows are painted brown. A sign is tacked to the worn-out wooden door that says, "Soup and More. 8-8."

"This place looks sketchy," I mutter, squinting against the sun to get a better look. "You sure you don't want to grab something to eat at your place?"

He laughs as he shuts off the car. "Come on, princess, you're going to be fine."

Rolling my eyes, I climb out of the vehicle, following my brother into the building. At first, the darkness of the building is such a contrast to the sunny outdoors that I find myself temporarily blinded, which has my heart hammering in my chest. But as I begin to adjust, I realize the restaurant isn't sketchy at all.

First off, it smells heavenly. A cooked garlic and onions scent permeates the air, making my stomach growl. There's a small counter that has glass displays filled with various breads and desserts. Behind it, a tiny woman around Mom's age roots around in a cabinet. The restaurant itself only has three tables and four booths. Along the walls, there are shelves filled with knickknacks, candles, and other small items that look to be for sale.

Soups and More.

I'm guessing all that stuff is the "more."

"Hey, kids," the woman says in greeting. "What can I get ya?"

Dempsey orders for the both of us and then ushers me over to a cozy booth near the big painted window.

"Why doesn't she scrape that paint off?" I ask, gesturing to the window. "I bet she'd get a lot more business."

Dempsey grunts and shakes his head. "Don't."

"Don't what?"

"Start trying to figure out a way to help this lady get business. I can see your wheels turning. Do not, for the love of God, put anything on your socials. I'm serious. If this turns into some stupid trendy hangout, I'll never forgive you."

The woman brings over the drinks Dempsey ordered

us—frothy rootbeer in frozen mugs—and promises to be back shortly with the daily soup special.

"I don't put restaurants on there," I remind him. "It doesn't fit my aesthetic."

"Thank fuck for your carefully culled aesthetic, whatever the hell that means."

It's no use explaining to my brother for the millionth time, so I ignore it and circle back to my terrible morning.

"I think I'm going to just drop the class," I say with a sigh. "You saw what a prick that guy was. And to have to be partners with him? Gross."

"I'm sure Dad will be so thrilled for you to drop out over a boy." He snorts with laughter. "Can I be there when you tell him?"

"You're as bad as Callum. Leave Dad alone. You know everything he does is out of love."

"Just saying," he continues, "I want to see his face when his little angel doesn't do something perfect."

"I hate you."

"Nah, womb mate, you love me forever."

"I just don't get why this weirdo decided to hate on me." I sip on my root beer and then frown at Dempsey. "He asked if I knew Mom. I think his beef is with her."

Dempsey straightens, face contorting into a scowl. "Mom? What the fuck?"

"Right? I was just sure he was one of Callum's old students or maybe you kicked his ass one time. You know, the usual Park family drama. But Mom? She's harmless and sweet. Everyone loves her."

"Callum doesn't."

"Because she dumped him to marry Dad. Understandable. But Two?"

"Two?"

"That's this guy's name. Two Sheridan."

"Who names their kid Two?"

"Focus, Demps. Why does Two have beef with Mom?"

He pulls out his phone. "We could call and ask her."

"No!" I say with a huff. "Don't call her. Because, if you do, then Dad will get involved. If Dad knows this guy is messing with me, who knows what he'll do."

"Hmm," Dempsey says in a teasing voice, "actually, I do. He'll hunt down the guy, destroy him financially, and then lock you in your room forever so it doesn't happen again."

The tiny woman brings us two trays. On each is a piping hot bowl of soup and a fat, crusty French roll. We thank her and then I glower at my brother.

"Exactly," I grumble. "I'll figure this out on my own."

"I could whip his ass." He shrugs as though that will go over well with his cop fiancée. "I could even recruit Spencer to help."

"Spencer would probably befriend him just to terrorize me."

We stop the conversation for a moment to sample the hot soup. It's savory, thick, and delicious. I see bits of rice, carrots, chicken, and other veggies. So tasty.

"Good choice," I say around a bite, burning my tongue in the process. "This is really good."

"Yeah, that's why you can't ruin it trying to 'influence' your cult followers." He makes quotations with his fingers, grinning stupidly at me.

"I'm just being a baby about this, huh?"

"You're always a baby, but you're *our* baby."

I flip him off, my mind still lingering on Two as I eat the tasty soup. The bread is warm and full of flavor. I can definitely see why Dempsey loves this place.

Eventually, we get on the topic of Beauty, Dempsey and Sloane's new puppy, and he tells me about how she chewed up a pair of Sloane's panties.

"She was pissed," he says with a grin. "They were her favorite period panties."

I curl my lip up. "TMI, Demps. Some stuff you just keep to yourself."

He cracks up laughing and then polishes off his bowl. "I'm going to grab us some dessert. Be right back."

As soon as he leaves, I decide to check in on my socials. I love looking at the analytics of each post or video to see how many people it reached and how many of those people interacted. Dempsey chats up the lady at the counter, so I decide to peek at my messages. Sometimes it takes me hours to get through them, so if I stay on it, checking in every couple of hours, I don't drown in messages. Sure enough, I have nearly fifty that need going through.

One catches my eye.

@TwoCanPlayThisGameX2

It's that creepy profile that messaged me yesterday. They created another account. I'm inclined to just delete and block without looking at the message, but curiosity has me opening it.

Online, you're anything but real.

Two's harsh voice fills my head. *Fake.* I'd been hurt by such a simple word. Being called fake is something that happens often to me, but it'd been extra brutal coming out of Two's mouth this morning.

Is this him?

Is he the one messaging me?

As much as I'd love to pin the weirdo as also being the creep, I know that's a reach. Two didn't know who I was until I introduced myself this morning in class. He wasn't impressed either.

Against my better judgment, I reply to the creepy account.

Who is this?

I tap my sharp nails on the table surface as I wait for a response. Seconds later, I get a reply that makes my blood run cold.

You'll know me soon enough.

"Best chocolate mousse pie this side of the Pacific," Dempsey says, dropping a piece of pie down beside my tray. "Cara guarantees it."

"Who's Cara?" I ask, distracted by the bone-chilling message I just received.

"Soup lady Cara. Over there. Pay attention." He snaps his fingers in front of my face. "This dude really does have you all fucked in the head."

For once, today, this isn't about Two.

It's about this person doing their damnedest to scare me. Maybe it's Spencer. This sounds exactly like something he'd do.

Or it could be something far more sinister.

I don't respond to the sender and instead block and delete like I should have from the beginning. This creep is probably sitting in his mom's basement in some other country far away from me. No need to worry.

"I'm fine," I say to Dempsey, tossing my phone into my bag and flashing him a brilliant smile. "See. All better."

He pushes the plate toward me. "Good. Now try the pie and report back."

He digs into his, practically inhaling it. Amused at his excitement, I follow suit and take a bite. An explosion of silky, decadent, rich chocolate assaults my taste buds in the most delightful way.

"Oh," I groan, "wow."

"Right? Will Sloane be disappointed if I dump her for Cara?"

We both crack up laughing. There's no way in hell Dempsey would ever let Sloane go. It's amusing to imagine, though.

When we're finished with lunch, we thank Cara and promise to come back in soon. It makes me a little sad that we were the only ones in there the entire time at what should be one of the busier times of day for a restaurant.

"We totally need to come back again soon," I tell Dempsey as we get back in his car.

"Hell yeah. I knew I'd have you falling in love with this place."

"Do you think it'll survive much longer?"

"Gemma."

"I know, I know. I promise not to tell the world about it. But seriously, though, if she ever mentions closing, I'm going to break my promise."

"Fine. Then and only then are you allowed to put this place on blast."

With my belly full and in the company of my obnoxious brother, I'm feeling tons better than this morning. Both the weirdo and creep who tried to ruin my day can go to hell.

I'm done being bothered by either one of them.

CHAPTER SIX

THIS BUILDING SMELLS LIKE FRESH PAINT.

It's giving me a headache.

Everything is so…new. Fresh. Perfect.

I instantly hate this new therapist on principle. He's probably some uppity dude who's going to want me to try eating organic or do some weird-ass light therapy.

Not interested.

The only reason I'm here is because Dad wants me to be. I'll sit in the office, bore him to death with my hobbies that hardly anyone cares about, and then bolt out of here just in time for my next class.

When I go to open the office door inside the building, it's locked.

Behind me, the building door opens and a young, sharply dressed man hurries in, a to-go coffee in one hand and a bag in the other.

"Oh my God, I'm so sorry," he says as he makes his way over to me. "The line at the coffee shop was insane. Jude thinks I need a coffee maker here in the office, but nothing tastes as good as when someone else makes it, am I right?" He grins at me. "Tate Prince. I'd shake your hand, but, you know, priorities."

I smirk when he holds up his coffee like he's toasting. "Two."

"I figured," Tate says, juggling his stuff to unlock his door. "Your dad told me all about you."

"I bet that was fun," I deadpan.

He laughs, pushing in through the door. "Your dad said a lot in our ten-minute conversation. A lot of really good stuff about you. I wish my dad had cared even half as much as your dad clearly does."

A twinge of guilt niggles at me. "What can I say? I'm his pride and joy."

As Tate sets his coffee, bag, and keys down on his desk in the corner, I take in the small space. Despite the building being new, his office is cozy. Rather than using stark paint, the office is decorated in wallpaper that's a throwback to another time period. I definitely approve of the selection and Dad would too. Instead of a leather couch like in all the movies or stiff chairs like at Dr. Wynn's, Tate's office has two plush chairs that sit in front of a plug-in fireplace.

"Can I offer you water or anything?"

"I'm good."

I take a seat in one of the chairs and then fiddle with the fireplace to see what kind of heat it puts out. I'm impressed when it immediately starts blasting me with warmth. Maybe I need one of these in my shop. My little space heater sucks… *when I actually remember to turn it on.*

Tate eventually joins me with his coffee. I note that he doesn't have his laptop or notebook. Dr. Wynn loved to write things all over her yellow notepad when I'd visit.

"Where's your stuff?" I ask, gaze darting back to his desk.

"Don't you, like, need to record everything to report back to Dad?"

Tate brings his coffee to his lips and takes a sip that makes him do a giddy dance in his chair. "Coffee is all I need. And everything we talk about is between us. Your dad doesn't get a report. If you want to tell him, you're more than welcome to."

I give him a sharp shake of my head. "Nah, I'm good. How old are you?"

"Everyone always asks me that," he playfully grumbles. "I just turned twenty-eight. Getting married in the fall, too."

Crossing my arms over my chest, I wait for him to hit me with a thousand questions. Nothing comes. Just sips and smiles. Awkwardly, I root around in my jacket until I find a lone butterscotch. I unwrap it and pop it into my mouth.

Still waiting.

"Park's Peak has a butterscotch latte. I'll bring you one next time. It's to die for."

I want to tell him there won't be a next time, but the drink does interest me, so I nod in approval. Maybe just one other time. The guy seems nice.

"Your dad says you're a bit of a historical restoration buff. That sounds super cool. My Jeep, er, my fiancé's Jeep, is a classic. Was that your Land Rover out front? Sweet ride."

I grin, unable to stop myself. "Finally. Someone who appreciates that damn vehicle besides me. Just today, some bratty girl at my school called it a hunk of junk."

He gasps. "Rude!"

"That's what I thought too." I move the butterscotch around my teeth, enjoying the clackity sound it makes. Tate doesn't seem bothered by it. "Dad says I'll get cavities from eating these things, but I've never gotten one."

"Good genes," Tate says with a chuckle. "I just had yet another root canal last month. Merry Christmas to me."

I bristle at the mention of genes. "Honestly, I wouldn't know. I'm adopted."

"Boy, I wish I were," he tosses in. "My dad was a shit parent. Mentally fucked me up, too. It's why I'm doing this here and now."

"You're allowed to cuss to your patients?"

"I can do whatever I want. This is my practice." He takes another sip. "Your adopted dad seems nice. You like him?"

"I love him and Pops more than anyone in the world."

"My heart." He pats his chest. "Jude wants kids. I know he does. I'm hoping we make our children feel as loved as your dads do you."

"Yeah, they're great."

Tate sits his coffee down on the small table beside him. "I'm sensing a mood shift."

I bristle, my hackles rising. "Your spidey senses are wrong."

"Nope. They're never wrong." He beams at me. "I won't push, but it does help to get things off your chest every once in a while. We're not meant to bottle everything up inside. My fiancé did for a long time. He's just now in the past year beginning to heal. Healing isn't a one and done, either. It's a long, torturous journey."

"I'd rather take the shortcut."

"You and ninety-nine percent of the world, including me. Some of us run from our problems." He raises a hand. "Guilty as charged. But when you stop running and face them head-on, something miraculous happens."

"What?"

"They're not as terrifying as we give them the power to be."

Knowing my dads could have had Gemma Park but got me instead is pretty damn terrifying, especially when I consider that there was so much disappointment and grief they must have felt. My dads are strong men, though, and put on a brave face to do the right thing by giving me a home. I hate that they must've felt so awful and devastated. I'm not exactly the best consolation prize.

"Listen, Two," Tate says gently, "I love helping people find peace and joy. It's something I never had growing up, so it soothes something deep in my soul. I'm not here for a paycheck—though money does help pay for my coffee addiction—or some other nefarious reason. I'm here because I want to be."

"Cool."

"Which means if you want to just be friends and talk about mundane, surface-level stuff, I'm okay with that. But as a friend, I'll push you when I feel like you need to be pushed. Never too much, though. I'm great at sensing what a person can handle and guiding them the right way."

"I'm not really good at talking about stuff."

"Oh no." Tate gasps, feigning shock. "You're the only person I've ever encountered who's that way."

I snort out a laugh. "You're sarcastic. Dr. Wynn smelled like cheese."

"I'm going to use that next time Jude's mad at me. 'You love me, mister, because I'm sarcastic and don't smell like cheese.'"

"Are you even qualified to do this?" I ask, mostly joking.

He doesn't get annoyed but instead brings a finger to

his lips. "Shh, don't tell anyone, but I'm totally winging it. Definitely don't tell your dad."

The conversation easily moves on to school. I tell him about my classes but sidestep the whole encounter with my number one enemy. Tate, sharp as a tack, narrows his eyes but doesn't call me out. Yet. Something tells me it'll only be a matter of time. Before long, the hour is up and I actually enjoyed myself.

"Let's meet on Wednesday," Tate says. "I'll bring your butterscotch latte and attempt to get here on time, though I'm not making any promises. Sound good?"

I'm already nodding because it does sound good. The latte, the fireplace, the company. I wonder if it makes me pathetic that I feel like I just made a friend.

You're paying him to be your friend, dipshit.

Ignoring that thought, I tip my head at him and slip out of his office. The smell of paint doesn't bother me this time and when I step outside, I'm pleased to see that he does, in fact, drive an older model Jeep. It's beat up with a dent or two but still a charming vehicle. At least Tate understands. Dr. Wynn drove a sleek, white Audi.

Maybe this new therapist is exactly what I need.

"I got her number," I say to Dax, not meeting his stare.

He nearly chokes on his bite of pizza. "What? Seriously? You legit got Hot Girl's number?"

"Gemma," I remind him with a sigh. "Her name is Gemma."

His green eyes sparkle with delight. "No fucking way. You *do* like her. This is awesome!"

I don't like her, but I'm definitely not going to tell him that. He's already a pain in the ass as it is.

"I saw a new therapist," I blurt out instead.

Dax's brows knit and he nods. "Okay. Already hate her?"

"Him. And he's cool."

"Cool? Like come grab pizza with us cool?"

"Maybe one day. He's not much older than us."

"About damn time. I can't believe you kept going to that walking corpse, Dr. Waxface."

"Dr. Wynn. And now that you say that, she kind of did look like a museum wax figure."

We both snort with laughter. My chest feels lighter after a helluva morning. I did need some best friend time despite my desperation to finish my project. Dax may annoy the shit out of me, but he's mine.

"Oh, some guys from class were going to meet up this Friday at the pool hall. I know you're on a deadline with Cedarwood, but I thought maybe you'd want to come along. Maybe bring *Gemma*." He waggles his brows at me. "Or not. It'll be fun."

When I'm focused on Dax, I notice things about him like the hope gleaming in his eyes. I still wonder why he sticks around to be my friend when I'm a bit of an asshole most of the time. I do like hanging out with him. It's just sometimes I get sucked into the void that is my mind. My only escape is my projects.

Maybe that's not completely true.

Right now, I feel calm and am enjoying myself, and we're not talking about Cedarwood.

"Yeah," I agree as I pick up another slice of pizza. "I'll go. I'm driving, though. Your car stresses me out."

He cracks up laughing. "That's just because it's fast. Your car hasn't ever seen over fifty miles per hour, old man. Well, except when you're trying to run over girls in parking lots."

I smirk. "I can't even figure out your door handle half the time. It's basically a damn spaceship."

We continue to joke around and eat pizza. Calm washes over me. When we finally finish, we abandon our table to try to see who's the better pinball player.

It's me, of course.

By the time we leave and part ways, the terrible feeling in my gut from seeing a certain someone this morning has nearly subsided.

Hopefully, I can ride this feeling until I'm forced to see her again on Wednesday.

Until then, I refuse to be tormented by her.

CHAPTER SEVEN

DIDN'T DROP THE CLASS.

After sleeping on it a couple of nights, anger settled deep in my gut. I'm not going to let some jerk who doesn't even know how to drive scare me away.

On Monday night, I sent him pictures of my notes. He actually responded, which was surprising, with "K," which was not surprising at all.

Asshole.

But it's been a couple of days and I'm feeling more prepared to handle Two this time.

As I pull into the parking lot at PMU for my building, I squint against the morning rays and hunt for a parking spot that my big beast of a vehicle will fit into. I see one several spots away and start forward. A flash of olive green darts out from between two cars. Despite slamming on my brakes, I'm not quick enough.

Thunk!

The person—I hit a freaking person—goes down and out of sight. This can't be happening. This can't be happening! With my heart in my throat, I throw the car into park and then jump out.

"Oh my God!" I cry out, rounding the front of my vehicle to inspect the damage.

What if they're dead?

I wasn't going that fast, right?

A man sits on his ass, rubbing at his shoulder. I drop to my knees in front of him, panic clawing at me, and desperately run my palms over his shoulder, looking for broken bones sticking out.

"I'm so sorry," I choke out, eyes prickling with tears. "I didn't see you and—"

I finally meet the stare of the person I hit and recognize the chilly light-gray eyes of Two. Of all the people to hit…

"Did you hit me on purpose?" Two asks, scowling at me. "That's fucked up."

I shake my head, scoffing. "What? No. You came out of nowhere! Seriously, what is it with you and parking lots?"

His eyes narrow. "I could ask you the same."

The initial shock of running into him wears off and irritation needles its way through me. "Are you hurt?" I demand, voice sharp. "Yes or no?"

His nostrils flare. "I'll live."

I hear people laughing nearby. I'm sure we're quite the spectacle. With a groan, I stand back up and offer my hand to help him to his feet. He reluctantly takes my hand, his freakishly large hand swallowing mine. Once he's standing, he jerks his hand out of mine like it's tainted with poison.

He stalks off without another glance in my direction. My heart continues to hammer in my chest as I climb back into my vehicle and park it.

I can't believe I hit Two Sheridan.

Even if he did deserve it…

If Dad ever finds out I hit someone, I'll be banned from driving forever.

So much for starting the day off feeling better than Monday. Somehow, this one is shaping up to be worse. What is it about Two that wrecks me so easily?

There's a coldness that emanates from him that I don't understand. Usually, when someone doesn't like me or my family, I can handle it with stride because it's always something stupid. This thing with Two, though, feels personal. As though we've wronged him on some visceral level that makes him despise me.

Why?

I'm going to figure it out. You can't hate someone so viciously for no reason. If there's a reason, and me or my family are the cause, then I deserve to know. Maybe I could fix it.

By the time I make it to class, my stomach is in knots. As soon as I enter the classroom, my eyes dart straight to Two. He absently rubs at his shoulder and I feel a pang of guilt.

I didn't mean to hurt him.

Mr. Pederson gives me a gentle smile as I pass by his desk. For some reason, he seems to like Two. He obviously knows a different side of him than I do.

I settle at my seat with plenty of time before class starts today. That helps ease the tension forming in my shoulders. After I pull out my notebook and pen, I turn to face him. Two stares straight ahead, cheeks still pink from the cold. His dark hair is in disarray and something tells me it has nothing to do with getting rammed by my Tahoe. He has a sharp jawline that, even I can admit, is pretty to look at.

Two may be a weirdo asshole, but he's definitely an attractive one in an unusual way. He's not classically handsome like his football friend. There's just something different about him—something you can't really put your finger on but know it's there. If we'd met under different circumstances, perhaps I'd have met a completely different version of him that I might have been immediately smitten with.

He cants his head to the side and eyes me warily. "What?"

Heat floods my cheeks. "Nothing."

"You're staring." He scoffs. "You didn't break me, Golden. Try harder next time."

Again with the Golden.

It's said with such disdain, I know it's meant as an insult. But, to me, Golden means beautiful and shiny and valuable.

"I wasn't trying to break you and you know it," I grumble. "I said I was sorry."

"I caught all kinds of grief Monday for almost hitting you, yet today, you want to be forgiven after actually hitting me. You're a piece of work."

Thankfully, Mr. Pederson greeting the class cuts our argument off. Arguing with Two feels like an unending circle that'll just keep making me spin around and around until I'm dizzy.

"Your semester project has multiple pieces. Because of the intricacies involved, I've taken it upon myself to assign each group a location." Mr. Pederson holds up a hand when a couple of people groan in protest. "These sites are vetted by myself and have the proper approval in place. Once assigned, there will be no swapping or trading or proposing a different location. Understood?"

I nod, eager to learn more about our project, which earns me an appreciative smile from our professor.

"You'll be researching the history of your site and proposing a plan for its preservation, restoration, or repurposing. This is one facet of your project." Mr. Pederson starts passing out a grading rubric for the project. "The other side of this project will be the public presentation. You'll not only be proposing this plan to the real site owners, but also in front of the Chamber of Commerce and PMU's dean, Dr. Skeller. This will give you practical application of what you learn in this course and prepare you for delivering these proposals in the future should you continue down this career path."

I skim over the grading rubric, slightly overwhelmed by the daunting scope of the project. I also vaguely remember meeting Dr. Skeller this summer on my tour of PMU. When I peek at Two, he doesn't even look at his paper. He's no longer rubbing his shoulder, which makes me feel a little better.

"This project," Mr. Pederson continues once he's back in front of the classroom, "needs to not just have the plan for preservation, but a solid professional presentation that includes relevant ideas for social media to reach a broader audience, a financial budget including possible grant opportunities, and a public engagement aspect that outlines any potential negative blowback from the community with ideas to circumvent that. Any questions thus far?"

No one says a word, clearly as intimidated by the project as I am.

"Okay, now for the assignment of locations. You won't be given class time this week to visit your locations, so you'll need to get with your partners at some point before Monday to do that. I'll expect you to turn in pictures and a summary of your location meeting by the next week."

The thought of going somewhere alone with Two is nauseating. Maybe it's not too late to try and convince Mr. Pederson to swap me out with another student.

But that means letting Two win.

He shouldn't get to throw a tantrum and get what he wants.

Mr. Pederson starts passing out the site assignments. When he sets our paper down, Two snatches it up with lightning speed to read what we got. I lean toward him, trying to catch a glimpse of the paper.

"Hemingford Hall," Two grunts in disappointment. "I wanted Cedarwood Mansion."

This dude really has a hard-on for that place.

"What's Hemingford Hall?"

Two snaps his head to look over at me. His gray eyes sparkle as he studies me. "How do you not know this?"

His attempt to make me feel inferior doesn't work this time. "Not everyone is a nerd like you," I hiss. "Tell me about it."

He presses his lips together. I wonder if he'll refuse just to be a dick. In the end, he releases a sigh and launches into an explanation. "Hemingford Hall was built in the early 1900s. Best friends and business partners, Alexander Heming and Edgar Ford, built an establishment for the elite. They held grand parties for the wealthy, famous celebrities, and even a few well-known politicians who eventually went on to become presidents."

"Where is it?" I ask after jotting down a few notes.

"It overlooks Park Mountain Lake on the north end. It's not open to the public anymore. A couple, Gregory and Paula Nordstrom, purchased the property with the intent on restoring the building back in the late nineties but have yet to do anything with it."

Mr. Pederson clears his throat. "I'll allow the next twenty minutes for you all to discuss and look up information about your sites on your phones, but then I'm going to lecture for the rest of the period. Use your time wisely, please."

When I start to pull out my phone, Two grunts and kicks the leg of my chair with his shoe, jolting me and nearly having me drop it.

"You won't find much there," Two reveals, crossing his arms over his chest. "Fortunately for you, it's one of the places I've researched for fun."

For fun?

Someone needs to redefine his idea of fun.

"Okay," I say with a huff. "Then tell me more about this place."

Two smirks as though he enjoys holding all the power. I'll do my own research later, but I may as well get all I can from him now.

"It's been rumored that Heming and Ford used to hide artifacts within the building. While at parties, they'd give each other clues to try and find them. If they weren't found by the end of the party, they were 'gifted' to the building. Their party trick would involve their friends and partygoers. Everyone would hunt for these hidden treasures."

"The place has treasure hidden?" I ask, brows lifting. "Valuable items?"

Two grins, eyes flashing wickedly. "That's the thing. Every single artifact was silly and worth nothing. Once, Ford hid a note that said Heming was a vampire. Heming did find that one and proudly hung it in his office until his death."

"It sounds like they had a lot of fun."

"My dad thinks they were gay, but because it wasn't something people at that time revealed about themselves, they kept it hidden away like their many shared treasures. It would explain why neither man ever married."

My heart patters in my chest. Thinking about these two playful friends, and potential lovers, from another lifetime feels like one of the historical romance novels Mom likes to read.

"Did you learn about this stuff from your dad?" I ask, unable to keep my sappy smile from tugging at my lips. "Maybe we could interview him as part of our research and—"

"No," Two snaps, eyes burning hot with anger. "You do not get to meet my family, Golden. Ever."

Hurt pokes holes in my chest. Once more, this mercurial man finds a way to stab at me for reasons unknown to me.

"Why not?" I ask, scowling at him.

Two opens his mouth to speak, but then Mr. Pederson interrupts to begin his lecture. I studiously take notes, attempting to not get distracted by Two's surliness. When class is over, I wait for more explanation, but Two bolts before I get a chance to ask him to answer my question.

There's a reason and I'll figure it out.

We're going to have to work together. If that means airing the dirty laundry, then so be it. Once I find out what his problem is with me and my family, hopefully, I can fix it so we can move on.

It's just a small hurdle, not a roadblock.

We'll get past this and maybe just maybe this class with Two won't be so freaking miserable for me.

CHAPTER EIGHT

Two

SHE WANTS TO INTERVIEW MY DADS.

Is she insane?

As soon as class was over, I had to get the hell away from that maddening girl. It's already dangerous enough having to interact with her in class, having been forced to pair up with her.

But to bring her home?

To the same house she almost got instead of me?

Fuck no.

I'm low-key looking forward to talking to Tate today. Not that I'm anywhere near confessing this shit to him, but it'll be nice to distract myself.

When I arrive, I'm somehow not surprised that his Jeep isn't there. Within seconds, though, he whips into the spot beside my car. I climb out and make my way over to the driver's side to assist.

"Oh, hey," Tate says, thrusting two to-go coffee mugs my way. "Can you carry these?"

Chuckling, I take them from him and wait by the doors going into the building. Once he's grabbed his bag and keys, he rushes over to me to open the door. I follow after him, hardly noticing the intense smell of paint because the scent of heavenly butterscotch billows from the small opening on one of the lids.

"Grab a seat," Tate instructs. "And for the love of God, get some heat going in here."

I find my usual seat—the thought oddly comforting—and set our cups down to fiddle with the fireplace. Once heat is blazing, I hand him his cup and bring my own to my nose so I can inhale it.

"I hope you love it," Tate says, watching me eagerly. "Making people love coffee is kind of my thing. My future brother-in-law was totally against coffee, but I converted him." He beams at me. "Go on. If this one isn't right for you, I'll find an even better one."

I blow into the hole and then take a tentative sip. Delicious, rich butterscotch and smooth coffee dance along my taste buds. Like Tate did the day we met, I can't help but do a little appreciative wiggle because it's that good.

"I knew it!" Tate cheers, offering me a hand to slap. "I'm really good at this."

I give him a high five and take another sip. This shit is amazing.

"Now that the important part is out of the way," he says, grinning at me, "tell me how your week's going."

"I got hit by a car in the school parking lot."

His eyes widen. "What? Is the Rover okay?"

"The Rover is fine," I say with a grumble. "My shoulder...not so much."

"Wait? Someone hit you with their car? How are you here and not at the hospital?"

"It was just a bump. Knocked me on my ass, though."

Concern etches over his features. "You should have

gotten it looked at. What if you injured yourself internally or something?"

"I really am fine."

Tate's eyes narrow. "Are you, though? That must have been terrifying. Even if you just got bruised or scraped up. Getting hit by a car isn't a small thing."

"It was just a dumb girl not paying attention."

"The same girl who called your car a hunk of junk?" he asks, head tilting to the side.

I blink at him in shock. He said he was good at reading people and pressing issues, but damn. Am I really that transparent?

"Yeah. How'd you know that?"

"You got the same exact tortured expression as you did on Monday when mentioning her."

I do?

Blinking several times, I wonder what else is clearly written on my face. Knowing my thoughts are visible on the outside has my heart hammering inside my chest. The last thing I need is anyone seeing inside my mind. It's a clusterfuck of pain and disappointment.

"And now you're afraid," Tate says gently. "You don't have to be. I'm here for you. This is a safe space to confide in."

Absently, I take another butterscotch-flavored sip of my coffee, wondering what's actually safe to say and what isn't.

"This girl. What's her name?"

"Golden."

He laughs. "Strange name and most likely fake, but I'll bite. What is it about Golden that you don't like?"

Tension coils around me, making me stiffen. "She's just a spoiled brat."

He nods, pursing his lips together, waiting for me to continue. Rather than spilling my guts, I bite on my bottom lip, refusing to say more. Finally, he gets the message and exhales.

"From what I know of Golden so far, which isn't much, she doesn't appear to be a spoiled brat. Could she have been teasing you about the hunk of junk comment? I'm sure her hitting you today was an accident. If it wasn't, I can refer you to a police officer who you can make a report to."

A laugh barks out of me. "She didn't do it on purpose."

"That's relieving," he says gently. "There's more to this story. Why don't you like this girl, Two?"

Let me count thy ways, Therapist Tate.

"She's my partner in class," I grunt out, avoiding the real reason. "She thinks she's perfect and snaps at me a lot. Now we're stuck for an entire semester having to do work together. It's stupid."

Tate nods as though he agrees, which makes me feel marginally better. "Working with someone you don't like has to be uncomfortable. Have you spoken with your professor to see if you could switch?"

"Pederson already made it known that we're not able to switch. The only way out of this partnership is if she drops."

"Why don't you drop?"

"Because that class is something I'm passionate about. It's an elective for her. She can literally take anything else and I'm sure we'd both be happier."

Tate takes another sip of his coffee, thinking in silence. Then he lifts a brow. "Do you want my honest opinion?"

"No."

His laughter is light and airy. "Too bad. I think you're being a bit hard on her. You barely know her. Perhaps if you took the time to learn more about her, your feelings of dislike wouldn't be so intense. It would certainly help make the rest of the semester go by more easily."

"It's not that easy…"

He leans forward as if he can draw the real reason out of me. "Why not?"

"Because." I take another blissful sip of my coffee.

"I didn't like my fiancé at first," he reveals. "He slammed the door in my face and fired me. It was humiliating."

"Sounds like a real dick."

"Totally a dick that day," he admits with a grin. "But I persevered. Behind his snappy, rude behavior, someone vulnerable hid deep inside him. That person behind the outward mask of his was enigmatic. I kept feeling drawn to learn more."

"Trust me. I don't want to know any more about Golden. What I know is already too much."

He nods, giving me a sad smile. "What if you're wrong? What if what you think you know is only the surface but there's more hiding beneath?"

Digging deep into Gemma Park feels like an exploration mission on Mars—dangerous and terrible and something that would suck the life out of me. Hard pass.

"My man was an asshole," Tate continues, "until I saw that he wasn't. He wasn't at all what he'd presented himself to be. Once I saw a tiny glimmer of someone else inside of him, I liked that person. A lot. What started out as hate morphed into love. Serendipity."

There's that word again.

"Sounds more like stupidity if you fell for your enemy."

Tate snorts with laughter, nearly dropping his coffee in

the process. "Oh, you'd really like Jude. A couple of grumpy peas in a pod."

"He probably wouldn't like me. Most people don't."

His amusement dies and the concern is back. "Why would you say that?"

"People don't get me. I'm too…weird."

"Weird? Explain."

"My hobbies, my clothes, my mood swings. People don't understand why I tend to get self-absorbed, hyper-focused on my projects, or just completely withdraw when I'm feeling overwhelmed, unloved, and misunderstood."

Tate nods like this isn't one of life's mysteries but something he understands. It gives me hope that someone in this world might get me.

"Two, have you heard of the Enneagram?"

"The what?"

He chuckles. "The Enneagram. It's a personality test. I'm pretty sure I know which one you are, but I think it would be helpful to see if you come to the same conclusion. You could also study all nine personality types. It might help you put family and friends into their categories, which would help you understand how to interact with them better. You might even start with Golden. See where she fits on the wheel. Then you can learn why you two seem to have friction."

"Sounds like another dreadful assignment."

"Oh, stop, drama king. It's not dreadful. It's fun."

"Says the therapist."

He rolls his eyes, looking far younger than his twenty-eight years. "Do it. For me. You owe me since I bought you coffee."

"Isn't that like an abuse of power or something?"

"Maybe if you're a normal therapist. We've established I'm not."

He sets his coffee down to go fetch his laptop. "It's actually enlightening, Two. Learning about what makes others tick is fascinating. Humans are all so different, but oddly enough, we all fall into these nine categories." Once he locates the site to take the test, he hands his laptop over to me. "Take the test. Once we find out what you are, I'll give you resources to first learn about yourself. Sound good? Now hold down the fort while I run to the restroom."

Since I'm being forced to, I oblige him and take the test. He comes back ten minutes later but sits quietly at his desk in the corner. Once I'm finished, I add my email to get the results.

"Done."

"Good. Check your email."

I set down the laptop to fish out my phone. Once I locate the email, I open it.

"The Individualist," I say, shrugging my shoulders. "Whatever that means."

Tate's grin is huge as he sits back down beside me. "Congratulations, Two, you're a Four." He hands me a stapled packet of papers that says Type Four at the top. "I knew it. Guessing people's Enneagram types is a gift of mine."

I take the papers from him and skim over the first page. Sensitive, withdrawn, dramatic, temperamental. "Nice. I'm an utter joy to be around."

"Absolutely." He beams at me. "You'll learn all about your strengths and weaknesses and how to interact with others. I think you'll really enjoy this once you dig in. Ready for homework?"

"For fuck's sake. A full load of college courses isn't enough?"

"Nope. You can handle more, Two."

"What then?"

"I want you to try to identify Golden, your dads, or anyone else close to you. You can even try to identify me. Sound easy enough?"

"When?"

"Friday. I'll bring coffee again. Want to try something new?"

"Nope. Get me the butterscotch truth serum."

He cackles with laughter. "I paid extra for a shot of that. Glad to see it worked."

"For the record," I grumble, "I don't like this."

"No one ever likes working on themselves," Tate reveals. "It's hard and uncomfortable. We learn things about ourselves that might be shameful to us or silly. However, when you put the work in, you grow."

"Is that a nice way of saying, 'Grow up, Two,'?"

"Again with the dramatics." He winks at me. "It means, let me help you flourish. You're closed up tight, wrapped up around yourself. We're going to peel back your layers so we can see all the intricate and beautiful parts that make you you."

"You worm your way in with people, don't you? Is that what happened with your fiancé?"

He nods, eyes twinkling. "And once I've chomped my way through, there's no getting me out."

His teasing words are comforting. Not many people, besides my dads and Dax, have stuck around for the long haul, continuing to put up with my eccentric shit.

"What if I stopped paying you?" I ask, testing him. "What then?"

He rolls his eyes. "Nice try. I'd help you for free. Now scoot along. I'm about to meet with my bestie at the craft store so we can pick out wedding favors. You're totally invited to the wedding since we're friends now."

We're friends now.

Just when I thought I could barely handle the only friend I have, I'm pleased at the prospect of having another.

CHAPTER NINE

H E'S BEEN A DICK TO ME BOTH TIMES I'VE SPOKEN TO him and then he randomly sends me some stupid personality test to take like we're besties?

Me: Ummm. I'm not doing this.

Tristan: It's the least you can do to repay me for my pain and suffering.

Me: Are you always so dramatic?

Tristan: According to this test, yes.

That piques my interest. If the test says he's dramatic, then maybe I need to see what I am for having to put up with him.

Me: Fine. I'm thinking about going to Hemingford Hall. Did you want to go with me?

Tristan: No. You won't get in. They allow private tours if you email them, but you won't get in on such short notice.

I refrain from sending him the eye roll emoji. He thinks he knows everything and it's super annoying. I'm a Park. Surely they'll let me have a look. It'll be nice to get started on the project rather than relying on Two for all my information.

Why does everyone get to call him Two, but I have to refer to him by his real name? God, he's so freaking weird. Feeling rebellious, I change his name on my contacts just because I can. Asshole.

Before I take a trip to Hemingford Hall, I pop over to check my socials. Rocks of apprehension sit heavily in my stomach as I brace myself for anything weird.

Another message.

The sender keeps changing the numbers at the end and creating new profiles. I don't know how they're getting past the bots that block this sort of thing. I'm definitely going to have to have Jude look into it if they keep it up.

You look sad lately. Overwhelmed. Maybe you need someone to hold you and promise it'll all be okay.

A shiver runs down my spine.

Yeah, this is definitely getting creepy. I want to reply back and tell the stalker to fuck off, but then I worry about it being a troll trying to entrap me. The trolls love pushing people until they break and lose their shit. I'm not going to give this person the satisfaction of a response.

Block and delete.

Before I can run off, I end up signing off on two different paid sponsorship contracts for a couple thousand each that'll be due by the end of the month. I mark it on my calendar and then finally close out my phone, eager to do something with all this pent-up energy.

Two: Well???

I huff at his impatience.

Me: I'll take the test in a minute if it means you'll leave me the hell alone.

Two: K.

Stupid, infuriating man.

I pull up the link to the test and then quickly fly through all the questions. Once it emails me the results, I pop it open and read my personality type.

Type Three.

The Achiever.

Me: I'm a 3. Happy?

Two: I'm a 4. No.

Ugh.

I put my phone on Do Not Disturb and shove it into my Michael Kors handbag. My nail scrapes along the zipper and chips the paint on one corner. For a moment, I wonder if I should take the time to fix it but then decide checking out Hemingford Hall, while it's still daylight, takes precedence.

"Gem, honey," Mom says from my bedroom doorway. "Everything okay? I was changing the sheets in Dempsey's room and heard you huffing."

I still don't know if it's sweet or creepy that she keeps his room exactly as he left it. He moved out and is engaged to her best friend. Not sure why we can't turn his room into a theater room or something fun.

"It's just my partner for one of my projects. Frustrating."

Mom smiles. "I'm sure you'll figure out a way through it. You always do." Her eyes dart to my purse. "Going somewhere?"

"Hemingford Hall. That's the project site. I'm going to see if they'll give me a tour."

"You're not going alone, though, right?"

I force a smile, lying through my teeth. "Of course not. My partner is meeting me up there. I'll be fine, Mom."

"I know you will," she says, eyebrows knitting. "Keep your phone on, though, so I know where you're at. You know how we worry."

Worry is an understatement.

My parents think every time I leave the house I'll be accosted and trafficked. While I know they do it because they care, I can't help but wish they'd give me some credit to navigate the world just as my brothers do.

I give Mom a quick hug and then hurry out the door before she can ask any more questions. Dad isn't around, which is a good thing. He's better at sniffing out lies.

Once I'm in my car and cruising on the main road, I sigh in relief, feeling as though I just escaped prison. It's not really a prison. I'm just being a brat. My parents go over and beyond when it comes to providing for us, but it doesn't make it any less suffocating.

Blasting my favorite playlist, I make a pit stop at the coffee shop and then follow my navigation to the address I'd found for Hemingford Hall.

The lake where the building is located sparkles in the afternoon sun. Despite being January, it looks deceptively warm out. I sip my warm coffee and attempt to release the tension in my shoulders. By the time I reach Hemingford Hall, I'm feeling more like myself.

"Wow," I mutter, looking through the windshield at the ancient, dilapidated property.

It's huge, bigger than all the houses on our property combined, but looks as though it might get blown over the next time the wind rushes down the mountain. The location, though, is gorgeous. It's a shame the owners haven't done anything with the place.

I pull up next to an old truck and turn off my car. I'm feeling both inspired and overwhelmed as I take in the state of Hemingford Hall. Me and Two really have our work cut out for us.

Were the two best friends who built this place secret lovers? Ever since Two mentioned it, I keep wondering, eager to learn more about them.

I eventually climb out of the vehicle and make my way up to the massive mahogany door with inlaid stained glass. So beautiful. I bet this place was quite a stunner back in the day.

After knocking, I attempt to peek inside through the colored glass but can't make out anything more than a few dark shapes.

"Hello?" I call out. "Anyone here?"

Nothing.

Well, Two did warn me I'd need an appointment.

I hate that he's right.

It won't hurt to take a quick look around, though, right? I start past the vehicles and begin peeking in windows. In some windows, the shades are drawn, but others reveal dusty rooms with sheet-covered furniture. Nothing too exciting or revealing. When I reach one end of the building, I turn the corner and walk along the shaded area. The wind whips along the side, biting into me through my stylish, but not exactly warm, leather jacket.

I should go home.

Another window reveals an office with ancient-looking books on shelves. I wonder if this was Alexander Heming's office? Maybe it was Edgar Ford's? Nothing from my vantage point discloses anything, so I keep making my way along the side until I reach the back of the building.

An older man with salt-and-pepper hair is chopping wood near a stump, his flannel-covered back to me.

I'm about to turn around and hurry back the way I came, but I'm busted when he looks over his shoulder, locking eyes with me.

"Oh, hi," I squeak out, waving at him. "Are you the owner of this place?"

The man frowns at me, holding the ax at his side. I'm assaulted with images of that movie Dempsey made me watch when we were younger where Ryan Reynolds chased after his family with an ax just like that one. I had nightmares for a week.

"Sorry," I say, taking a step back. "I can go."

"Come here, girl. Speak up. I can't hear a damn thing you're saying."

He's no more than thirty feet away. Why can't he hear me? Slowly, I approach him, nerves zinging through me. Maybe it's just a ploy to chop me up and I'm falling for it.

"Hi, uh, I'm Gemma Park. I'm a student over at PMU."

The man's eyes narrow. "What do you want?"

"I'm doing a project on this property. Mr. Pederson said—"

"I don't know a Mr. Pederson," the man says, cutting me off.

"Well, uh, he said that this project was cleared by the owners. I'm sorry," I say, taking a step back. "I can leave."

The man huffs and tosses the ax to the ground. Thank God. "I just don't know anything that goes on around here," he mutters. "My wife gets us into some shenanigans we have no business being in." He gestures at the building. "Hence this shithole."

"Oh." I give him a shaky smile. "I can come back another time."

"She'll be back here in just a few if you want to wait." The man skims his gaze over my body before stopping at my face. "You're freezing out here. We could wait inside together. I could give you a tour."

I'm not easily scared by things, but I'm certain it's never a good idea to go into a creepy building with a strange man alone. That might get me killed. Then Dad would raise me from the dead just to kill me all over again for being stupid.

Parks are not stupid.

"I appreciate that, but I have to get home now." I give him an awkward wave. "Thank you for your time!"

He scowls at me, but I don't wait around for a response. I power walk back the way I came, trying not to break out into a run. The man probably thinks I'm insane. When I round the corner to the front of the house, I see a black sedan speeding away.

Was that his wife?

I should have flagged her down and talked my way into a tour. These people are probably super nice. I'm just paranoid because of Dad, who thinks the world is out to get me.

With a heavy sigh, I head back to my vehicle. The hair on my arms stands on end when I see the door sitting open.

I closed it.

But I didn't lock it.

I'd just shoved the keys into my jacket pocket, all too eager to get a closer look at this place. What if that person stole my new purse?

I rush over to the vehicle, my eyes darting over to my purse, which sits exactly in the same place. Relief floods over me until I see a cut, yellow buttercup-looking flower sitting in the cup holder. Beside it is an envelope.

After looking into the back to make sure nobody is hiding, I settle into my seat, close the door, and lock it. I turn the engine over to get heat pouring out of the vents. I'm tempted to sip my coffee, but what if the person who left this stuff for me poisoned it?

Quickly, I roll down the window and dump out the contents of my cup. Once I'm safe inside again, I pick up the envelope and tear it open.

You can block me all you want on social media, but it's not so easy to block me in reality.

- The One Who Admires You the Most

Nausea roils in my gut, souring the coffee I did manage to consume.

This creepy stalker isn't some strange person in their mom's basement halfway across the world.

No, this person is here.

They know what I drive, who I am, and know exactly how to find me.

This just went from annoying to terrifying.

CHAPTER TEN

Two

Golden: I got us an appointment for this afternoon at 4. Do you mind picking me up?

I continue to stare at the text even after she sends her address.

Golden: Please.

Me: You have a car. Remember? You hit me with it.

Golden: Fine, I'll pick you up then. Where do you live?

In a house with two men who were almost your daddies…

Me: I'll drive.

I glance at my watch and am annoyed to see I'll need to go now. I'm knee-deep in wallpapering the foyer of Cedarwood Mansion, which will be a bitch to try and pick up where I left off, but Hemingford Hall is more of a priority at the moment. With a huff, I close everything up and turn off my space heater. This project will have to wait for another day.

Rather than dealing with questions from my dads, I avoid the house altogether and head straight for my car. Once inside, I have to try the engine four times before it turns over.

"Good girl," I say, patting the cracked leather on the dash. "You purr like a kitten."

The heater doesn't work great in my car, but I don't need it. My military jacket keeps me warm. As I drive, my thoughts drift back to yesterday when Gemma told me she was a Type Three.

I did a deep dive last night, digging into everything that went into a Type Three Enneagram personality. Basically, they're obsessed with success, accomplishments, and their self-image. From what I know of Gemma, it seems spot-on.

I'll see Tate again tomorrow between classes. This time, I'm going to get his cell number. I have tons of questions about this shit that I think he can answer.

My phone GPS barks at me and I turn down the road that leads to Gemma's house. It's the biggest and fanciest one on the street. Her black weapon of a Tahoe sits in the driveway. My shoulder now sports a big-ass bruise thanks to her.

Rather than going up to the door, I lay on the horn. Seconds later, she rushes out of the house, glaring at me.

I don't acknowledge her irritation, choosing to fiddle with the radio instead. There's a local station that plays rock from the fifties that I really like. Settling on that station, I wait for Gemma to climb in.

The door squeaks in protest when she opens it. Some trash I forgot to take out gets whipped out and tossed into her yard. Whoops. They're paper napkins. Biodegradable. The earth will be fine.

"Drive," Gemma huffs, slamming the door once she's inside. "Otherwise, Dad will come out here and give you the third degree."

I'm not about to talk to her parents, so I put the Rover in reverse and cruise back down her road to the main one.

"Your car is a mess," she says, shoving one of my filthy boots out of the way with her pristine black one. "How can you deal with this?"

"It's not that messy."

"Two, you littered my yard when I opened my door. It's a dumpster."

"Tristan."

"Here we go." She sighs heavily. "I'd rather not go into all this with you today. Can we call some sort of truce? I had a bad day yesterday and I'm on edge."

This intrigues me. "Why? Because of me?"

She smirks at me. "You wish."

Kind of. It's satisfying to know I get under her skin as much as she gets under mine.

"I went to Hemingford Hall by myself," she says softly, looking out her window. "The guy was weird. Made me feel uncomfortable."

At least I know why she wanted to go together this time.

"Most people aren't happy when you show up unannounced at their place of residence."

"I know." She glances back over at me. "That wasn't even the bad part."

I wait for her to elaborate. "Just spit it out already, woman."

"Someone followed me there. They left me a flower and a note."

"I'm sure it was your boyfriend."

"Boyfriend?" She shakes her head. "I do not have a boyfriend."

"You just grope dudes in parking lots for fun then?"

"What are you—oh. That was my twin brother, you idiot. Gross."

Twin brother.

Would he have been living in my room too had Jamie not changed her mind?

"Looked intimate."

"It wasn't," she grumbles. "It's a stalker."

I snort out a laugh. "Golden has a stalker?"

"This isn't funny. It was scary."

"Well, next time you'll listen to me. I told you not to go there."

She crosses her arms over her chest, clearly fuming at my words, and refuses to say another word. Shrugging, I turn up the music a bit and enjoy the beat of the next couple of songs on our drive. By the time we turn off on the road that takes us to Hemingford Hall, she's relaxed again and eagerly taking in the sight of the stately building perched on the side of the lake.

An old truck and a maroon minivan are parked out front. I park beside the minivan and shut off my car. Gemma doesn't immediately get out, instead glancing over at me beneath her thick lashes.

"Will you stay close?"

It's on the tip of my tongue to tell her no because riding in the car was close enough for me, but real trepidation shines in her eyes. She may be my nemesis, but I won't let some random guy make her feel uncomfortable. That's *my* job.

"Yeah, Golden, I got you."

She grins at me, a megawatt smile that nearly blinds me. It's unfortunate she's so fucking pretty. My dick twitches in agreement. That line of thinking needs to go out the damn window because I will *not* get distracted by her glossy perfection.

I climb out of the vehicle to avoid her disarming smile. An older woman with her blond hair in a messy ponytail greets us from the porch.

"You two must be the PMU students," the woman says, beaming. "You'll have to excuse my grouchy husband. Gregory prides himself on scaring everyone away. I'm Paula Nordstrom."

"Gemma Park and Tristan Sheridan," Gemma says for both of us. "Thank you for letting us come over on such short notice. We're both eager to get started on our project."

Paula's eyes twinkle. "I remember being just as excited as you two when me and Gregory purchased this place. Somewhere along the way, we got overwhelmed. Mr. Pederson assured me his students are really good at what they do. Perhaps, after this project, we'll have a plan of action we can finally take."

"We'll do our best," Gemma vows, turning her charm up to what feels like an obnoxious level to me. "We may have to come over multiple times as Mr. Pederson may or may not have mentioned. We promise not to intrude. Just tell us where we're not allowed to go and we'll respect that."

"You're welcome anywhere, darlin'," Paula says, gesturing for us to follow her. "Gregory may give you a little grief, but you just have to ignore him. That's what I do."

Gemma shoots me a quick look and it's the uneasiness in her gaze that once again has me feeling stupidly protective over her. This Gregory dude can fuck off as far as I'm concerned.

"I'd give you the grand tour, but I have a feeling you'll do a lot better if you explore on your own." She points toward an open doorway. "I'll be in the main sitting room with Gregory at the end of this hallway. This place is too big to heat, so we tend to stay in the front of the building as much as we can. Just holler if you need anything."

I give her a nod and the two of us wait until she disappears down the hallway and into the main room. I'm itching to start going into each room one by one, but Gemma stops me when she grabs onto my wrist.

"When I was here yesterday, I think I saw an office. It could have belonged to Heming or Ford. Seems like a fun place to start." She smiles at me and then starts tugging me behind her. "This place is freaking amazing, right?"

I stiffen but don't pull my arm away from her, allowing her to lead the way. Her hand projects warmth through my jacket that radiates up my entire arm.

"I'm shocked you also find it amazing."

She snorts out a laugh. "I'm more than a pretty face, Two."

I don't chide her for calling me Two. Her face is indeed pretty, but the more than part is yet to be discovered. I'm not exactly eager to go on a Gemma Park exploration mission, digging for hidden treasures beneath her shiny surface. But I do love this class and I definitely love this place already.

"I'll accept the truce," I say with a grunt. "While we work on our project, I mean."

She gives my wrist a squeeze. "Thank you. This is going to go a lot smoother without you hating me with everything in you."

Though she's probably right. I still have my guard up. I'm not going to allow her to burrow her way under my skin, making me forget everything about my past that haunts me and the fact she's basically responsible.

Technically, her mom is, but still.

Jamie's name wasn't on that wall. Neither was her twin, Dempsey.

No, it was Gemma.

Just Gemma.

"Here," she exclaims, voice pitched with excitement. "Wow. Look at this place."

I follow her into the office. She finally releases her hold on me. We both take in the ancient room in awe. It's covered from floor to ceiling in dust, wallpaper has peeled off the walls in some areas, and a few bookshelves have shelves that have completely collapsed. This place is a mess—a wonderful, beautiful mess.

"Do you think there are artifacts hidden in here?" Gemma asks, practically giddy as she bounces on her heels. "What if we find love notes? How freaking romantic would that be?"

Listening to her babble reminds me of Dad. Whenever he's passionate about one of his interior restorations, he can't contain his excitement. He also bosses Pops around and tells him what sort of hard shit that needs doing. Pops always does it with a gentle smile on his face.

"The artifacts they hid were silly things like jars of random stuff. Edgar once collected hundreds of dead moths, put them in a jar, and then hid them someplace in Hemingford Hall for Alexander to find."

"That's so sweet," Gemma says, grinning. "Right? You know they were in love."

Again, she reminds me of Dad, finding romance in

everything. My gut twists at the thought of her being more like him than me. Fate, in an epic plot twist, gave him me instead.

"Perhaps," I say, "or maybe they just liked to terrorize one another."

"My nephew, Spencer, is always pestering his woman," she reveals, "and he's wildly in love with her. Maybe they can be friends and lovers. It's a thing, you know."

Actually, I don't.

My experience with lovers is one person, one time, and we didn't exactly stay friends after.

Dax sleeps with lots of his friends, but I think they all want to be longtime lovers after. He's never interested in more than a few nights of fun.

"Where do you think they hid their artifacts? Surely they weren't in difficult places like beneath the floorboards," she says as she closely inspects a bookshelf. "Their guests who would go on these hunts with them wouldn't like having to destroy the floor to find their prize. It had to have been obvious."

I nod, letting her giddiness bleed into me. "Like hidden in a false book?"

Her eyes widen comically and she starts checking the books on the shelves, gently tapping on their spines as she goes along. Since I'm much taller, I mimic her actions but go for the ones that are out of her reach. A few minutes in and I thump one that feels hollow.

"Bingo!"

She squeals and rushes over to me. "Hurry. Pull it down."

Definitely bossy like Dad.

I pluck the book from the shelf, coughing when a plume of dust flutters down on my face. Before I have a chance to open it, she takes it out of my hand and gently flips it open.

It's indeed a false book, but there aren't love notes inside. A tiny golden key sits in the bottom.

"What do you think this opens?" she asks, voice filled with awe. "This is so much fun!"

I can't help but grin at her. It *is* kind of fun. I've never known anyone besides my parents and Mr. Pederson who agrees with me.

"If I had to guess," I say, forgetting for a moment that I hate her, "it opens a secret compartment in that desk."

Her eyes glimmer as she beams. "We're going to find where it goes. Our project is totally going to be the best, right? How can it not be?"

"Hell yeah, it is."

For once, I actually agree with her.

CHAPTER ELEVEN

Gemma

W E'VE BEEN KICKED OUT.

Who knew exploring an old building could be so much fun? It was *so* much fun, in fact, that Two and I overstayed our welcome. It was nearly nine when Paula kindly asked us to go home.

"I think we should do a miniature replica," Two says as he attempts for a third time in a row to get his car to start. "It will help the client visualize the outcome during our proposal. Plus, I'm skilled at this. No one else in our class will come close."

"Like your Cedarwood model?"

"You remember me talking about that. Interesting." The engine finally sputters to life and he glances my way, his face dimly lit by the glow of his dash lights. "You think that's stupid or something?"

His voice is tight and defensive. When Two was in Hemingford Hall with me, he was a totally different person. Someone I enjoyed being around. Now he's back to his usual prickly self.

"No," I say with a sigh. "I wanted to see it. You shared your pictures with Mr. Pederson and sort of lit up when you spoke about it. I thought maybe—"

"You really want to see it?"

I smirk at him. "Yes. I want to see your model. There's no ulterior motive, Two."

"Fine. I'll take you to it."

My brows lift in surprise. "I get to see the real one? Not just a picture?"

"If we're going to be partners in this project, you need to see what I'm capable of." He glances my way as he backs out of the lot. "You can't go into the house, though. If you have to pee, hold it."

He's definitely a strange, cantankerous man, but I'm slowly learning not to let it rattle me. Two just says whatever is on his mind, not caring how people interpret it. Me, on the other hand, care too much about what people think.

"I'll hold my pee," I promise, making a show of crossing my heart. "I'm excited to see this thing."

He straightens at my words. As he drives, I can see the tease of a smile tugging at his lips. I know he wants to hate me, but he's having trouble right now. That makes me stupidly happy like I achieved something truly difficult.

While we ride through town to his house, I shoot Mom a quick text to let her know I'm still working on the project with my partner but we're moving locations.

My stomach growls when we pass by a fast-food joint. Two looks over at me and then checks his watch. The next restaurant we see, he pulls into the drive-through.

"I can eat later at home," I tell him. "We don't have to stop."

"We both missed dinner. It's fine. You have money, right?"

"As long as it's under ten dollars, then yes."

He whips his head my way. "All you have is ten dollars to your name? I saw your house. You're loaded."

"It's not about that. I just don't want to waste my money on food."

"Food is never a waste of money." He rolls his window down and looks at the lit-up menu board. "If you go over ten bucks, I'll cover you."

We tell the person on the speaker what we want and then I hand Two my crinkled-up ten-dollar bill. He shakes his head as though he can't believe all I have is ten dollars.

"Do your parents not give you an allowance? What about a job? Do rich girls even have to get jobs?"

"I have a job," I say dryly, swatting at his arm. "I'm not this girl you've painted me out to be. Honestly, I don't understand what you have against me."

He glances my way as he drives to the next window. "What is it?"

Just like when I talk about my job to my brothers, embarrassment washes over me. It's not like Two will understand it. He'll just give me a hard time about this too.

Luckily, I'm saved from answering as he pays for our food. Once he's passed my drink and our bags over to me, we're on the road again.

"Stripper?"

I almost choke on my sip of Pepsi. "W-What?"

He cackles with laughter, the sound pleasant enough I instantly forgive him. "You should see the look on your face. Do you have something against strippers?"

"No," I grumble. "Ugh. Why are you so difficult?"

"It's fun watching you squirm."

I roll my eyes and take another refreshing sip of my drink.

"If you absolutely must know, I'm a social media content creator. I have over a million followers."

"Be for real."

"I *am* being for real." I pull out my phone and access my main account to show him. "See. Million-plus."

He peeks over at my phone at the next stoplight. "They pay you to do what?"

"The followers don't pay me anything," I explain, trying not to bristle at his insinuation that it's for something sinister. "Because of my reach and my original content, I'm approached by many brands to help me advertise for them. If the brand's products align with my values and aesthetic, I entertain doing a collaboration with them. It has to be a good fit, though, and something I can easily incorporate into my usual content or I won't do it. Before we met up, I signed two contracts for two grand each."

Two gapes at me, not moving when the light turns green. Someone honks, zapping him out of his stupor. "Two thousand for what?"

"One is for a hair mask. They sent me some freebies to try. I absolutely loved how it made my hair feel. We've negotiated that I'll do an ad for their product on my page and I'll be compensated for it."

"Two grand for a hair mask." He shakes his head, voice filled with awe. "This is a legit thing? They're not scamming you? Or are you scamming them?"

I snigger. "I'm not scamming anyone. And yes, it's a legit thing. Welcome to the future, Two. So glad you could join us."

He scratches at his cheek with his middle finger, which makes me grin. Though he's still a complete asshole most of the time, I'm learning to navigate the treacherous depths of Two.

Our conversation is cut short when he pulls into a long driveway that takes us to an updated-looking farmhouse. I wish it were daylight so I could see it properly.

"My workshop is around back. We have to be quiet."

We get out of his car with our food and drinks, and I follow him into the darkness on the side of the house. The moon illuminates a decent-sized shed. He has me hold his drink while he fiddles with the door.

"Ignore the mess," Two says as he flicks on the light. "I do."

As soon as I can see inside the shed, I'm in awe. Shelves line the walls and are covered with various tools, boards and textiles, and stacks of old magazines. There are several work-tables, but one in particular seems to be the one that gets the most use as it's the cleanest and has a model in progress sitting on top. Two leans over the table and flips on a space heater before returning to take his drink back from me.

"This is Cedarwood Mansion," he says, motioning to the model. "I was in the middle of wallpapering when you texted."

I set my drink and our food bags down on a clear spot on the table so I can take a closer look at the replica. The high level of detail on such a small thing instantly captivates me.

"Holy shit," I murmur as I take it all in, "this is so cool."

"Ideally, I'd have liked to repurpose materials found in Cedarwood for the replica, but the owners wouldn't let me."

"Rude," I tease.

"That's what I thought." He picks up a thin piece of wood from the table. "Most of the material I use is leftover stuff from when my dads remodel places. They have a ton of stuff in their shop. Dad uses a lot for inspiration when he's coming up with design ideas."

The pride with which he speaks about his parents softens me toward him. I may complain about my family, but I love them dearly. They mean everything to me. It sounds as though he feels the same about his parents too. It makes me like him a little more.

"Do you think Paula will let us use stuff from Hemingford Hall for our replica?" I ask, turning to look at him.

He's crouched near me, also taking in the sight of the model, so our faces are close—so close I notice flecks of dark green in his chilly gray eyes.

"We're going to ask," he says with a crooked grin. "And if that doesn't work, we'll beg."

We both grin before turning to inspect the piece some more. He goes through each part, showing me tiny details like the brass doorknob on the front with the initials CM carved on top.

"The real Cedarwood Mansion has this," Two explains. "All of my replicas are as exact as they can be."

"I love this," I tell him, truly meaning it. "It's so impressive and well thought out. You should be proud."

He pulls back and refuses to meet my stare, shrugging. "Hungry?"

"Yup." I stifle a sigh of frustration. Just when I thought we were making progress, he pulls away again. "Do you make the furniture and stuff too?"

He drags another stool over for me to sit down at. After he's seated, we dig around in our bags, and once our burgers are out, he takes a huge bite of his, dropping shreds of lettuce all over his jeans. Messy, messy boy.

"I make everything," he says around a mouthful of food. "Even the stuff that goes in the cupboards."

I shove a napkin at him so he'll deal with the ketchup on his lip. "Really? You must have tiny tools, huh?"

He nods, snatching up one of the little tools with his free hand. "The hardest part is finding the right tools for jobs like this. I've collected a lot of these over the years."

"You should see my nail art arsenal." As soon as I blurt it out, I freeze. Everyone in my family knows I do my own nail art, but it's not something I tell my followers. They always ask where I go to get them done and I just tell them it's a secret. My nail art is my hobby that feels sacred and something I don't want to share with the world.

So why did I just tell Two about it?

"Nail art?" His eyebrow arches high.

"Yes," I tell him with a smirk as I grab my phone. "This isn't easy. It's intricate and takes a lot of time. You of all people should get that."

He takes my phone from my hand when I thrust it in his face and starts scrolling through the photo album. "You did all of these?"

"Yup."

"Interesting." He lifts his gaze for a moment, locking his intense eyes on mine. "What do your followers think of this?"

"They don't know about it," I mumble. "It's *my* thing."

"I share my thing with anyone who will listen to me about it," he challenges. "Why don't you show your zillion followers what you can do? It's actually pretty good."

"I don't know," I admit. "Because I'm not great at it. What if they think it's stupid? What if they start expecting me to share about nail art all the time? Worse, what if they hate it and yell at me to share more makeup and hair stuff?"

"You really do worry about what others think. Just like the Enneagram website says."

Oh great, we're back to this.

"I guess I do." I shrug my shoulders and sigh. "That's dumb, right?"

"You said it, not me." His grin is back. "Maybe I'll let you do something on the replica since you've clearly got skills."

I gape at him in mock surprise. "Ooh, I get to help on our project? You're so generous, Two."

He simply laughs, which makes my heart stutter a bit. Tonight feels like we've made progress. I actually had fun, too. Maybe this class won't be so bad after all.

CHAPTER TWELVE

Two

SHE MAKES IT DIFFICULT TO HATE HER.

Having her in my space last night and showing her Cedarwood was…nice. Even Dax doesn't have the patience to sit and listen to my ramblings. Gemma, to her credit, took everything in that I said and then asked questions that proved she was interested.

Of course the first girl to not think me and my hobbies were freakish would be my mortal enemy.

You're being dramatic again, Two.

I try to ignore the warring thoughts in my mind. On one hand, I want to ignore her and pretend she doesn't exist. Each night since I met her in the flesh, I've lain awake in bed, thinking about that picture with her name on the wall. It hurts being around her. Knowing her. Talking to her.

On the other hand, she's clever, quick-witted, and clearly talented. I like that she puts up with my bullshit and keeps squaring off with me, no matter how much of a dick I am. It means she's a worthy adversary. A challenge.

This morning, in class, we actually talked about our project and there was no animosity. Afterward, she even waved and said she'd call me later. My chest tightened and my dick perked.

Finding her attractive is my biggest problem right now.

I just can't go there with her.

"So sorry I'm late," Tate cries out as he hops out of his Jeep. "They were out of butterscotch flavoring. I was so upset that they allowed that to happen!"

"You got me something else?"

He nods as he hands me a coffee. "Not butterscotch, but it's buttered caramel. Probably as close as they could get. I took a sip and it's tasty. If you don't want it, I'll drink it too."

The man is already buzzing on caffeine. The last thing he needs is an extra helping. Nah, I'll take one for the team, even if it's nasty as fuck.

Luckily, I sip it and actually like it.

"It'll do, donkey."

Tate sniggers, clearly getting my Shrek reference, and leads the way to his office. Once inside, we do our thing— him setting all his crap down on his desk and me getting the fireplace going. Finally, a few minutes later, we sit down by the fire to chat and enjoy our coffees.

"Update on Golden," I say, not meeting his stare. "She's kind of cool."

Tate chuckles and leans forward, eyebrows lifted in a way that shows he's delighted about this revelation. "Do tell. I want the tea."

A smile tugs at my lips and I shrug, hoping I can make it go away. "We went to our project site. Spent a lot of time there. Got kicked out. I took her back to my place and—"

Tate gasps, covering his mouth. "You what? Tell me!"

"Not that," I say with a chuffed laugh. "We ate dinner and I showed her Cedarwood Mansion. She liked it."

"It sounds like you're taking the time to get to know her. I'm proud of you, Two."

"I don't know." I sip my coffee and stare at the fireplace, drifting back to last night. I'd stolen glances of her as she marveled over my model. She really is pretty. "She could just be fucking with me."

Tate's lips press together and he sets his coffee down. "Why would she be doing that? What would her motive be?"

"Make me feel stupid?"

"That's your insecurities talking," Tate says gently. "Could it be that she's really just a nice girl and you two got off on the wrong foot?"

"Maybe," I mutter grumpily.

"Why is it so difficult for you to like her? There's something I'm missing here."

Unease sours the coffee in my gut. "Call it intuition."

"That doesn't sound like intuition. It sounds like your mind is trying to self-sabotage this relationship for you." He reaches over and pats my knee. "What makes it so hard to let people in? You let me in and we're practically best buds now."

My lips curl into a grin. "Yeah, I guess we are."

"She could be another friend, you know. You just have to allow her to be. It doesn't have to be romantic. Having a good, solid, supportive friend is just as important as any romantic relationship. It fills a need your heart aches for. Denying yourself like this is cruel to *you*, Two."

"I just…" I bite my tongue. I seriously don't want to get into the whole ordeal with him. Maybe one day. "I'll try."

It sounds vaguely like a lie, but I do mean it.

If I can make nice with Gemma for this project, it'll make things go a lot smoother. When the semester is over, she'll be out of my life again, this time for good.

"I'm proud of you," Tate says. "You're in charge of your

own happiness. It's okay to ease into it little by little. I know you're capable of this."

Thankfully, I'm able to steer the conversation away from Gemma and back to the Enneagram. We spend the rest of our session discussing the different types. He gives me some more handouts and resources for me to read up on. I also get his phone number so I can text him whenever. Sure, Dad is paying him, but I can already tell Tate is someone I could be friends with even outside of our therapist/patient relationship.

"Have fun this weekend," Tate tells me when we're finished. "If you meet up with Golden again, I want to hear all about it."

I wave him off, ignoring the tightening in my chest.

I'm looking forward to seeing her again, maybe locked away in my shed with me. The fact that this is a stupid fantasy of mine makes me cringe.

A weekend off from Gemma is more than needed.

She's working her way under my skin.

The pool hall is busy as fuck tonight. Cars are jammed into every spot and it's only by pure luck that we snag a place in the damn lot when someone leaves. Dax is his usual chipper self, dressed to impress. If he's on the prowl for a hookup, it'll happen.

I, however, am not.

The last thing I want is to date or be with someone.

That shit sounds exhausting.

Dax hops out of my Rover and leads the way, giving a chin lift to a group of girls. I ignore them altogether, striding to catch up to my eager friend.

"Why are you in such a hurry?" I demand. "It's just pool."

"I want you to meet my friends from class," Dax says, bumping me with his shoulder. "I told you. Time for you to get out of your shell and meet some people."

"Can't it just be us?"

"It'll always be just us," Dax says with a boyish grin that reminds me of our childhood, "but we can also hang with other people too to spice things up."

I grunt at his response, following him into the pool hall. It reeks of beer. The clacking of balls, loud hum of chatter, and offensive country music on the jukebox all nearly have me turning on my heel to hightail it back to my car.

But then I see her.

Gemma fucking Park.

I recognize her long, sleek dark hair and the animated way she talks with another girl around her age. Her artsy nails—nails I now know she did herself—move wildly as she talks, clearly with both her hands and her mouth. The blonde next to her sees me staring and shoots me the bird.

It reminds me of middle school. Dax suddenly became one of the popular kids while I was still his weirdo best friend who went everywhere with him. While Dax didn't care, the other popular kids did. They always did shit like smart off to me or flip me off or fucking sneer when he wasn't looking.

And even though I act like that doesn't hurt, it does.

It always fucking does.

Gemma turns to see where the blonde is looking and when her eyes latch onto mine, she doesn't flip me off. No, her gaze brightens and she beams at me. The sting in my chest is immediately soothed. How Gemma of all people made that happen, I have no idea.

"Holy shit," Gemma says, bouncing over to me. "How weird for us to run into each other here!"

I'm stunned when she launches herself at me and hugs me. I remain stiff with my arms at my sides, but I do inhale the scent of her hair. I wonder if it's the hair mask. Definitely worth the two grand.

She pulls back and grins. "Me and Aubrey were holding a table for Dempsey and Spencer. You two should play with us until they get here."

Dax nudges me with his elbow and mutters under his breath, "Hang with your girl, man. I'll be right over there."

Before I can beg him not to leave me alone, he's gone. Gemma frowns after him and then grabs my wrist like she did at Hemingford Hall. Of course I can't help but go willingly. This weird magnetic hold she has on me is alarming. It makes me want to run the other way, but I can't.

"One of your followers?" Aubrey, the bitchy blonde, asks. "She's famous, but you already knew that."

"Don't be a brat," Gemma says, shooting her friend an exasperated look. "Two's my partner in school."

Aubrey softens and guilt twists her features. "Sorry. I'm just in a really bad mood. My baby, Rue, kept me up all night. Spencer said he'd bring me garlic knots from that pizza place I love so much, but he's late. Not only am I cranky from lack of sleep, but I'm hangry and about ready to start eating innocent victims if they look at me wrong."

Gemma stands beside me, putting an arm around my waist. "Don't eat my friend. We're going to have the best project and I need him."

She needs me.

My heart hammers in my chest.

Gemma releases me and I instantly dislike the feeling. She racks up some balls and then grabs a cue stick. I discreetly check out her ass in her skintight dark denim jeans as she bends over to take the first shot. Aubrey catches me staring and shakes her head, rolling her eyes.

I continue to watch Gemma land ball after ball in whatever pocket she's aiming for. I've played pool some with Dax, but I'm not a goddamn shark like she is. Finally, she misses, and from what I can tell, on purpose, and hands me the stick.

"Your turn."

I take it from her, noticing a tingling sensation where our fingers touch. Gemma watches me, grinning happily as I scratch the ball on my turn.

"Oh," Gemma cries out, clapping, "this is too good. Look, Two, I think I may be better at something than you!"

Her words are said in jest, but the usual insecurities creep back in. Golden versus second best. Story of my fucking life.

I want to abandon the game and her, but my feet remain rooted to the floor. Like a fly caught in her web, I watch helplessly as she takes more flawless shots. Again, she purposely misses before handing the stick to me.

"My brother is really good," Gemma explains as I contemplate my shot. "I really do have the upper hand here, but that's not your fault."

"Hmph."

The cue ball cracks into one of my stripes, barely landing in the corner pocket. Gemma walks over to where I plan to shoot my next ball, standing there with her hands on her hips. I can't help but dart my gaze up her front. A sliver of her stomach shows beneath her black sweater and a glimmer of a bellybutton ring catches the light.

Fuck, how I'd love to see it up close.

With that thought and my dick chubbing, I miss the cue ball completely, the end of the stick scraping across the green felt. Gemma and Aubrey both crack up laughing. Heat floods my cheeks as I attempt to shake away the embarrassment.

"Cheater," I grunt out, waving at Gemma to move. "That should earn me extra moves."

Thankfully, she moves out of the way and I retake the shot. I miss, naturally, and then Gemma cleans up the rest of the table with flawless shots. It's nearly impossible not to look at her. Hell, me and every other man with a working dick in here can't keep our eyes off her.

"Another game?" Gemma asks, smirking.

"Nah, losing is boring. Not interested."

Before I lose my will to walk away, I turn on my heel and stalk away from her to go find Dax. That was an asshole move, but I'm feeling way too out of my element here.

When I make the mistake of looking over my shoulder, I find Gemma in the same spot, staring after me, a pouty frown on her lips.

I ruined her good time.

Why the hell do I feel so damn guilty about it?

CHAPTER THIRTEEN

Gemma

Two: We have a date for Hemingford Hall. I'll pick you up in a few.

I rub the sleep out of my eyes as panic sets in. How long ago did he send this text? Thirteen minutes ago. Crap!

Flying out of bed, I manage to throw on jeans, a hoodie, and my sneakers before I get another text.

Two: I'm waiting, but not for long. I have donuts. On me since you're food poor.

Oh my God.

I don't have time to be annoyed. The last thing I want to do is drive myself to Hemingford Hall. I rush into the bathroom, brush my teeth and then my hair before pulling my long locks into a messy bun.

There's no time for makeup.

What if one of my followers sees me?

Panic starts to set in as I contemplate grabbing my makeup bag to put it on in the car, but then Two's blasting my phone again.

Two: Come on, Golden!

Two: Sixty seconds…fifty-nine…fifty-eight…

"Asshole," I hiss, storming out of the bathroom. I snatch

up my backpack and purse, nearly crashing into Mom as I exit my room.

"Whoa, sweetie," Mom says with a chuckle. "Where are you headed off to in such a hurry? Coffee date with Tate?"

"Uh, no, sorry. Off to work on my project with my partner."

She opens her mouth, ready to ask more questions, but I quickly kiss her cheek and rush down the stairs.

"Be careful! Let us meet this girl soon!"

Girl?

Oh crap. They'll probably freak once they learn I've been running around with a guy. I'll save that drama for another day.

Dad is in his office when I pass, but thankfully, he's on the phone. I blow him a kiss and then run out the front door in a frenzy.

And, as promised, Two is already halfway down the road.

He freaking left me!

"Hey!" I holler, chasing after his stupid junk mobile. "It hasn't been sixty seconds, asshole!"

He hits the brakes and waits for me to catch up. By the time I climb into his vehicle, I'm sweaty and pissed off.

"Rude!" I shriek, damn near on the verge of tears from frustration. "You can't do that to me!"

Emotion clogs my throat and I feel like I'm going to cry. Over a stupid boy! But it's not just him. It's everything. School, my family, work. I've just got a lot on my plate and I'm starting to feel overwhelmed. The last thing I need is Two adding more stress. My bottom lip wobbles and I bite on it.

"You like butterscotch coffee?" Two asks in greeting. "Hope so."

I stare at the coffee in the cupholder from my favorite

place. Rather than yelling at him more or crying, I pick the coffee up and sip it. It's sweet and delightful. "Thank you."

He gasses his car and we barrel down the road. "Sorry for being a dick last night. Is that why you're about to cry?"

Last night, he did hurt my feelings. However, it wasn't out of character for him. Dempsey and Spencer showed up right after he walked away, so it was a good distraction.

"I'm not about to cry," I grumble, though the tremor in my voice says otherwise.

"Liar."

Anger flares in my chest, chasing away the hysteria. I sip on my coffee and peek over at Two. Today he's dressed casually like me in a PMU hoodie and jeans. Except instead of a messy bun, he's wearing a worn ball cap to cover his chaotic hair.

"We're twins," I say with a snort. "Of course we are."

He bristles and ignores the statement. Whatever. I'll be able to handle his surly ass a lot better after coffee. By the time we make it to Hemingford Hall, my coffee has done its job and I've devoured two chocolate-glazed donuts.

Two doesn't say anything as he parks and shuts off the car. He grabs his coffee and backpack before striding away toward the front door. I follow after him, my short legs unable to keep up with him. He's already inside and gone by the time I reach the landing.

"He said he wants to look in the attic," Paula says in greeting. "Good morning. You guys are up early today."

"Just excited," I tell her and mean it. "Do you think we could have any scrap material we find for our miniature model?"

"Of course. Take whatever you want as long as it's nothing of value. I trust your judgment."

I thank her and then hurry to find Two. When I reach the second floor, I find him at the end of the hall, pulling down a ladder from the ceiling. He's dropped his belongings haphazardly in the middle of the floor. I take a moment to move his stuff to the wall and then add mine. By the time I finish, he's already disappeared into the attic.

With a sigh, I crawl up the rickety ladder and into the dark, musty space. I sure as hell hope nothing jumps out at me. If I see a mouse, I'll legit die.

I shudder just thinking about the time Dempsey found a dead mole in the yard and chased me around with it. He shoved it into my shirt. When I finally got it out from under my clothing and gathered the nerve to pick it up, I nailed him square in the nose with it. Made him bleed and everything. He deserved it one hundred percent.

Rodents are not my thing.

A dim light flickers on overhead and I see Two standing hunched over, his tall frame unable to be fully upright without hitting his head on the rafters. The space is littered with boxes, old furniture, and other treasures I'm eager to explore.

"Paula says we can take whatever we want for our project as long as it's nothing of value. I think we should run everything by her before we actually take it just in case."

He nods as he scans the boxes. "Where should we start, Golden?"

I dust off a velvet footstool and plop my ass on it. "Maybe catching our breath?"

His gray eyes lock on mine as he studies me. "Climbing a ladder winded you?"

"No, but frantically running since the moment I opened my eyes has."

He cocks his head to the side. "You're not wearing makeup. Where are your fake lashes?"

Wincing, I look away. I'd hoped he wouldn't notice. I rarely go anywhere without makeup. Now I feel exposed and vulnerable.

I don't say anything, wondering if I'm going to actually break down and cry today. It feels imminent and Two is supercharged today with his antagonization. It's only a matter of time.

He crouches down in front of me, grabbing my chin with his long, bony fingers. "I like it better. You can see your freckles."

My belly twists delightfully at his words. Did Two just compliment me? No way. "You should feel proud. Not everyone gets to see the real me. I'm apparently showing you all the goods."

His thumb strokes along my jaw, sending a shiver down my spine. "Why are you showing me?"

Good question. Why am I letting Two see these parts of me? He's been a maddening thorn in my side since the day I met him. Of all people, he doesn't deserve to see past my carefully applied layers both inside and out.

"I don't know. You just feel safe, I guess."

He frowns at my words, drops his gaze to my non-glossed lips, and then scrambles away like he just saw a rat. I squeak, darting my head all over, looking for the beast.

"What did you see?" I demand, hugging my middle. "If it was a mouse, tell me. I don't like them."

With his back turned to me, he grunts and waves me off. "No mouse. We just need to get to work."

I stay annoyed for about three seconds until he opens a box with old pictures. Then I grin back at him, eager to see what awaits us.

◎

Paula let us borrow a few pictures, but we have to bring them back. However, she did let us take some of the torn-off wallpaper in the office, some dusty floorboards we found, an entire box full of old clothing, and a bunch of other random stuff. Now, we're on our way to Two's to work on our model.

"We should stop by this cool place on Main Street for lunch," I say, pointing in the general direction. "We need fuel to keep working."

"Let me guess," he grumbles almost playfully, "I'm buying."

"Naturally unless you think they'll accept the change at the bottom of my purse."

"You've got problems."

I crack up laughing. "And you're one of them."

The vibe between us is no longer tense like it was this morning. We both fell into mutual states of bliss when we started discovering all the cool stuff in the attic. Despite it being winter, the attic got hot quickly and we both got filthy and sweaty. I suppose it was a good thing I didn't waste my time on hair and makeup.

Two cruises down Main Street and then parks in front of Soup and More once I point at it. He doesn't make a face or comment on the front of the building. After we climb out, I lead the way into the dark building. It's busier than when me and Dempsey came, but there're a few open tables.

With Two standing beside me at the counter, ready to pay for my food, I suddenly wonder if this is how it would feel to be on a date. Sure, I've liked guys over the years, but I haven't ever been allowed to date any of them. Dad drilled into me that lots of guys are after two things—money and sex—and that I should deny them both until I know they're the one.

We order our food and then settle at the same table me and Dempsey sat at. Two's eyes bore into me from across the table. Then, to my surprise, he reaches across the table to wipe at my cheek.

"Dust is smudged on you," he says, voice a low, guttural growl. "All better."

I smile at him. "Thanks. What do you think of this place so far? Pretty cool, huh?"

"It's definitely a hidden gem." His eyes dart to mine and lock into place. "Pretty cool."

My flesh heats because I think maybe he's referring to *me* being the hidden gem. That I'*m* pretty cool. Or I could be feeling super vulnerable and reading into it. Ugh.

"Today was a success."

He nods. "It'll be even better once we get back to my place."

Heat coils in the pit of my stomach. I'm definitely reading into everything he says. Why, of all people, does it have to be with Two?

"I don't like to lose," Two says, darting his gaze to the table. "That's why I bolted after the pool game. Plus, your friend didn't like me."

"She's family. And it was just a game, Two. You win some, you lose some."

"But I don't like losing to *you*," he grits out. "It fucking sucks."

I recoil at his words. "Oh."

His panicked eyes land back on mine and he curses under his breath. "Sorry. I'm being dramatic. Supposedly it's my thing."

"I'm feeling a bit dramatic too today," I admit with a shrug. "Can we just be dramatic together and know neither of us is going to leave the other in the literal dust? We're partners. I like that I can let my guard down with you."

He softens as he reaches over to touch my hand. "More dust."

There was no dust. He just wanted an excuse to touch me.

Another shiver dances down my spine.

"I'm glad you're my partner for this," he murmurs, thumb gently rubbing at the pretend dust on my hand. "No one else is as serious as we are."

"I'm an achiever, remember? I like to accomplish my goals and be the best. Even if I feel like a total fraud the entire time."

He studies me for a long beat. "Is it hard being perfect all the time?"

I don't fake a smile or spin a lie to make him think better of me. I give him the truth. "So hard. This morning, you almost saw the breakdown. Sometimes, when it's all too much, I just come crashing down. It takes a few days to pick myself up and put all my armor back on."

"Sounds heavy."

"It is."

THE TORMENT OF TWO

"Leave your armor at home, Golden."

Tears well, but I don't let them fall. "Okay."

The woman who owns the place—Cara—delivers our delicious food a little while later and it's only then that I realize he's held onto my hand the entire time.

I'm not reading into this.

Two likes me whether he likes it or not.

The feeling is mutual.

CHAPTER FOURTEEN

Two

THINK WE JUST HAD A DATE.

Sure as fuck felt that way.

The urge to touch Gemma again is overwhelming, but thankfully, we're done with our food. I bolt out of the booth and storm outside, not bothering to wait for her.

If I wait, I might try to touch her again.

Her skin was so soft. I want to touch her hair next.

There can't be a next time, Two.

I burst out of the building, hightailing it to the Rover. When I see a flyer fluttering under the windshield wiper on the passenger side, I slow to a stop. Tucked in next to it is a winter aconite flower—a hearty yellow flower often seen popping up through snow.

Gemma sucks in a sharp breath of air as she stops beside me. She starts forward, but I race her over to it. Snatching the paper out before she can, I bring it to my face to read.

No one adores you like I do. Especially not him. The way he touches you is wrong. When I touch you, it'll be more than right. It'll be perfect. You'll see.

Anger swells up inside me as the letter crumples in my fist. Gemma, with her soft, small fingers, pries it out of my ferocious grip. Her shoulders hunch after she reads it.

"Who the fuck is doing this?" I demand, feeling

shockingly protective over her. "This is more than a super fan, Gemma. This is psychotic."

She throws the yellow flower onto the street and stomps on it, completely distracted by the act of destroying it. "You called me Gemma."

I grunt in frustration. "Focus. We need to go to the cops."

"No," she hisses, whirling around to face me, shaking her head. "It's not a big deal. They're just trying to scare me."

People are starting to stare at us and this shit is none of their business.

"Get in," I bark out as I open her car door. "Now."

She scowls at me but obeys. Once I've climbed in on my side, I attempt to turn over the engine. Naturally, it doesn't start.

"You're downplaying this," I growl, relieved when the engine starts on the second try. "Why?"

Gemma huffs and shrugs. "Because if my dad gets wind of this, it's going to suck. He'll go into overprotective mode and watch me like a hawk. I barely just got my freedom when I started college. I can't have it taken away over some stupid person trying to scare me."

I back out of the parking spot and gas it, making sure to watch my rearview mirror in case anyone is following us. "What if it's more than a scare tactic? What if it's a warning? A fucking promise. I don't like this."

"And you think I do?" Her voice is shrill. "I'm worried, Two. My family has dealt with not one but two abductions in the past few years. I know the Park name draws attention and freaks are always out to get us. But I also can't let these people dictate my life."

"You're not even going to tell your parents?"

"Nope."

We drive in mutually irritated silence. I think she's being stupid as fuck not reporting this to anyone. It makes me realize she needs protection. Right now, I'm the only protection she's got.

Unbelievable.

When we reach my house, I'm happy to see both my parents' vehicles are gone. Saturdays are a busy day at work for them. Sometimes they even recruit me to come help, though they do try to hold back doing that while I'm in school. Summers are always fair game, though.

After shutting off the car, we collect our bags and make several trips to bring all our findings from Hemingford Hall into my workshop. Neither of us is speaking to one another at the moment. I'm still pissed and apparently, she is too. I have half a mind to text Tate and ask him how I deal with this girl since he's the professional and all.

"It's cold," Gemma mutters, hugging herself and shivering.

I crank up the dial on the space heater. "Sure it's just the cold and not adrenaline?"

"Can we just drop it? I want to work on our project, not analyze this stupid stalker. If we can pretend it's not happening, it'll make things a lot easier."

Prowling over to her, I frown. "You can't just pretend it away, Golden. That kind of thinking is stupid. You'll be more vulnerable that way."

She lifts her chin, bottom lip slightly quivering. "Please."

"No." Before I can stop myself, I reach up and touch her. Again. Gently, I stroke my thumb along the bottom of her chin. "I'm not going to let some asshole terrorize you."

Her lips curl into a devilish grin that has my dick thickening. "I already have some asshole terrorizing me. What's one more?"

She licks her dry bottom lip. The action trips a wire inside of me. My mouth descends upon hers. I don't stop to think or talk myself out of it. I simply put my lips on her perfect ones I can't seem to stop staring at.

"Oh," she mutters, voice soft but not alarmed.

As her lips part, I dart my tongue into her mouth, eager to taste her. She moans and fuck if it doesn't scramble my already messed up head. I slide my fingers into her ultra-glossy hair, tugging her closer so I can devour her sweet mouth.

She's not supposed to taste so goddamn delicious.

Why does this kiss feel like something I've been aching for my entire life?

Her palms skate up my chest over my hoodie and then her fingertips are probing the sides of my neck. We kiss with fire a thousand times hotter than the steady warmth pouring from the space heater. All the animosity I have for her feels forgotten in this moment. She feels like mine right now and I want to savor her.

My hands roam down her body until I find her narrow hips. She squeaks when I lift her, setting her on a nearby stool. Then, to my delight, she spreads her thighs, welcoming me to stand between them. From this angle, I can own her mouth with mine, exploring all the soft, slippery corners of it. Her whimpers and gasps are music to my ears and a motherfucking tease to my dick.

She freezes when my cold hand slides beneath her hoodie. Her flesh is hot and silky. I can't help but caress it with my thumb, desperate to explore more of her.

How did we get here?

How do we stop?

A mewl rattles out of her throat as I tease my fingers up higher and around to her back. The clasp of her bra easily comes undone. By the time my palm is back to her front, sliding over her naked breast beneath the cup of her bra, we're both panting. Her nipple is hard and small like a pebble. I crave to have it between my teeth.

"Two," she murmurs. "Two, stop."

With a grunt, I pull back, letting go of her and stepping away. Her lips are swollen, red, and parted. It's her eyes that do me in. Her pupils are blown and the look in them says she wants to do *anything* but stop.

Reality seeps in, rushing over me like a frigid avalanche. My dick deflates as I realize who I'm here with and what I'm doing with her.

It's Golden.

Number one.

The first choice.

Shuddering, I stagger away from her until my ass hits another table behind me. She winces and then awkwardly fidgets for her bra clasp under her hoodie.

What did we almost do?

How could I have been so stupid?

"I just wanted to talk for a second," Gemma says, eyes pleading. "Stop looking at me like I'm roadkill right now. Please."

As she approaches, I sidestep toward the door, one hand out in front of me. Her brows knit together and hurt flashes in her eyes.

"Why are you this way toward me?" Her voice trembles

and fat tears well in her pretty blue eyes. "What's so wrong with me?"

Guilt infects my every cell. Knowing what I know about her thus far, not being adored and seen as perfect is really hard on her. Yet, here I am making her feel like shit.

"Tell me, Two. It's not fair. How can I fix it if you don't tell me?"

I scrub a palm over my face. "You can't fix it, Golden. It just is."

"*What* is? Explain."

She slowly makes her way over to me and then gently steps into my space. Automatically, my hands encircle her waist. So much for showing some self-restraint.

"Two," she begs. "I feel like we can be something. You just have to let it happen. It won't with this big boulder between us. Please."

Unable to help myself, I nuzzle the top of her head with my nose, inhaling her sweet scent. My palms find her ass, settling there, like they were made to hold her. She relaxes against my chest, hugging me tight.

This feels good.

Too good.

"You really want to know?" I ask, voice hoarse. "You're not going to ridicule me or run off after?"

"I've put up with you thus far. I think I can handle whatever you dish out."

I smile against her hair, but it quickly vanishes when I think about the picture I found all those years ago. Pain lances its way through my heart.

"I'm adopted," I say softly. "My dads adopted me when

I was two. It's the only word I could say at the time, so the nickname kind of stuck."

She squeezes me again to encourage me to keep talking.

"My guess is that people wanted a baby and would ask my age a lot. I was probably always picked over for adoption. Not like I can remember it anyway."

"Oh, Two."

"I'm not being dramatic either," I say with a defensive grunt. "It's just the way of life." A heavy sigh escapes me. "All was good until I was nine. My dads were the best. I love them so fucking much."

"I can tell," she murmurs. "I think it's sweet."

"Dax told me there wasn't a Santa. Said he could prove it. One day, I went searching through Dad's things, looking for presents, and found a trunk. Inside it were the adoption papers and…"

I shudder at revealing the most hurtful thing that's ever happened to me. To the perpetrator no less.

It's not her fault, dumbass.

"I learned I was their second choice," I choke out, voice strained with emotion. "They had a picture of a nursery set up for someone before me. A baby. A little girl." I clear my throat and spit out, "Gemma."

She freezes and then pulls back to look up at me. "What?"

"You. It was you."

"It couldn't be," she whispers. "I was never going to be put up for adoption."

The devastation in her expression has me stalling. I didn't think this might hurt her. She wasn't the victim. I was. But she's learning that she was almost given away.

"Never mind."

She shakes her head in vehemence. "No. Do not do that. Finish your story."

"The letter was from Jamie. Your mom. Said she was working things out with Nathan and that she wasn't going through with the adoption. She apologized profusely and said she'd honor my dads by keeping the name they'd chosen for a little girl."

A tear streaks down her cheek. Then another. Another. Before long, the dam breaks and Gemma is boo-hooing in her palms.

Fuck.

I did this.

I broke her.

For years, I dreamed of this moment and now it fucking sucks.

"I always felt second best," I manage to whisper despite the pain cutting into my throat. "You were always the one. And then..." I trail off and shudder. "I met you in class, put two and two together, and realized I was forced to work with the person solely responsible for my pain."

She lowers her hands, face red and splotchy. "Two, I am *so* sorry."

I blink in shock when she throws herself back into my arms. This time, as she sobs, I feel my own cheeks growing wet. It's not the first time I've cried over this shit, but it's the first time I've done it with someone else.

"We're going to get through this," Gemma vows, breath hot against my chest. "I promise."

Hope prickles at my chest. "But I hate you."

"You might once have, but it won't last."

"How can you be so sure?"

She tilts her head up and then stands on her toes. Her mouth connects with mine. The fiery connection from before is reignited. Both of us shamelessly try to out-devour each other.

She's right.

The last thing I'm thinking about right now is hate.

CHAPTER FIFTEEN

Gemma

Kissing Two Sheridan feels good. Really good. I'm not sure how we got to this point, but I'm not hating it one bit. Neither is he, no matter how much he wants to.

We have chemistry.

There's no denying that.

My face feels raw from his scruff and my eyes burn from my tears. There's no stopping this kiss, though. I ache for him to slip his hand under my hoodie again. This time, I won't stop him.

He pulls away almost angrily, a growl rumbling from him. "We have to stop."

I lean toward him, silently begging for another kiss. "Why?"

"Because if I keep kissing you like this, I don't know what's going to happen." He steals another quick kiss. "I want things I don't have any business wanting."

I groan, tugging at his hoodie to pull him nearer. "I want it too."

My heart races inside my chest. Do I? I've never had sex before. Do I really want my first time to be with Two? A guy who hated me until now?

Yes.

"I'm serious," Two says, voice firm. "I need time to think about this. So do you. Can we just work on our project for a bit?"

Rejection washes over me. He's right, though. I know he's right. In this moment, kissing him feels right. But how will I feel later when I'm alone. Will I regret this moment?

It's definitely possible.

After what he told me about Mom and the adoption stuff, my mind is a mess.

Two reaches up and cups my cheek, his gray eyes searching mine. "I like kissing you, Golden."

I can't help but grin at his words. He doesn't give me time to preen at them because he's already breaking away. As he suggested, he begins unloading our boxes we filled from Hemingford Hall onto one of the tables, getting straight to work.

The kiss is soon pushed aside as we distract ourselves with our project. While Two assembles the supplies, I work on taking pictures from my phone of the different pictures we brought with us. One picture is of Alexander Heming and Edgar Ford looking dapper in their fancy old-timey suits, both of them grinning with mischief.

They were definitely a couple.

I can tell by their clear affection for each other in the picture.

Our plan is to use the pictures for our model, scaling them way down and printing them for miniature picture frames we'll be making. Two made a list of all the tasks for our model and is starting on that while I work on some of the other aspects of our project. We spend hours making progress, neither of us letting our buzzing phones distract us.

It's just me and Two and all things Hemingford Hall.

Headlights flicker through the window, jolting Two. He jerks his head up, glances down at his watch, and then curses.

"What?" I ask with a yawn. "Who is it?"

"Probably Dad." He strides over to the window and peers out. "As soon as he goes into the house, we have to leave."

I frown at him. "Why?"

"Because," he hisses, gesturing at me. "He can't see you."

Reality seeps its way back into my brain. It makes sense now why he didn't want me meeting them in the first place. Two is protecting his dads from the hurt my name and face will bring. I suddenly feel sick to my stomach.

"Fuck, someone's coming."

"I'll hide," I tell him, ready to crawl under one of the tables.

"No, it's fine. I'll deal with him."

He steps outside and then I hear his voice along with another, though I can't make out what they're saying. I check my messages to find that I've missed a lot of them.

Tate: Coffee date with me and Willa?

Tate: We had to go without you because you never answered.

Willa: I miss you. Come see me and Bane soon!

Dempsey: Want to go to Seattle with me next month for an art thing? Sloane has to work.

Spencer: Rex learned how to say shit. Dad's not happy.

Mom: You're working really hard lately. I'm proud of you but you need to take some time for yourself. Spa day soon, sweetie?

Dad: Bring your project partner in the house next time so we can meet her. Your mom says you're spending a lot of time with her.

Mom: Packages arrived for you today from Sephora and a couple of other places. Let me know if you want me to open them for you.

Jude: Dad wants me to vet out your friend. What's her first and last name?

Dempsey: Beauty shit on the couch! How do you get shit out of fabric? Ask Mom! Hurry, I have to get this shit cleaned up before Sloane sees!

Dempsey: Never mind. Mom's coming over to help me. Thanks for all your help, womb mate.

I don't even know where to start on responding to them all. If my text messages are this out of hand, I can't begin to imagine what's going on with my socials. Knowing I'll need to get on tonight and do a live at the very least feels exhausting.

The door to the workshop reopens and Two steps back inside.

"That was too close. I got Dad off my back, but we need to leave." Two starts gathering his backpack, frantically throwing stuff into it. "Come on, Golden, we don't have all day."

I bristle at his grumpiness but know he's just stressing out. My presence won't be received well by his parents. Just thinking about bringing them pain too has my stomach knotting.

Two is so focused on practically dragging me to his car that he doesn't notice the note taped to my window. As soon as he leaves me to go to his side, I snatch it off and shove it into my pocket. It's cold in his car and I shiver while he tries to get it started. After the fourth attempt, it fires to life. Two rummages around in his console, eventually retrieving a couple of butterscotch candies. He offers me one and I accept.

As soon as the candy hits my tongue, I'm reminded again of our kiss. He tasted buttery and rich, just like the candy. He loudly clacks his candy around in his mouth as he drives. I think it must be a nervous habit or something. Neither of us speaks while he drives in the dark back to my house.

When we arrive, Two is stiff and won't look at me. I'd hoped for another kiss, but it's clear he's on edge. I reach over and give his arm a squeeze.

"I had fun today with you."

He grunts. "Same."

"Can I call you later?"

"Not sure I'll answer. I'm behind on Cedarwood Mansion."

"Oh." Deflated, I grab my things and fling open the door. "I'll see you in class on Monday then."

He reaches across and takes hold of my hand before I can escape. "I'll answer."

"Okay." I give him a quick smile before tugging from his hold.

I've barely made it to the door before he takes off down the road. Being alone outside creeps me out, so I rush into the house. My parents are curled up on the couch, watching a movie together.

"Hey," I say, waving at them as I pass.

"Where are you off to in a hurry?" Dad asks. "We've barely seen you in days."

"Busy with school stuff," I mutter. "I'm tired."

He starts to say something else, but Mom tugs on his shoulder. "Good night, Gem."

"Night."

I flee the living room before they can interrogate me more. Once I'm safe in my room, I strip out of my clothes and start my shower. It's not until I'm about to get under the hot spray that I remember the note. Without a stitch of clothing on, I tiptoe back into my room and dig around in my hoodie until I find the paper.

He likes you, but no one will ever cherish you as much as I do. He's a boy. I'm a man. There's a difference you'll one day understand, my sweet, innocent angel. Don't have sex with him. You'll be disappointed. I'll be disappointed too. When the time is right, I'll make you mine.

A shudder ripples through me, making my teeth chatter. This guy is insane. Two's right. I do need to tell someone. Tomorrow, I'll talk to Sloane about it. Maybe even Jude. This is getting way too creepy.

After a long, hot shower where I attempt to chase the chill of my stalker away, I get into my coziest pajamas. I make a couple of posts using content I'd pre-recorded and saved in my drafts. I'll do a live another day. Once work is done, I crawl into bed, mind still racing.

Mom considered adoption. I know she was a young mother and was dealing with the stress of secretly being with Dad even though her boyfriend was Callum at the time. Did she feel overwhelmed like I do half the time? Like she wanted to give up and quit?

I want to talk to her about it, but I'm afraid it'll open a can of worms I'm not ready to deal with. Plus, she and Dad may forbid me from seeing Two or going to his house. The thought of suddenly being denied his presence is gutting.

I like him.

He's annoying and weird and sloppy and the total opposite of me, but I like him.

It's crazy, but I already miss him.

I dial his number and wait for him to answer. He said he would even after he said he wouldn't. On the second ring, his deep voice fills the line.

"Hey."

"Hey," I parrot back. "You answered."

"I told you I would."

"No Cedarwood?"

"Figured you needed me more."

A thrill shoots through me and I'm unable to suppress a grin. "I did."

He covers the phone for a second, his voice muffled, and then I hear a door close. "Dad's being nosy tonight."

"Mine too."

We both chuckle quietly.

"Our little secret, huh?" I murmur, letting my eyes fall closed as I listen to his breathing.

"Yeah. Our secret."

"Like Alexander and Edgar?"

He snorts. "Except we're the opposite sex."

"But we're totally like them, right? Hiding our feelings from those around us."

"Yup."

"I know you want to hate me, Two, but I'm glad you can't."

His breath rattles through the phone. "Me too, Golden. Me too."

"Tell me a story about you."

"Why?"

"Because I want to know more about you."

"I annoy most girls."

"You annoy *me*," I remind him with a smile. "But I keep sticking around for some reason. You've grown on me. Like a fungus. Now tell me a story."

"Perfect little Gemma Park is tainted by Two."

"Story time."

He grunts at my persistence but then proceeds to tell me a dramatic tale about how one time he and Dax nearly drowned in the creek behind his house when they tried to ice skate on it. I listen with rapt attention, enjoying the animated way he tells how they were able to escape the chilly waters. When he finishes, the air between us feels lighter.

"Your turn. Tell me about your brothers. I always wanted a brother. Dax is the closest thing to one I have."

We spend the next several hours on the phone, talking about everything and nothing. With each passing moment, I fall deeper and deeper into the abyss that is Two Sheridan. Learning silly things like his favorite song or foods he can't stand intrigues me. Sharing real details about myself with him is something rare for me to do. It's refreshing. Needless to say, I'm enjoying the man whose guts I hated a week ago.

"The sun's coming up," Two says with a yawn.

"Guess we better go to sleep." I pause and then ask, "I'll see you Monday in class?"

"Nah, Golden," he murmurs. "I don't think I can wait that long."

My heart does a somersault.

Keeping Two a secret is going to be really, really hard.

CHAPTER SIXTEEN

Two

I T'S DARK BY THE TIME SHE CAN ESCAPE HER FAMILY dinner. She'd told me via text today that it's a weekly thing for them and there's no way of avoiding it. It's been torture waiting all day for this moment to see her.

She slips out the front door and runs to my idling vehicle. Chilly air nips at me when she opens the car door. I'm already backing out of her driveway before she can get the door closed or her belt on, eager to be alone with her.

"Hey," I say, gassing it down her road, barely able to keep my gaze fixated ahead of me.

"Hey."

When I reach the end of the road, I put the vehicle in park, unable to resist for a moment longer. Like two magnets drawn to each other, we both meet for a frantic, desperate kiss.

I'm so fucked over this girl.

She whimpers and tugs at my jacket as she tries to pull me closer to her. I could kiss her all fucking night.

Her phone starts buzzing and she curses. Once she pulls away, she answers.

"Hi, Mom." She chews on her bottom lip and shoots me a small smile. "What? Oh, yeah, we're leaving. Nothing's wrong. Okay, bye."

"What?" I demand as soon as she ends the call.

"She clearly followed me onto the porch, trying to catch a peek, and then noticed we stopped at the end of our road. Hurry, let's get out of here."

I don't have to be told twice. Gunning it, I take off onto the main road. Both my dads are home, so we can't go there. I end up driving us to a lookout point on Park Mountain. Since it's dark, most of the bikers or trail walkers have gone home. As soon as I put the vehicle in park, Gemma unbuckles and climbs over the console.

My hands find her hips, guiding her into my lap so that she straddles me. She's wearing thin, stretchy leggings that give me access to the shape and feel of each curve of her body. There's not much room between her back and the steering wheel, so she's forced to press her chest against mine.

"Hey," she murmurs, hot breath tickling over my lips.

"You already said that." I squeeze her ass, drawing her closer to me. "Why do you smell so good?"

"I smell good?"

"Fucking delectable."

She grins and brings her lips to mine. I kiss her hungrily. Now that I know how she tastes and I've stepped over the invisible line of "I really shouldn't fucking do this with her," I'm eager to have more.

"We were supposed to think this shit over," I grunt between kisses. "Not dive right back in."

"I thought about it. I want it."

It's a terrible idea, but I can't find it in me to argue with her for once. I'm also down to make out without a care in the world.

"What did you tell your parents?" I ask, pulling away

slightly so I can see her pretty eyes in the dimly lit vehicle. "How did you escape?"

"School stuff. They think you're a girl."

I snort out a laugh. "My parents think I'm hanging with Dax."

"I won't be able to hold them off forever," Gemma says with a sigh. "They're already demanding to know more about my class partner."

Our lips find each other's again and there's no time for talking. We kiss and kiss until it's too hot in the Rover. My nuts feel like they're going to burst and it doesn't help that she keeps rubbing her lithe body over my dick.

This time, when I slip my hand under her hoodie, she arches into my touch. Like a madman, I start yanking at the fabric and before I know it, it's tossed somewhere in the passenger seat floorboard. Moonlight licks over her silky flesh, making my mouth water. Her breath hitches when I unlatch her bra. Then I tug it away, freeing her glorious tits.

"What if someone sees?" she mutters, breath hot and body quivering.

I cover both of her juicy tits with my hands. "I'll keep them hidden, Golden."

This thing between us is burning hot and fast. It's stupid to keep letting my dick run the show, but I can't help it. I fucking want her right now more than anything.

"Two," she whispers. "Please."

I don't know what she's begging for, but I pray to God I can give it to her. Releasing one of her tits, I replace my hand with my mouth. Her whimpers turn into breathy moans as I suck on her pebbled nipple. I slide my other hand between us, finding her pussy through her thin pants. A gasp of shock erupts from her when I find her clit.

"You like that, Golden?"

"Mmhmm."

I gently bite down on her nipple and tug before releasing it. "Want me inside you?"

"Y-Yes."

Warning bells are blaring inside my head to slow the fuck down, but I ignore them. I fucking ignore them. The only thing that matters right now is me and Gemma. Our mutually tangled pleasure. My hand finds its way into her pants, bypassing her underwear to get to her pussy. We both make strangled sounds when my fingers reach their destination.

"So fucking smooth," I rumble, almost angry at how perfect she feels at my touch. "How?"

"Spa day," she murmurs. "I went this morning with Mom. We like getting waxed."

At this point, my dick is straining against my jeans, desperately needing to be touched. The thought of slipping and sliding along her slick, smooth pussy lips is nearly maddening.

"I like it," I growl, easing a finger into her tight body. "A lot."

She stiffens with my finger inside her and stares at me. "I don't know what to do. I've never done anything like this."

Pre-cum leaks from my dick at her words. Comparing what happened when I was sixteen to now is a difference between night and day. That time was an act. This time is fucking everything. Everything's so much more alive, hotter, lost to madness.

"I don't know much either," I admit, slowly fucking her slick hole with my finger. "I just want to make you feel good."

She groans and starts meeting the thrust of my finger as she bounces her hips up and down. "When you go deep, it—ah!"

The spongy place inside seems to make her writhe with pleasure, so I reach my long finger to press and massage it. This has her jolting and her body spasming.

"How does this feel?" I ask, mouth resting on her pert tit.

"So good." She whimpers. "I think I might be able to get off like this."

I want to strip her down and fuck her right here, right now in my Rover. Somewhere in the depths of this steamy haze, I have the sense to pull back the reins.

Not tonight.

If we go too fast, too soon, we're going to crash and it could get ugly.

"Come on my finger," I say and then suck her nipple into my mouth. "Fuck, I can feel you clenching. I bet that's going to feel fucking fabulous on my cock."

She moans, clenching harder and quicker. Then she detonates. My dick is throbbing almost painfully in my pants. I ache for some sort of friction. As she trembles with her orgasm, I slowly fuck her with my finger until she collapses against me.

"Oh," she breathes. "I can't believe…wow."

"Yeah, wow."

I slide my hand out of her pants and then grip onto her hips. She quickly catches on that I still need to feel her. With deliberate movements, she rubs her pussy over my dick. The sensation feels so fucking good.

"I'm going to come in my pants," I say with a grumble. "I don't even care right now."

Our lips fuse together again as she continues on her mission to make me come too. It doesn't take long before my balls are tightening. Then my cock pulses with thick ropes of cum soaking my underwear.

I've never felt so alive in my entire life.

This "dry" sex was a thousand times better than the real sex I had a few years ago. A lot fucking wetter too.

Gemma shivers in my arms. I hug her to me, warming up her back with my palms. She snuggles against me and I feel her smile on my neck. It makes me smile too.

"That was amazing," she whispers breathily against me. "Thank you."

I stroke my fingers through her silky hair. "I want my dick to recover so we can do it again."

She cracks up laughing, which makes me laugh too. We're lost in our own little world. So much so that when someone knocks on the window, we both scream.

A flashlight shines in the window, causing me to squint away from the light.

"Ma'am, please put your clothing on and step out of the car."

The man turns around and when my eyes adjust, I realize a damn cop caught us.

"Oh my God," Gemma hisses. "Oh my God. My dad is going to kill me!"

"Get dressed," I instruct. "I'll handle it."

She snorts as she throws on her bra. "No offense, but I think I better handle it. You're not exactly great at peopling."

She has a point there.

Still, I don't like her facing this cop alone.

"We'll go together, though."

"Deal."

She pulls on her hoodie and then we both climb out. Once she's safely tucked into my side, I clear my throat.

"We're decent."

The cop turns around, frowning. "You can't have sex up here. How old are you two?"

We both state our ages—legal ages—and the cop relaxes a bit.

"We were just fooling around," I explain. "Not having sex."

"Not for lack of trying," the cop grunts. "Ma'am, you were topless. What's your name?"

Gemma is silent for a beat and then sighs. "Gemma Park."

He shines the light rudely in her face. "As in Nathan Park's daughter?"

"The one and only."

"Holy shit." He laughs but plays it off as a cough. "Sorry, this is just…unexpected."

"Can you please just let us go with a warning?" Gemma asks, voice small. "Me and my boyfriend just wanted a little privacy."

Boyfriend?

I know it's part of her innocent act, but it fills my chest with stupid pride.

"Public indecency is a crime, Miss Park. I could haul you in."

A growl rumbles out of me. "Don't be a dick, man."

"Excuse me?" the officer clips out. "I think you best remember who you're speaking to."

"He's just being protective," Gemma rushes out. "Please, sir. We didn't mean any harm."

The officer stares at her for a long, uncomfortable minute without saying a word. I'm getting antsy when he finally speaks.

"I'll let you go," he finally says, "but if I ever catch you naked again in public, I'm arresting you and taking you to the station. Got it, little girl?"

I crack my neck, not loving the way he's speaking to her. My mouth opens, ready to tell him just that, but she nudges me with her elbow.

"Got it, sir. My boyfriend will take me home now."

My fingers clutch into her hip, drawing her impossibly closer to me. I don't like the way this dude in uniform rakes his gaze over her.

"What's your name, Officer?" I demand through gritted teeth. "And how did you suddenly stumble upon us?"

The man stiffens and narrows his eyes. "I'll be asking the questions around here, young man."

"Officer…" Gemma says, lifting her hands in a placating gesture, waiting for him to fill in the blank.

"Brandt," the officer grunts. "I patrol this area."

"Thank you, Officer Brandt, for being so nice about such an embarrassing thing. I swear it won't happen again."

He keeps his eyes trained on her face for another long couple of seconds before nodding. "Off you go, sweetheart. I'll even keep this from your daddy."

With a wink and a nod, he starts back for his police cruiser. I have the urge to go after him and kick him in the balls. Gemma must sense this because she places a palm on my chest.

"I think I better go home now," she murmurs. "I'm sorry this turned into a mess."

I slide my palm to her ass and give it a squeeze. "Yeah, Golden, let's get you home. Some of us need to change our goddamn underwear."

She giggles and it's music to my ears.

Fuck Officer Brandt for raining on our parade.

It wasn't a total loss, though. We both got off, and apparently, she's my girlfriend. I'd say it was a pretty good evening after all.

CHAPTER SEVENTEEN

Gemma

EVERYTHING WAS FINE UNTIL THIS MORNING.

I'd skated past Mom and Dad's questioning about why I was back so soon. Me and Two didn't get into any serious trouble. We also spent all night talking again over the phone.

Despite being exhausted for school today and dragging out of bed, everything was fine.

As I was drying my hair, I got a text.

Unknown: Public nudity is beneath you, sweetheart. Luckily you were caught before things escalated.

I can't keep ignoring this guy, which is why I'm making a pit stop by the police station before school. Sloane will know what to do.

Tara, the receptionist, waves as I enter. I give her a bright smile despite the anxiety simmering in my gut. Sloane is sitting at one of the desks in the middle of the station, arguing with another guy one desk over.

"Hey, Sloane," I greet as I approach. "Is this a bad time?"

She shakes her head but glares daggers at the other guy. "No, just the usual from my partner."

"Ethan Montgomery," the guy says, grinning my way. "She's just so easy to rile up."

"Come on," Sloane says, rising from her chair. "I need coffee. I've finally figured out how to use the new machine."

I follow her into the break room where she sets to making two coffees. She makes mine like she makes hers, which is presumptuous, but after a sip, I decide I definitely like the way she makes it. She gestures for us to sit at one of the tables.

"What's up? Dempsey okay?"

"Yeah, of course. You see him more than I do nowadays."

Her smile is dopey and nothing like the bitchy cop expression she had on when I first arrived. "I guess I do."

We both take a moment to sip our coffees and then she speaks again.

"What can I help you with? I can see the worry in your eyes."

I set my paper cup down and inspect my nails. Last night, while on FaceTime with Two, I did a cool effect on my nails using some of the extra Hemingford Hall wallpaper clippings I'd stuffed into my purse. The Victorian look is pretty cool. Two thought it was awesome.

"I think I have a stalker."

She sits up. "You think or you know?"

"I know." I meet her gaze. "It started off with strange messages online, but it's progressed to letters left on my vehicle. The person has been following me and knows about…things."

"Things?"

"Personal stuff," I say quickly, not eager to tell her about Two since I can barely explain it myself. "This morning there was a text from them."

I dig around in my purse and hand over the notes I'd collected. She rises from her chair and fetches a Ziplock bag for me to put them into. Once it's sealed, she sits again.

"What does the text say?"

"Personal stuff."

Sloane's blond eyebrow arches up in a questioning way that makes me squirm. "Gem, sweetie, you're not telling me something. I can't help you if you leave parts of the story out."

I puff out a heavy breath. "It's embarrassing."

"It's between us. I won't tell your brother or mom or Ethan in there. Spill."

"I got caught making out with my, er, boyfriend last night. Without my shirt." I wince at saying those words, waiting for some sort of disgusted reaction from her. I get nothing aside from the expectant look on her face as she waits for me to continue. "A cop discovered us and gave us a tongue lashing. But then, this morning, well, here."

I swipe open my phone, locate the text, and thrust it at her.

She reads it and then uses her own phone to take a picture of it. "I'll run the number, but more than likely it's a burner. However, since they have your number and know where you always are, it has to be someone who knows you. Run into any weirdos at school who might have a crush on you?"

Literally ran into one, but I have a crush on him back.

"No." I shrug, glancing down at my coffee. "My parents don't know I'm seeing someone. You know how protective they are."

"I do," she says gently.

"The person doing this is probably just trying to scare me, right? They're probably harmless."

I wait for my sister-in-law-to-be and newly appointed

detective to assure me I'm overreacting. Of course she's a no-bullshit kind of gal.

"It's worrying." She reads the text again. "I'll do some investigating on my end. You let me know immediately if anything new happens and try not to touch the note. I'll come to you. These are probably riddled with your fingerprints."

"I just don't know of anyone who could be doing this. If I did, I could confront them."

Sloane shakes her head. "Please don't do that. If you have a hunch, you let me know. I won't have you putting yourself in harm's way." She casts a look past the break room and then back to me. "If they message you online again, though, let your brother take a peek. He has more resources and means to uncover someone's online presence. Don't delete and block next time."

She's not talking about Dempsey, either.

My brother Jude is the whiz with technology and his hobby is basically hacking anyone and everyone who poses a threat to our family.

"I will," I assure her even though the thought of talking to Jude about all this makes my gut clench. It's bad enough talking to another woman about it.

"What was the cop's name?" Sloane asks, voice dipping low. "The one from last night?"

My blood runs cold. "You think he's my stalker?"

"I'm not saying that," Sloane murmurs, "but this station already had one bad seed. I'll always keep my eyes and ears open. You never know."

"Brandt. We asked how he stumbled upon us, but he didn't give an answer other than he was on patrol."

"Where was the location?"

"One of the lookout points on Park Mountain."

She relaxes. "We patrol those areas frequently. Teenagers like to go up there and neck."

I snort out a laugh. "Neck?"

"I'm not that old, Gem. Necking? Never heard of it?"

"Like making out?"

"Yep, it's official. I *am* old. Thanks for pointing that out, kid."

My phone, that's still in her hand, buzzes. She looks down at it, reading a text, and then hands it over to me.

"Who's Two?"

Heat floods my face and neck. "The boyfriend. You swear you won't tell anyone?"

"Promise. Be careful, though." Her brows knit together. "Trust me. I have a reckless sister. If you're hiding who you're seeing, there's a reason and it's usually not good."

"My parents," I say lamely.

"If Jamie can get over her best friend being engaged to her son, I think she can handle her daughter dating someone. Promise me if this is serious between you and your guy, you'll open up to your family about him."

"I will," I rush out. "Just not right now."

"Go on and get out of here. The boyfriend awaits, and I quote, 'in the parking spot right in front of where you hit me with your car.'"

I groan as I read the text he sent. He's never going to let me live it down.

"Thanks, Sloane."

We hug and then I down my coffee before hightailing it to campus. I'm nearly late, but as promised, Two is leaned against the grill of his Rover, waiting for me. I pull into the spot next to him and leap out, eager to kiss him.

He pulls me into his arms, rakes his fingers through my freshly washed and dried hair, and then crashes his lips to mine. Already, this morning, he tastes like butterscotch. I kiss him, eagerly roving my tongue over his to sample the rich, buttery flavor. Before it can get too hot and heavy, he pulls away and then grabs my hand.

Walking into the building holding Two's hand feels right. Like we're a united front. I always had my brother on the same "team" if you will, but then he moved out to be with Sloane. I didn't realize how lonely I was until now. Two fills a void my brother left, and not in some sicko perverted incest way. Two's not just the object of my every lust-filled thought, but he's my friend too. Yes, he's weird and annoying and brash at times, but I like that about him. It endears me to him.

"I went by the police station this morning," I say, glancing his way. "Talked to my future sister-in-law. She's a detective."

"About last night? The asshole cop who was following you?"

"Yeah, uh, that. But also the text from this morning."

He jerks to a stop and comes to stand right in front of me. "What text?"

I pull my phone out and show it to him. His jaw clenches and his gray eyes gleam with anger.

"It's that cop. It has to be."

"Sloane says it's normal to patrol up there. I think the stalker was just following me and saw the cop with us."

He tears his gaze from mine to scan the parking lot. When he doesn't see an immediate threat, his eyes are back on mine. I'm pulled into his arms for a tight, quick hug that does wonders to soothe my erratically beating heart.

"We need to be more aware of our surroundings," he murmurs, kissing my head. "This guy's gotten the upper hand too many times. If I ever catch him, I'll…" He trails off, letting his warning hang in the air.

"You'll bore him to death talking about the original flooring of an entertainment hall built in the early nineteen hundreds?"

He pulls away, smirking at me. "For most people, it's torture. You're just a weirdo who likes it. You have a Victorian kink."

I give him a playful shove. "I do not. Okay, maybe I do. I keep wondering where Alexander and Edgar had their sordid affair. Was it in the quiet, secluded attic? Or did they boldly make love on Alexander's desk with the drapes open?"

His chuckle warms me to my core. "We're not including this"—he waggles a finger at me—"in our project. This is factual, not fiction."

He brings my hands up so he can admire my nail art and then surprises me when he kisses one of the knuckles. "It's going to be hard keeping my hands off you during class."

"I won't complain if you can't," I say with a teasing grin.

The smile on his face falters and he releases my hands. "I know, but we can't. There are people, including Mr. Pederson, who know my dads. Sorry."

I can't help but shiver from his tone. Reality is a harsh reminder that our fun, steamy romance is something we must keep secret. His dads could truly be crushed by this news and my parents would have a fit if they knew who I was seeing.

To his credit, Two doesn't dart ahead of me but walks

by my side, even remembering to open the door for me. Sometimes he does romantic stuff, and other times he takes off in his vehicle with my legs still dangling out the car door. He's multidimensional like that.

Once in class, he gets into an animated conversation with Mr. Pederson about Cedarwood Mansion updates. I note that he glosses over the fact there haven't been any real updates because all his free time has been spent with me and our project.

I check my phone and there aren't any new strange texts, nor are there any stalker messages on my socials. In my email, I find several new offers for collaborations with brands, including one that pays a whopping fifteen grand if I'll go on a hiking trip with them and do a live showcasing their survival gear.

Um, no.

Some people should actually look at my overall aesthetic before contacting me. Beauty and hair products, yes. Survival gear, no.

Unless it's some ploy by my stalker.

My blood runs cold.

Would this guy try and get me alone in the woods?

Maybe I'm just overanalyzing everything.

Rather than keep it to myself, I take a screenshot and text it to Sloane. She gives me her work email and asks for me to forward it to her. I have another email from the dean of PMU, Dr. Skeller, talking about an event coming up soon that they'll be accepting applicants for. My skin continues to prickle and I hate that this stalker has me paranoid about school emails too.

I have Sloane on this and Two will protect me when we're together.

I'm tired of being made to feel uneasy and afraid.

Hopefully, soon, I'll learn how not to let this stuff affect me.

At least Two's a great distraction.

As he strides over to our table, he flashes me a hot, secretive grin that makes my insides melt.

Yep, he's a fantastic distraction because I can't think about anything right now aside from the way he made me come in his truck.

CHAPTER EIGHTEEN

Two

"I'M GOING TO BE LATE," I MURMUR, UNABLE TO KEEP my tongue out of her mouth long enough for her to give a response.

After class, we found our way into my car since we had a few minutes to spare before I needed to leave for my appointment. A few minutes turned into several and now I can't stop kissing her.

Finally, Gemma has the strength to break away, flashing me a sweet smile that promises more later.

How much later?

Where will we go so we're not bothered by anyone?

"Hemingford Hall later this afternoon?" I ask, voice raspy with need. "So we can work on our project."

Truth is, our project is coming along nicely. The past couple of nights spent talking all night, we also worked on it. Our other classes may be suffering from our heated romance, but not my favorite one. It's most definitely just an opportunity to spend some alone time with her.

"I'll meet you there this time," she says, nodding. "Mom is getting nosy."

I cup her cheek with my hand. "Drive in circles if you have to if someone is following you."

"I will. I'll be careful."

My eyes drop to her lips and she licks them, making the growing need for her spike to unhealthy levels. Before I can maul her again with my mouth, she gives me a small wave and climbs out of the vehicle. The slamming car door jolts me out of my Gemma haze. Surely I'll get her out of my system soon and can think straight again.

She presses her nose to the glass of my driver's side window and makes a silly face. I playfully thump the glass where her nose is earning a loud laugh that has me grinning.

Okay, so maybe I'll never think straight again with her in my presence.

I wait, despite being super late, for her to get into her vehicle. Once she drives off, I follow her out of the parking lot and then head for my appointment with Tate. This time, he's already there. I bound out of my vehicle and rush inside, chasing the scent of coffee and butterscotch. When I reach his office, I'm glad to see he hasn't turned on the fireplace and is just setting his stuff down.

Not that late.

"Hey," I greet as I make my way over to the fireplace. I crank it up despite the fire burning in my chest. "Bring me something good?"

Tate walks over to me and thrusts a cup at me. "Your fave." He pauses to look me over. "You're…different today. What's up?"

I bristle at his observation and take my time sipping the butterscotch goodness. "Nothing."

Tate snorts out a laugh. "Liar! Your hair is messier than usual and you have pink lipstick all over your mouth!"

Bringing my hand to my lips, I try to hide a smile at the thought of her leaving her mark on me. She was certainly mussed up when I was done with her. Apparently, she did the same to me.

"Please tell me it's Golden," Tate says, practically bouncing in his chair. "Please."

"It's Golden."

He shrieks with happiness, making my ears hurt and my entire body cringe. Tate continues to do a giddy little dance in his chair, pleased as punch.

"I knew it." He waggles a finger at me. "I'm great at reading people."

"I didn't like her at first," I argue, though the attempt is lame. "She grows on you."

"Trust me, I know the feeling." He takes another sip of his coffee, eyes twinkling with delight. "Tell me how you got from Friday to today and everything in between."

So I regale him with all the details, leaving out some of the moments like her shirt coming off and us getting caught. I also don't tell him about the stalker because it's none of his business. By the time I finish, we're nearing the end of our session and he's glowing with happiness. I guess I am too.

"This is great," Tate says. "You really put yourself out there with her and got to know her. She sounds like a sweet girl."

"Yeah, I suppose she is."

Tate, the emotional hound dog, leans in with his eyebrows furled together. "I'm sensing a but. Or maybe some hesitation on your part still. There's more you haven't told me, right?"

The last thing I want to do is go into the drama of all *that*.

"This thing between us," I say with a huff, "isn't ideal. It's kind of fucked up, really. Our parents can't know."

As soon as I blurt the last part out, I wish I could reel it back in.

"She's not eighteen?"

"No, she is," I grunt. "It's other stuff."

"Hmm." Tate studies me long enough for me to fidget in my seat. "Other stuff you don't want to tell me about?"

"Not really."

"Two," he says slowly, "are you sure you're not making it out to be a bigger deal than it is? This other 'stuff'?" He reaches over and touches my arm. "Imagine, just for a moment, the worst-case scenario. You introduce her to your dads. What does that look like for you?"

I close my eyes and imagine me and Gemma kissing in my car. Then I see myself holding her hand as I bring her onto the porch. Dad greets us at the door, thrilled that I've actually brought home a girl. Pops is waggling his brows at me from behind him, letting me know she's cute and I did well. I'm proud to have her beside me.

Until I introduce her.

Gemma Park.

The Gemma they almost had from their past.

My twisting gut has my eyes popping back open. "They'll be hurt. I can't bear seeing pain in their eyes. It's too much."

"Okay," Tate says in a soothing voice. "It's okay. We'll explore this some more Wednesday if you'd like. Maybe we can figure something out that doesn't hurt the ones you love."

Ideally, I should just break contact with Gemma and put this whole thing behind me. But I don't want to do that. I actually like kissing her and talking to her and spending time with her. That's what makes this all so fucking stressful.

"Think about it," he urges. "I think exploring this and

working it out is important for your happiness. Holding it all in and keeping it a secret is going to become a heavy burden causing strain on your mental well-being."

He has one thing right.

I'm feeling the strain and it sucks.

◎

"Which do you prefer?" Dad asks, showing me two different wallpaper samples. "Understated or bold?"

I bounce my gaze between the two samples and then hand him the bold, geometric gold pattern on black. "I like this one."

Dad grins. "Me too. I was hoping you'd say that. Your father, on the other hand, is going to be miffed. If we go with this design, then I'm going to have him replace their tub because it's black and clashes with the matte color of the wallpaper."

"Where is Pops?"

"He's out doing a bid. We were thinking of grabbing Chinese later and watching movies on Netflix. You joining us?" He clasps his hands and places them under his chin before batting his lashes at me. "Please, please, please, please."

I smirk at him. "Your theatrics don't work on me. Plus, I have project stuff to get to this afternoon."

"Fine," he grumbles, "but we'll find time to sit down as a family again here soon. Being busy is understandable. However, we both miss you. Make some time for your dads."

"I will," I promise and mean it. "So what did you need me to stop by the shop for?"

Dad's playful nature fades and he narrows his eyes, watching me for any tells. "How are you liking Tate? He won't tell me anything other than the fact you make your scheduled appointments."

I stifle a sigh of relief. "I like him. A lot. He's easy to talk to."

Dad's gaze softens and he reaches across his desk to take my hand. "I'm so happy, Son. There's something different about you lately. Did you meet someone? A girl? A guy?"

"Not into guys," I say with a grunt. "No offense."

Dad chuckles. "None taken. So it's a girl then?"

Guilt churns in my gut as I avoid his probing stare. "Just my project partner."

"Who's a girl?" Dad asks, lifting his brows.

"Yeah, uh, Golden's a girl."

"Golden," Dad says, frowning. "What an unusual name."

"Yup."

"When do we get to meet her?"

I stiffen and then jerk my hand away from his to run my fingers through my messy hair. "Um, she's shy. Yeah. Really shy. Doubt she'll want to meet you."

Hurt crosses over his features and I feel like a dick for putting it there.

"Are you sure it's not just you being embarrassed of us?" Dad asks, wincing slightly. "Me and Pops will be on our best behavior. I promise."

"I'm not embarrassed of you guys," I grumble, not meeting his stare. "It's just…awkward."

Not a total lie.

"Well, when you're ready, we'll be thrilled to meet her."

"Sure," I mutter. Then I change the subject away from Gemma. "Tate's really cool. Drives an older model Jeep, so he appreciates a classic. He brings me coffee for each session. Butterscotch lattes."

Dad's eyes twinkle with happiness. "I'm so glad we switched you to him. I can already tell a difference in your mood. For a while there, you had me and Pops really worried. Dax too. You're still taking your medicine properly, right?"

It's times like this I feel like a kid again.

"Yeah, Dad. I'm all good." I stand up and stretch. "I need to get going. Meeting Golden to work on our project."

Dad also stands and comes over to me. He hugs me tight, nearly crushing my ribs. "I love you, sweet boy. So damn much."

Emotion balls up in my throat and my eyes sting as I hug my dad back. Tate wanted me to imagine a scenario where my dads meet Gemma. Well, that's a horrible thought. The look of betrayal on my parents' faces would be too much to bear.

And they'd feel so betrayed.

I'm knowingly carrying on this sordid affair with the little girl they wanted to adopt. It would be heartbreaking for them on so many levels.

Finally, I manage to leave the shop and Dad without cracking under the weight of my guilt. On the way back to my car, I find some missed texts.

Golden: I'm at HH. Paula made extra for dinner and invited us. Meet me in Alexander's office when you get here.

All the awkwardness fades away as I anticipate seeing

Gemma again. Talk about a rollercoaster for my emotions. Another text I missed is from Dax.

Dax: Mom is being SO overbearing, man. I know you're like not in any rush, but I think I'm going to get my own place after the semester is over. We could be roomies.

Dax: Don't make me beg.

Dax: I bet we can rent a house with a shed or something so you can do your dollhouse shit.

I respond back to Dax first.

Me: It's not dollhouse shit.

Dax: Whatever, 2. I need out from under that woman's constant criticism. You're lucky you have two dads and no mom. Just saying.

I am lucky to have my two dads.

Knowing just how almost unlucky I was is a constant reminder that plagues me.

Ignoring Dax for the time being, I shoot out a reply to Gemma.

Me: No one followed you to HH? Gregory's not creeping on you either? Maybe Gregory IS your stalker.

Gemma: TWO! Don't freak me out! Get your ass here and protect me from that cantankerous old man!

We text back and forth each time I get stuck at a red light, but I like knowing that as long as she's texting with me, she's safe.

Maybe moving in with Dax is a great idea. I could see

Gemma and my parents would never have to know. When I park at Hemingford Hall beside Gemma's Tahoe, I text Dax back.

Me: I'm in to move this summer. Won't hurt to start looking at places now.

He sends me a fuckton of unnecessary heart eye emojis that have me chuckling. I love my dads with everything in me, but it would be nice to have Gemma all alone whenever I wanted with nobody to get upset over it.

Suddenly, May seems like forever away.

CHAPTER NINETEEN

Gemma

TWO FINDS ME IN ALEXANDER'S OFFICE AND IT'S LIKE we've been apart a lifetime. With a barely stifled squeal, I rush over to him and throw my arms around his neck. He grabs my ass and lifts me, encouraging me to wrap my legs around him too. His pleased grin warms me from head to toe.

"Missed me, huh?"

"Kinda." I run my fingers through his messy hair. "Did you miss me?"

"Who are you again?"

I roll my eyes and huff, but he chases away my annoyance with a starved kiss that has me forgetting my own name. When we finally pull back for air, he gives me a dopey smile that makes my heart melt.

"Yeah, I missed you, Golden."

Paula's voice can be heard nearby, which is the only reason we pry ourselves apart. I doubt she'd be too thrilled to have us making out on her watch. That's not what we're here for.

"What are we doing today aside from stealing kisses whenever we can?" I point toward the bookcase. "We can look for more hidden artifacts if you want."

Two seems eager to do just that because he starts tapping on book spines, clearly hoping to get lucky finding a hollow one. As he does his thing, I stand back and inspect the massive bookcase that takes up the entire wall.

There's just something about this bookcase that keeps stealing my focus.

I know there's something here.

More artifacts or letters hidden away in empty books?

While Two continues his search, I step out of Alexander's office to explore the space next door. It's a simple, narrow room that's currently being used as a catch-all for boxes and Christmas decor.

The room on the other side of that one is a sitting room with furniture hidden beneath sheets. This room is larger and more like Alexander's office in size.

But something feels off.

Hemingford Hall is full of secrets, so I'm learning to let my gut lead the way. Right now, it's telling me to go back to the second room. I inspect the walls and ceiling before checking both the third room and Alexander's office.

There's at least a six-foot thickness between the office and the catch-all room.

A hidden room?

I walk back into Alexander's office and begin inspecting each bookshelf for a hidden latch or knob, starting with the far end by the windows. Two, equally engrossed in his task, ignores me as he pulls books and reshelves them with efficient speed. I skip past him to check the other shelves. When I reach the last one and find nothing, I let out a sigh.

Maybe I'm imagining it.

"What's wrong?" Two asks as he saunters over to me, eyes narrowed. "What did you see?"

"It's what I didn't see." I blow a strand of hair away from

my face. "There's a space between this room and the next one. I think it's a hidden area."

His eyes light up. "Seriously?"

As though he has to confirm it himself, he leaves me to inspect the other room. Then he strides back in, a huge grin on his face.

"You're brilliant," he murmurs, capturing my face in his hands. "So fucking brilliant."

Our hunt is soon forgotten as he crashes his lips to mine once more. I climb my Two tree again, happy to hang onto him like a koala. As our kiss heats up, he leans my back on the bookshelves.

That are collapsing under our weight.

I suck in a sharp gasp of air as I fall backward, him on top of me. The bookshelves didn't collapse. I think we just found the door to the room.

We both scramble to our feet, aware that we've uncovered a dark, dusty hidden space. Two pushes on the bookshelves that seem to pivot on some sort of rolling mechanism. It clicks softly into place, bathing us in complete darkness.

"What if there's a dead body in here?" I hiss, shivering at the prospect.

Dim light from Two's phone shines on his face. "That'd be unfortunate but also quite an interesting find."

I snort because he'd find that interesting. He mashes the flashlight button on his phone while I pull mine out of my pocket.

"Holy shit," he mutters.

By the time I get my own flashlight on, he's stepped ahead of me into the narrow passage. The area can't be any bigger than six feet wide and twelve feet long. The ceiling is the same height as the other rooms.

It's what this room contains that makes it so interesting.

"There's a bed," Two states, shining his light on the small, ancient, rumpled bed. "Were prisoners kept here?"

I push past him to discover a small table beside the single bed with an oil lamp on top. When I try the drawer, I discover it's locked.

"Need a key?"

I turn to catch Two's delighted grin as he wiggles the key he's been carrying around with him ever since he found it in one of the false books on the bookshelves. He's tried every lock in this building. Every lock except this one.

He hands me the key and I make quick work of opening the drawer. Inside, I find a stack of letters, written on brittle paper from another time period.

E,

You are everything to me.

A

Oh my God.

"I knew it," I shriek, turning to show Two the top letter. "They were lovers!"

He studies the letter, eyes widening. "This was their…"

"Love nest."

Finding this hidden room where the two men kept their biggest secret feels surreal. My heart aches at the thought of them hiding their love from everyone around them.

"We can't put this in our project," Two mutters under his breath.

"Why not?"

"Some secrets are meant to stay hidden."

Though I disagree, I don't argue. I like the idea of just the two of us knowing it exists. Maybe Paula and Gregory do too, but they never mentioned it before.

We continue to inspect the small space until footsteps can be heard approaching.

"Dinner's ready! Where'd you two go?" Paula calls out from close by. "Attic?"

My eyes meet Two's and he covers his lips with a finger, signaling me to be quiet. I give him a nod and remain still as we wait.

As soon as she's been gone for a few moments, we scramble to find our way out of the room. It's as simple as pushing on the right side and the bookshelf unhooks from its latch in the middle, swinging like one of those rotating doors you see at the airport. Once we're back in Alexander's room with the shelf pushed into place, we share a knowing grin.

We just made an awesome discovery.

Together.

It's late by the time Paula kicks us out. Neither me nor Two is eager to leave after what we found earlier, but it's not like we have a choice. Once outside in the chilly night air, Two takes my hand in his, squeezing it.

This whirlwind between us keeps growing in intensity. It makes me wonder if this is how Willa felt when she started seeing Callum. Or if Dempsey felt consumed by Sloane like I do Two.

My thoughts are on Two's ravenous kisses making the

cold much more bearable. But also, because of it, I completely forgot about my stalker.

Until now.

A bone-chilling shudder ripples through me when I see a yellow flower quivering in the wind, barely pinned by my wiper blade. Beneath it, sits a small, torn off piece of paper with a note for me written in neat, black scrawl. Two snatches it up and holds it where we can both read it.

I hope it's not too late. From what I've gathered, you're still very much an innocent. However, with each second that passes, you're getting closer to losing that precious innocence because of that boy. I wasn't ready to have you as my beloved guest yet, but perhaps I need to move up my timeline.

Whoever wrote this must be privy to me and Two's budding romance. Are they watching our every move? Is it someone I know or a complete stranger?

It's not until Two gathers me in a fierce hug that I realize I'm trembling. He murmurs sweet assurances against my hair as he rubs my back. I melt in his embrace, thankful to have him on my side.

"We're going to find out who this fucker is," Two tells me vehemently. "He's not taking you anywhere. Ever."

I wasn't ready to have you as my beloved guest yet, but perhaps I need to move up my timeline.

Bile creeps up my throat. This person is unhinged. Do they mean they're preparing a place for me? Some hidden room like the one behind Alexander's office for them to have me whenever they want?

"I'm scared," I admit, blinking back tears.

"Me too, Golden. Me too."

I've been on edge all week. Aside from the threatening note my stalker left on my car Monday night, it's been crickets ever since. Two, true to his word, has stuck by my side whenever I'm not at home. I've been tempted to let my guard down a few times, but then the thought of being someone's prisoner always finds a way to creep its way back into my head. Even my job is suffering as I've been apprehensive about freely putting myself out there for the world to see—for my stalker to see.

"What the hell, Gem!"

Dempsey bursts into my bedroom, huffing with fury. I shrink into my covers, my heart clawing its way up my throat with the jump scare he just gave me.

"I was almost asleep," I bite out, squinting against the lamplight when he turns it on. "Why are you here? It's late."

Two went out with Dax this evening, so I was left to be bored out of my skull all night, hence my going to bed early.

"I'm here," he grits out as he sits on the edge of my bed, "because Sloane told me you have a goddamn stalker."

I knew it was only a matter of time before she let that one slip.

"I'm handling it," I hiss. "Keep your voice down or our parents will want to know what's going on."

Dempsey's nostrils flare. "Oh, they know something's going on because I just bust through the front door looking for you."

I scramble to sit upright and smack his shoulder. "You can't tell them!"

"Why the hell not?" he demands.

"Because you know how Dad gets. He won't ever let me out of the house."

"Maybe you need to be locked away where it's safe!"

Gaping at him, I sputter, "Seriously? You're going to take his side? Since when?"

"Since the threat of you getting kidnapped. For fuck's sake, Gem!"

"No one is kidnapping me." I dart my gaze to my doorway to make sure my parents aren't there. "Plus, your fiancée is investigating."

"It's probably that freak at your school," Dempsey says, eyes narrowing on me. "What's his name again?"

"It's not him."

"Your problems started when he came into the picture!"

"Demps, it's not Two."

"Two. That's right. Who the fuck is this guy anyway?" He pulls out his phone. "I'm going to look him up. What's his last name?"

I knock his phone out of his hand and onto my bed. "It's not Two."

"How the hell do you know for sure?"

"Because he's my…he's my…" I bite on my bottom lip and then cringe. "Boyfriend?"

Dempsey stills, cocking his head to the side. "Since when do you have a boyfriend? And why do you say it like it's a question?"

"It's…we're…" I sigh heavily. "Complicated."

"Because he's hiding something?"

Yes.

"No," I rush out. "It just is. Can you leave it be?"

He gapes at me like I've lost my mind. "There's someone

leaving notes for you, threatening to take you, and then you drop a boyfriend bomb on me when you've legit never dated anyone before. I'm supposed to just let all this be? Fuck that. I want to meet this guy so I can vet him myself."

How did this go from the stalker being the problem to Two being the problem?

"Fine," I rush out. "You can meet him. As far as the stalker, I'm handling it. Just don't involve our parents. Please, Dempsey. I'm begging you. I'll never get to leave the house and I…" I trail off. "I really like Two. If I don't get to see him, I'll be miserable."

Dempsey scowls. "Did you have sex with him?"

"What? No! Why do you even care?"

"Because we don't know anything about this guy," he growls. "He could be using you."

"Get out," I snap, thrusting a finger at my door. "I'm done talking about this. If you breathe a word of it to our parents, you're dead to me."

He flinches at my words, clearly stung by them. Well, I'm stung too. I don't appreciate being woken up getting the third degree.

"Promise me you'll be careful. I'll back away as long as you promise me that."

I relax and give him a nod. "I promise. Now what's our cover story for you bursting in here so late?"

Dempsey flashes me a devious grin. "I'll just tell them I didn't know where pregnancy tests are sold and thought you might know."

"You're a dick on so many levels."

"It'd be kind of funny to see Mom's face twist into one of horror imagining me already knocking her best friend up."

"You haven't really knocked her up, though, right?"

"Fuck no. A puppy is hard as hell. A baby? That sounds like torture."

He ruffles my hair, making it all go in my face and earning an agitated sigh from me before he saunters out of the room.

I wasn't lying when I told him I'd be careful.

If it means spending all my time with Two or Dempsey or my parents to keep me safe, I will. I just want to have options. If Dad finds out, I'll have none.

CHAPTER TWENTY

Two

HER BROTHER WANTS TO MEET ME.

Officially.

And apparently, I should be scared.

Gemma fidgets nervously in the passenger seat of my car. She checks her phone for the millionth time.

"He's not going to beat me up," I say, gassing it when the light turns green. "You can stop panicking."

"You don't know Dempsey. He's a punch first, ask questions later kind of guy. Plus, he's super protective over me. Our only saving grace is Sloane will be there to run interference."

I reach over and take her hand in mine, squeezing it. "It'll be fine. If shit gets tense, I'll start talking about Cedarwood Mansion. That usually does the trick to put the mere mortals to sleep."

She snorts out a laugh. "Turn there. And you're right. I can imagine the utter look of boredom on my brother's face. He slept through most of his classes in high school. Just pretend you're his professor."

I'm glad that she seems to lighten up as we make our way through her brother's neighborhood. Our final destination is a small home with Dempsey's nice-ass car parked out front beside a police SUV.

We're barely out of the car when a dog comes barreling

our way, barking animatedly. I scoop the hyper little thing up and hug it to me.

"Hey there, pup."

"That's my niece, Beauty," Gemma says, scratching the dog behind the ears. "She was so tiny weeks ago and now she's this giant thing. They say she'll keep growing too."

The dog seems to be a mix of Golden Retriever and something else. Maybe a husky. Either way, she's cute and goofy. I love her immediately.

All happiness at the furry greeting fades as tension pulsates behind me. I turn around, Beauty still in my grasp, to find Dempsey several steps away, glowering at me.

"Be nice," Gemma growls.

Her growls are as vicious as this goofy pup's probably are.

"I didn't say anything," Dempsey growls back, definitely with more promise of a bite.

"Two, this is my twin, Dempsey. Demps, this is my, uh, boyfriend, Two."

I glance over at her, unable to keep the grin off my face at how she introduces me.

"'Sup," I say with a lift of my chin.

A blond woman comes up behind Dempsey, steps past him, and offers me her hand. "Sloane."

Her clipped, brisk tone makes me bristle more so than Dempsey's asshole-ish one.

"Detective," Dempsey adds smugly.

Gemma smacks her brother and then gives Sloane an exasperated look. "He's rubbing off on you, girl. Be nice to Two. He's good people. Can we go inside now?"

The intensity crackling in the air dissipates quickly as we start herding our way inside. I'm grateful for the pup, who won't stop licking my jaw like it's a lollipop. She's a sweet distraction from this uncomfortable encounter. Once inside, my stomach grumbles with hunger. The scent of decadent garlic and cheese fills my nostrils.

"Damn," I mutter. "Smells good in here."

"Demps is a fantastic cook," Sloane says with pride, no longer playing the grumpy cop lady part. "It's the only reason I agreed to marry him."

Dempsey chuckles, his hackles also no longer raised. "I can think of another big reason."

Sloane gapes at him, cheeks burning pink. "Go check on the bread, Troublemaker."

I glance around the small, homey living room. It's nice but not as nice as I'd expect for someone in Gemma's family to live. Hell, my house is nicer than this one and we're not millionaires like the Parks. Regardless, I like the space. It's decorated with cool artwork on the walls—a few pieces are of people, one of which is Sloane in a navy-blue dress.

"I like your art."

Sloane grins at me, wide and beautifully. Even though she's a lot older than Dempsey, I can see why he's attracted to her. "Dempsey. He's a man of many talents."

Beauty yelps and squirms, so I put her down. Then I walk over to admire the illustration.

Gemma takes my hand and leans her head against my shoulder. "Sorry for the less than friendly introduction. They're good people, I promise."

I squeeze her hand. "I'm good, Golden. Swear it."

A moment later, Dempsey announces dinner is ready. I wash up at the sink to rid myself of the puppy smell and then take a seat across from Dempsey at the square table with

Sloane on my left and Gemma on my right. I take a moment to scan my gaze over the spread. Lasagna, Caesar salad, garlic cheese bread. My stomach grumbles again.

"Mom's a way better cook," Dempsey states, "right, sis? But I learned a few tips and tricks from the old lady."

Sloane gasps. "Call her old again and I'll haul you in for elderly abuse."

He cracks up laughing and I can't help but smile too. Gemma, used to her brother's antics, just rolls her eyes as she starts making a plate. The conversation is light and friendly as we all make grabs at the delicious-looking food. Once I take my first bite of lasagna, I decide I can get along with Dempsey so long as he cooks for me again.

"This shit is good," I say around a huge mouthful of food. "Really good."

Dempsey starts cackling and it's aimed at Gemma. "Where'd you find this one? A barn?"

I flip him off, fully aware that I'm shoveling food in and dribbling sauce down my chin. I've always been a messy eater. It's part of my charm, what can I say.

"We're still working on domesticating him," Gemma says, tossing a napkin at me. "He's a good boy, though. Aren't you, buddy?"

I flip her off next.

Sloane starts to laugh, so I go ahead and give her the bird to make it a trifecta.

Despite all the ribbing, all of it aimed my way, I find myself relaxing. Dempsey is just protective of Gemma and I have no issues with that. Sloane is a cop, so it's in her nature to be suspicious. I like both of them and will make an effort because of Gemma.

"Just wait until Mom and Dad see him eat," Dempsey says with a chuckle. "I'd pay money to capture Mom's stunned reaction."

I stiffen and Gemma tears off a piece of her bread, not making eye contact with her brother.

"What?" Dempsey demands, humor dissipating immediately.

"We're, uh, not ready for the whole 'meet-the-parents' schtick." Gemma shrugs her shoulders like it's no big deal.

Sloane's eyes narrow as she studies Gemma. "You're awfully secretive lately. You know you can tell us anything."

Gemma's guilty expression gives her away. Before she can continue to dig herself deeper, I throw myself on the grenade for her.

"It's because of me," I blurt out and then shove another bite of lasagna into my mouth. "I don't want to meet them."

"Oh God," Gemma grumbles under her breath.

"Why the hell not?" Dempsey demands, fire in his tone.

"I don't want to." I shrug, swipe the napkin over my lips, and take another massive bite. "That simple."

Dempsey's fork clatters to the plate as he glares daggers at me. "You've got a fucking attitude, you know that?"

"Demps," Sloane says softly, touching his arm. "Chill."

"It's not that simple," Gemma states, rushing in to my aid now. "His parents know our parents. It's a whole thing. We're not that serious anyway. No sense in bringing the whole family into our relationship when it may not last the semester."

I flinch at her words, blinking at her. "Right. Good to know how you really feel, Golden."

She deflates, hurt pinching her pretty features.

"It is serious, dumbasses," Dempsey argues. "Don't play

me for stupid. There's something either of you isn't saying. Out with it already. Stop bullshitting us."

Gemma bites down on her bottom lip and shrugs. "It's not my story to tell."

Except it is her story to tell.

She is the story.

"I'm seconds from wringing both their necks to get them to talk," Dempsey utters to Sloane. "Got any interrogation tactics that might be more effective?"

Sloane ignores him, eyes boring into me. I shift under her unnerving stare.

"What's the 'whole thing' between your parents? Elaborate." Sloane abandons her fork to cross her arms over her chest. "May as well come clean and get it out in the open. Tate says talking—"

My scowl falls away as a grin tugs at my lips. "You see Tate too?"

"He's my therapist, so yeah," Sloane says.

"And he's our soon-to-be brother-in-law," Gemma and Dempsey both say at the same exact time, creeping me out with their "twin-ness."

I recover from that to realize the depth of their words. "Wait. Tate's family to you?"

The three of them nod in unison.

Betrayal burns hot in my chest, licking at my cheeks. The lasagna in my belly roils violently. Was this all some sort of trick? Have they all been playing me?

"You know Tate too?" Gemma asks slowly, eyes darting all over me in concern. "What's wrong?"

I don't sense anything other than curiosity in her tone. Maybe they're not all out to get me and it's just a huge fucking coincidence. Story of my life. Gemma is a walking, talking example of that.

Scrubbing my palm over my face, I sit back in my chair and look up at the popcorn-textured ceiling. Dad would shit his pants if he saw the ceiling and would have Pops out in no time to scrape it away.

The thought of my parents further sours my gut.

"Tate's my therapist. I, uh, told him all about Golden—er, Gemma. I didn't realize you all were connected." I drop my chin and meet Dempsey's probing stare. "I really liked him too, dammit."

"You can still see him," Sloane says gently. "He's not one to talk about his other patients. You can trust him."

We'll see.

My trust in Tate went from ten to one in a matter of minutes.

"I'm adopted," I blurt out, returning my stare to the hideous ceiling. "My parents adopted me when I was two, hence the nickname."

The table is silent. Gemma reaches over to touch my hand. I want to jerk it away, the hurt of my past making me raw, but I draw strength from it instead. She threads our fingers together and squeezes my hand.

"When all the stuff was going down with Dad and Callum," Gemma interjects softly, "Mom considered giving her baby up for adoption."

"Of course she did," Dempsey huffs. "I bet it was me, huh? They were going to keep you?"

Sloane shakes her head. "Jamie knew she was pregnant but didn't know about the twins until much later on. Let them speak, Dempsey."

For his credit, he clamps down, jaw muscle ticking, and nods my way.

"She must have got in contact with my dads somehow, though I don't know all the backstory, and promised them a baby," I explain, skin prickling with embarrassment. "Dad named her Gemma—this baby girl they were hoping for."

"Oh," Sloane murmurs. "She didn't even tell me she considered adoption when she found out she was pregnant. Jamie was probably terrified—even too terrified to confide in her best friend." Sloane slumps as though that thought physically wounds her. Maybe she can talk to Tate—the therapist for every-fucking-one—and sort that emotional shit out later.

"Your dad came through and they decided to keep the baby. Furthermore, to honor my parents, they decided to keep the name, Gemma, if it were a girl." I rub at my temple that's now throbbing. "You know how fucking crushed they must've been? They had a nursery set up for her. I saw the pictures."

Dempsey watches me with pity.

Hell, they all do.

Gemma, for her part, also looks guilty.

This dinner with my "not really that serious" girlfriend has gone down the toilet all too quickly. I'm eager to get the hell out of here.

"Damn, dude," Dempsey rumbles. "That's…so fucked up."

Unable to deal with their expressions any longer, I push back from the table, the wood legs screeching across the floor.

"I need a breather," I grunt out. "I'll be in the car, Golden."

Without another word, I bolt.

CHAPTER TWENTY-ONE

Gemma

BEAUTY DECIDES THAT TWO'S ABRUPT EXIT IS HER cue to hop onto his vacated chair and help herself to the rest of his lasagna. While Dempsey and Sloane both simultaneously start hollering at my precious fur-niece, who was just hungry, I abandon my own meal to follow after Two.

Before I can get the front door open, he's barreling back through it with a familiar yellow flower in one hand and a note in the other.

My stalker strikes again.

Coldness seeps into my every cell. This creep followed me to my brother's house and left me another message while we ate. I feel so violated.

Sloane, sensing my mood change, abandons scolding Beauty to come over to us. "What is it?"

Two trembles with fury or fear—I'm not sure which.

"My stalker," I say sharply. "Wherever I go, they go."

"Set it on the coffee table," Sloane instructs. "Let me grab some gloves."

Two drops both items onto the table as if they're riddled with disease before tugging me into his arms. All the drama moments ago is forgotten as something far more sinister greets us.

Dempsey manages to clean off Beauty's face, though her fur is stained from the sauce. She gets the boot into the backyard where she pitifully yelps at the door as if to plead her case.

By the time Sloane returns, Beauty has stopped complaining to no doubt wreak havoc on some part of their yard.

Sloane sits on the edge of the table and first inspects the flower before picking up the letter. She unfolds it and her eyes dart across the paper as she quickly reads it.

"Hmm."

"What does it say?" Dempsey demands.

"'Must be getting pretty serious if you're showing him off to the family. Tell your boyfriend to keep his dick in his pants. Or else.'" Sloane frowns. "That's all it says."

I shudder at the warning. "Or else what?"

Sloane goes into detective mode. "Any jealous ex-boyfriends or people who might want to be with you that you can think of?"

"No," I say as Dempsey blurts out, "Only the entire Internet."

I scowl at him. "Not helping."

"Just stating the obvious," Dempsey says with a shrug. "You have like a billion followers. It could be anyone."

Despite my being visible to a million-plus people, I don't think it's one of them. Clearly, it's a local. Someone who knows me and has easy access to me.

"We've spent a lot of time together," Two interjects. "I haven't seen anyone who stares a little too long or anything. The creepiest thing that happened was when that cop caught us."

Dempsey tenses. "Caught you doing what?"

"Irrelevant," Sloane barks out. "The cop's been cleared. I checked his patrol car driving logs and the vehicle hasn't been to your school, home, or Hemingford Hall. He may have been creepy as you claim, but he's not the stalker. Your stalker is staying hidden for a reason."

"Because he's a pussy," Dempsey growls. "If he comes out of hiding, I'm going to kick his ass."

"You and me both," Two agrees.

"That means," Sloane continues, ignoring the spike in testosterone levels, "either they're small or incapable of carrying out their threats, which could mean a girl you might know could be trying to scare you. Or…"

"Or," I urge her to continue. "I don't know of any girls who could have it out for me."

"And we're sure *this* guy didn't plant it just to freak you out?" Dempsey tosses back, jabbing a finger at Two. "Convenient he was the one to find the note."

"Fuck all the way off," Two barks. "Get off my back, man. Your fury is pointed in the wrong direction."

"Dempsey," Sloane says with a sigh. "Give Two a break. It's not him."

Two shoots Dempsey a smug look that has my brother's face reddening.

"What is your other thought, Sloane?" I ask, bringing the topic back to where we started. "If it's not some mean girl. Who then?"

"Someone with a reason to stay under the radar. A person in a position of authority perhaps? A prominent figure? A friend of your father's?"

The room goes silent as I process those words. Imagining it could be one of Dad's old guy friends has me cringing. Hard. I think I like the stranger idea better.

"We have to get Dad involved," Dempsey says softly. "It's the only way to keep you safe."

"I actually agree with him," Two chimes in. "I know you don't want to, but he might be able to give us better insight into who's doing this."

My stomach twists. All my freedom will be gone. Dad will go into protective papa bear mode and I'll be kept under lock and key. Not literally, but it won't be good.

"I won't get to see you," I say, closing my eyes and nuzzling against Two's solid chest. "Unless you meet them, which I know you don't want to do."

Two stiffens momentarily and then relaxes. "If it helps keep you safe, I'll meet them. I can't exactly say I'll be happy about it, but if it's what we need to do, then I'll do it."

"We *are* serious," I mutter. "All this hiding and pretending is too much. I'm sorry I said it wasn't earlier because it's not true."

I can feel Sloane's and Dempsey's eyes on my back, but I ignore them. Two strokes his fingers through my hair in a comforting gesture that does wonders for calming me down.

"We just *had* to start liking each other, Golden," Two says dryly. "Really made a mess of things."

Grinning, I squeeze him tight. "Nothing can be messier than the way you eat. I think we can handle this. Together."

We stand on my front porch, hand in hand. I've yet to open the door and head inside because my gut keeps twisting with nerves. Mom was confused when I texted her that I was coming home with a guest and for her and Dad to be presentable. The whole drive from Dempsey and Sloane's back home was fine, and I was feeling good about coming clean, but now that we're here, I can't seem to pull the trigger.

Will it get ugly?

My parents don't even know I have a boyfriend. I'm not just going to drop that bomb on them but a few more for grins and giggles. Ugh. I really want to rewind tonight and erase this stupid idea.

"Let's get it over with," Two says, glancing down at me. "If I could handle your brother, I can handle your parents."

It's different, though.

Mom and Dad aren't going to be eager to kick his ass. They'll come in hard with their overprotective parent speeches, followed by new rules I'll have to follow. My freedom to run off with Two at any time will screech to a stop.

"Will you be okay meeting…her?" I ask softly. "Because of…"

Because of the fact she's responsible for your family's pain?

"I'll be okay," Two vows.

Before I can chicken out, I step forward and open the door. The lights in the living room burn brightly and both of my parents are sitting on the love seat with glasses of wine. Dad's expression is impassive and cool, but Mom's eyebrows are at her hairline.

I guess they weren't expecting a boy.

"Hey," I chirp, feigning a carefreeness I don't feel one bit. "I figured I'd come clean and introduce you to my boyfriend, Two."

Dad rises from the love seat to extend a hand to Two. "Boyfriend, huh?"

Two shakes my father's hand and then pulls back, not bothering to greet my mother at all.

"Yeah, it's a long story," I blurt out. "Come sit, Two."

I guide him over to the couch and we both take a seat. My parents' eyes bore into us. Dad finally sits, downs the rest of his wine, and sets it down on the end table with a loud clink.

"Long story," Mom parrots, hurt shining in her eyes. "How long have you been together? I can't believe you kept this from me."

I'm really close to my mother. Sometimes it's like having a built-in best friend. I hate the curdling feeling of shame in my belly.

"It just kind of happened," I say, waving my hand in the air like it's no big deal. "We met at school. He's my partner."

My parents exchange a quick look of panic, both of them no doubt calculating all the times I've been out gallivanting with my partner. I'm sure they're imagining sordid details of things that didn't happen.

Okay, well, some probably did.

"Me having a boyfriend isn't the big deal here," I tell them. "There's more."

Mom's face pales. "You're pregnant?"

Two snorts as if this is funny. The glower on Dad's face says it isn't.

"What? No. Mom, I'm still, uh, a you know…"

Virgin.

Don't make me say it.

Both of my parents relax as though my virginity is something sacred that needs protecting at all costs. I can lose my virginity and be just fine. My life, though, that's another story.

"Well," Mom encourages, a practiced smile on her face. "What's going on?"

"Two's real name is Tristan Sheridan."

Dad doesn't seem to register the last name, but Mom's eyes widen in immediate horror.

"He, uh, is—"

"Oh my God," Mom croaks out. "Oh. My. God."

Dad tenses and shoots me a questioning look. "Explain."

Two decides it's his turn to speak and launches into it before I can stop him. "I'm the second choice baby. You know, the one my dads got when they couldn't have Gemma here."

I'd wanted to deliver this delicately, but Two doesn't do delicate. Finally, Dad understands. He goes from confused to pissed in an instant.

"Gemma," Dad growls. "What the actual fuck?"

"Nathan," Mom chides.

It's not the first time I've heard Dad curse, and it certainly won't be the last. I shift in my seat, feeling awkward about this whole conversation.

"Are you doing this to hurt us?" Mom asks, eyes welling with tears.

"What? No, it was seriously a coincidence that we were partnered up," I rush out, panicking at the idea she thinks this is all some big production to upset them. "How could you even think that?"

Mom deflates. "Wow. It's a lot to take in."

"Well, I, for one," Dad bites out, "don't feel comfortable with you running off with some boy all hours of the night. It's not safe, Gem."

"I know," I blurt, "and I'm sorry. That's why I'm coming clean right now."

"Do your dads know?" Mom asks Two, pain gleaming in her eyes. "How did they take it?"

"Nope," Two hisses, "and I plan to keep it that way."

Mom shakes her head in disagreement. "Two, honey, they need to know—"

"I said no." Two's voice is sharp like a blade, broking no room for argument. "Tell them the rest, Golden."

My parents gape at me, shocked that there could be more. There's a big ol' stalker cherry to set on top of this screwed-up conversation.

"Someone's been, uh, following me and leaving me notes," I say, not able to hold Dad's stare. "It's a little creepy."

Two snorts again. "Someone? It's a stalker. You have a stalker. He knows where you live, where I live, where your brother lives, where you go to school, and where Hemingford Hall is. He even knows your phone number! It's more than a 'little creepy,' Golden."

Dad jumps to his feet, eyes darting all around in panic. "Why am I just now hearing about this? How long has this been happening?"

"A few weeks," I admit, cringing. "Sorry, Dad."

"I need to know everything," Dad barks out. "I'll have Jude search and Sloane—"

"Sloane knows," I interject, "and she's investigating."

"It's one of those followers," Dad says, shaking his head in disappointment. "I thought your social media stuff was harmless. Apparently, I was naive. I want you to delete your accounts immediately."

"Dad!" I shriek, also rising to my feet. "You can't just take away my business—my job! It's not one of my followers!"

"Until we've caught this sick piece of shit," Dad snarls, "I won't take any chances with my baby girl."

Two also stands. "Sloane thinks it's one of *your* buddies, man."

Dad goes still and glares at me. "What?"

"They're keeping their identity hidden for a reason," I tell him with a sigh. "She thinks it could be a friend of yours or someone in a position of power in this town. Someone who can't risk their reputation."

Silence befalls the living room as Dad processes my words. Mom also stands, taking hold of Dad's hand.

"Two, I think you should leave," Mom says gently. "We have much to discuss with our daughter."

"Yep," he grunts, already striding for the door. "See you around, Golden."

I hate that I don't even get a hug or kiss goodbye, but now's not the time to push my parents. They're about to explode.

"A friend of mine," Dad utters, shaking his head. "We're going to find this asshole and I'll ruin him in every way possible."

As happy as I am to be out with my secrets and have Dad fighting for me, I know it won't come without new restrictions.

I just hate that my freedom with Two is about to be yanked away.

CHAPTER TWENTY-TWO

Two

"**W**AKE UP."

I blink away my grogginess to find Pops standing in the middle of my bedroom, arms crossed over his barrel chest and a furious expression on his usually easygoing face.

"Hey," I say, sitting up and rubbing the sleep out of my eyes. "What's up?"

His nostrils flare and he motions out of my room. "Get dressed. Meet me in the living room. We need to talk."

"About what?" I ask, heart rate kickstarting to life.

He doesn't answer as he stalks out of my room.

What the fuck?

Did I run over Dad's rose bush again?

I hope I didn't leave the space heater on in the shop.

I barely give myself time for a piss and to brush my teeth before I'm throwing on a T-shirt and jeans so I can find out what's going on.

The house smells like cinnamon rolls, making my stomach grumble. I don't dare go hunt down food, though, since Pops is clearly angry about something. In the living room, I find both my parents already there. Dad is curled up under a blanket sniffling and Pops is pacing in front of the couch.

Oh fuck.

Dread coils in my gut. Deep down, I know what this is about. But how? How do they know?

I glance over at Dad, who's clutching a used tissue. He won't look my way, which stings, and his eyes are red and swollen from crying.

This can't be happening.

I freeze, unable to sit or move, fixated on the crushed expression Dad wears. He's always so fierce and strong. Seeing him like this is gutting. And Pops? He never gets angry. Like ever. His face is a dark shade of red going on purple like he might burst at any second.

"Sit," Pops commands, voice harsh.

I jolt out of my haze and stumble over to one of the armchairs. Everything aches in me to sit by Dad, but I don't think he wants me there. Years and years of self-doubt and feelings of inadequacy claw at my insides.

"What's going on?" I murmur. "Tell me."

Pops cracks his neck before turning his glare on me. "How about you tell us, Tristan."

I dart my gaze over to Dad, who's begun crying again. Disgust at myself and the entire situation suffocates me.

"I don't know what you mean," I lie, tearing my stare from Dad to my hands. "I don't."

Liar, liar, liar.

Pops lets out a huff of disbelief. "Who the hell are you anymore? It's like I don't even recognize the man in front of me."

My shoulders hunch at his words. If I could crawl into a hole right now to hide from this confrontation, I would.

"How do you know?" I still can't look Pops in the eyes, but I need answers too. "Who told you?"

"Jamie Park," Dad whispers. "We had quite the conversation this morning."

Seriously?

Anger quells up inside me, chasing away the crushing sadness. She called my dad up and tattled to him? "Of course she did."

I feel both my parents' stares on me and finally glance up to look at them.

"What does that mean?" Dad asks, bottom lip trembling. "Two, how did we get here? Explain. Please."

Scrubbing my palm over my face, I let out a heavy sigh. "Do we really have to do this?"

Pops growls—seriously growls like a goddamn dog. "Yes, Son. We really do."

Okay, so no avoiding it.

I really wish Tate were here to mediate this shitshow.

"Did you know Tate's fiancé is Jude Park?" I cock my head to the side, looking Dad's way.

"We did." Dad purses his lips while he and Pops share a weighted look. "Jude hired our company a while back to repair his porch and add a wheelchair ramp. When I learned Tate was a therapist and a very nice young man, I wanted you to see him."

I cross my arms and lean back in my chair. "I'm surprised you even took the job after that family…"

Dad swallows and his eyes water. "After what, Two? What do you *think* you know?"

"Think?" I say with a scoff. "Dad, I found the letter from Jamie. I saw the picture."

"You went through my things?"

"Believe me," I spit out. "Never made that mistake again."

Dad flinches at my words. "What has gotten into you?"

"Exactly when did you find the letter and picture?" Pops demands, railroading right over Dad's question. "Why didn't you talk to us about this?"

Memories of being nine years old and curious about Santa assault me. Why did I have to go snooping? I found so much more than I'd bargained for.

"I was nine."

Dad starts to cry again and Pops storms out of the room. A door slams somewhere within the house. Guilt and anger and sadness swirl around inside me like some fucked-up typhoon ready to suck me up and spit me out.

"Nine," Dad rasps out through his tears. "Oh my God. This explains so much."

It does?

Before I can probe him, Pops returns with the offending letter and picture in hand. He slaps them down on the coffee table before landing in a heap beside Dad. His anger is still there like a live electrical wire, but his eyes shine with abject despair.

I knew this would happen.

I knew if it ever came to light, they'd have to revisit the horrible, devastating memories.

Jamie Park is a witch.

How *could* she?

Why would she?

Hasn't she done enough to torment my dads?

"There's so much to unpack here," Dad says with a humorless laugh. "So much."

Pops leans forward and stabs a finger at the picture. "Tell us everything."

I press my lips together, not eager to get into this. There's no hiding it now, though.

"Two," Pops clips out. "Cut the bullshit and speak."

"Dax told me Santa wasn't real and he could prove it." I run my tongue over my bottom lip, wishing I'd grabbed a handful of butterscotch candies so I'd have something to distract myself with. "I told him he was wrong. Went hunting and discovered that stuff instead."

"Oh, honey," Dad croaks. "You must've been so confused and hurting."

"To say the least," I mutter.

"So you sought her out?" Pops asks, jaw muscle flexing. "To punish us?"

Dad gives a sharp shake of his head. "Grant. Cool off before you say something you can't take back."

"I just want to understand how it is our son is apparently dating the girl we almost adopted." Pops pinches the bridge of his nose. "All scenarios as to why this has happened in my head are bad ones. What did we do to ever deserve this betrayal by our own son?"

"Betrayal?" My voice rises several octaves. "How betrayed do you think *I* felt when I discovered I was your second choice?"

Tears of anger and years' worth of pain form in my eyes, blurring my parents' figures. I press the heels of my hands against my eyes, trying to get them not to leak. A ragged sob rips from my throat anyway. So much for that.

Hands are suddenly on either side of my head as Dad kisses the top.

"You weren't a second choice, honey," Dad says with

a broken voice. "You were the best decision we ever made. Instalove. The second we laid eyes on you, you were ours."

His words prickle their way into my aching heart.

"But you wanted Gemma. Enough to name her and fix up a nursery for her," I argue through my tears. "She was your number one. I was the backup option after Jamie broke your hearts."

Dad pulls back and kneels in front of me. "Eyes here, Two." He motions at his red, teary ones. "*You* are our number one. *You.*"

Pops comes over to join, sitting on the arm of the chair. "You really thought we were pining away all these years over Gemma?" His strong hand clutches my shoulder. "Son, from the second we got you, you've been our entire world."

"Did you start dating her to get back at us?" Dad asks. "Because of how you were feeling?"

I swallow hard and shake my head. "No. As soon as I learned who she was, I hated her instantly. I didn't want to like her, Dad. I fucking swear it. It just happened."

Pops chuckles. "Sounds like when I met your dad. We weren't ever supposed to be a thing, but it just happened."

"Once you realized you weren't exactly straight," Dad reminds him with a goofy grin. "Had to convince you a few times until you understood."

They join hands, sharing in their moment, gazing happily at each other. It gives me hope that this whole Gemma thing won't completely destroy them.

"How'd you meet her?" Dad finally asks. "If you didn't seek her out, how did it happen?"

"In class. She called my car a hunk of junk."

Pops scoffs and Dad sniggers. Since the vehicle is

Pops's old car and Dad made him retire it, their reactions are appropriate.

"Then she hit me with her car!"

Dad's humor is wiped right off his face. "She *what*? On purpose? What the hell? Are you okay?"

I let his rapid-fire questions penetrate my aching heart. He loves me. They both do. Their concern and care have always been so overwhelming in a good way.

"It was an accident. I'm fine now. Just got bruised at the time." I can't help but grin. "I was such a dick to her. Naturally, I got partnered up with her for the Hemingford Hall project."

"Gemma's your project partner? Jamie failed to mention that part." Dad's eyes widen comically. "Gemma was here, wasn't she?"

"Yeah," I admit, feeling terrible. "She's actually cool, though. Not at all a bitch like I'd assumed."

A smile tugs at my lips as I think of her pretty glossy lips and sassy personality.

"Well, I'll be goddamned," Pops says with a chuckle. "Our boy is in love."

Dad squeals—legit squeals—making me and Pops both wince.

"You're being safe, right?" Pops continues. "I know we've had the birds and the bees talk many times before, but I feel like we might need to have a refresher course."

"Pops, no," I say with a grimace. "I know everything there is to know about sex. I'm a grown-ass man in case you forgot. Besides, we aren't even there yet. Damn."

"Thank God," Dad says, shaking his head. "Take things slow. Get to know each other before you make commitments with your bodies."

"Dude," I grunt. "I really don't want to talk about this with you guys."

"Condoms?" Pops asks, completely ignoring my request. "You have them just in case?"

"I'll put them on the grocery list," Dad interjects. "Should we buy more lube?"

Fuck my life.

Now they're just tormenting me.

A blossom of warmth fills my chest. This wicked, ugly secret is now in the open and we're all teasing and laughing, sitting close by each other and touching.

They do love me.

I'm their whole world, they said.

"How did you know Jamie anyway?" I ask, still needing to know more about their past. "There seemed to have been some sort of relationship there."

Dad glances up at Pops. "You want to tell him, hon? This is more your story than mine."

"She was just a kid I knew from the neighborhood I grew up in," Pops explains, sadness in his voice. "Her family was full of assholes who used to whip up on her. Your grandma would always invite her over to eat supper with us. I kind of thought of her as an annoying little sister, but deep down, I knew she needed the break from those horrible people."

"We later invited her to our wedding," Dad cuts in, "but she never showed. The girl really did live a troubled life. Then, one day, she reached out to us to tell us she was pregnant and wouldn't be able to keep the baby."

"Except she did keep the baby," I grumble. "Screwed you over in the process."

"She was young," Pops states in her defense. "And scared.

Yes, we were hurt by her changing her mind, but we also were realistic from the start. At the time, we weren't actively looking to adopt, but after things fell through with Jamie, we both realized there was so much love in our hearts. We needed to share that with someone."

"That someone was you, Two," Dad croons. "Our perfect, precious baby boy. Still are."

Something tells me I'll be forty and my dads will still treat me like their precious baby boy. Something tells me I won't hate it either.

"I know it would be awkward for you guys to meet her," I start to say, but Dad cuts me off.

"Honey, no. We really, really want to meet her. Not as some little girl we never adopted but as our son's girlfriend. The girl our beautiful, funny, smart-as-a-whip son is crazy over. I know we've been busy with work and you with school, but please make time to bring her over to dinner one day so we can properly meet her."

At one point, I wondered what it would be like for Gemma to meet my dads. I imagined heartache and tears. Now, though, I can imagine the four of us having a really good time.

"Yeah, okay. I'll bring her over. She really wants to meet you guys."

Dad grins and pulls my head toward his to kiss my forehead. Pops squeezes my shoulder again in an affectionate gesture he's done my entire life as far back as I can remember.

"I'm sorry I snooped," I say, coming down from my momentary high. "I should have talked to you about it. Once I tell Tate this is what I've been carrying for so long, something tells me he's going to beat my ass for not telling him sooner so we could talk it out."

Dad cracks up laughing. "Good. We pay him well to beat your ass."

A weight tumbles off my shoulders and shatters on the floor around me. Who knew talking about this could feel so good? I've been spending years and years bottling it up inside. Releasing it is so…freeing.

CHAPTER TWENTY-THREE

Gemma

I'M UNBELIEVABLY PISSED AT MY MOTHER RIGHT NOW.

She called Two's dads this morning and tattled.

How could she?

Is she trying to ruin my life—ruin this good, sweet, tender thing between me and Two?

When he texted me this morning to let me know what she'd done, I'd been humiliated and horrified. Luckily, he said his parents were handling it well. Just wanted me to know.

If I weren't terrified of getting abducted by some creeper, I'd take a drive far away from this house just to calm my mind and get away from Mom. Instead, I do the next best thing. I go next door to visit Willa and my little buddy Bane.

"Knock-knock," I chirp as I enter my brother and sister-in-law's house.

Bane babbles from somewhere within the home. I follow the sounds of my nephew's adorable little voice to find him in his room in his bed, clearly just having awoken from a nap. His parents' bedroom door is closed.

Ew.

They're probably making more babies.

"Don't worry, I've got him," I say to the baby monitor, knowing they can hear me. "Keep doing your thing, big bro."

I hear laughing from their bedroom, which makes me grin. Bane's blue eyes sparkle with delight when he sees me.

"There's my Baney-boo," I croon as I scoop him into my arms. "Did you miss me?"

He continues making cheerful, loud sounds that warm my heart while I snuggle him to me. With Bane, I can almost forget I'm angry at Mom. Almost.

At least over here, I don't have to see her. Mom doesn't exactly come over to Callum's that often. I mean, she tried to ruin *his* life too…

Guilt assaults me. I know that's unfair. Mom had her own terrible struggles when she was younger and vilifying her won't help the situation. I just need a break from her.

I feel Bane's diaper and decide he needs changing. I'm no expert at this job, but I can do a better job than all my brothers combined. Bane's only peed on me once. After I change him, I pick him back up and carry him into the living room to wait for Willa to stop being bred by my brother.

Minutes later, they both hurry into the living room. Willa's face is flushed, with beard burn from my brother's scruff. Callum wears a smug smirk. They both smell like sex. Yuck.

"What's up?" Willa asks, sitting beside me. "Everything okay?"

She's always been one to read people well, especially me.

"Not really." I shrug like it's no big deal. "Just Mom trying to ruin my life, is all."

Callum plops down in the recliner, nosing his way into our conversation. "She's a master at that shit."

No matter how much time goes by or how happy Callum is, he'll never truly let it go that Mom left him for our dad. Truthfully, I'd be pissed too if I were him.

I then proceed to word-vomit everything to Callum, Willa, and little Bane. By the time I finish, Willa's eyes are wide as saucers. Callum studies me with a pensive look.

"So you have a boyfriend and never told me?" Willa asks, hurt lacing her tone. "I gotta admit. I'm a little stung by that."

I sigh as I reach over to squeeze her hand. "I know and I'm sorry. It was just a weird thing, you know? I didn't want anyone to know. Now, apparently, *everyone* does."

"Bring him to family dinner tonight," Callum suggests. "Let's see if he passes the brotherly test."

"Oh, he totally won't," I say with a silly smile. "Two's his own weird person. Doesn't ever say or do the right thing. While I find it endearing, it's put him on the bad side of every family member he's met thus far."

Callum's smile curls into something a bit wicked. "I like him already."

Bane grabs hold of some of my hair and hollers as if to throw his two cents in as well. I kiss his fuzzy head and squeeze him tight. I love this little guy.

"Tell us more about this stalker," Callum says, growing serious. "You said Sloane thinks it's someone Dad knows. Hell, that could be anyone. He's friends with everyone in this town."

"If I know Dad, he's probably already making a list for

Jude," I say with a frown. "She also thought it could be a girl just trying to scare me."

"And it's definitely not that cop?" Willa asks. "He seems like a suspect to me too."

"Sloane doesn't think so," I say with a shake of my head. "It's creepy to think some old man Dad knows could be doing this."

"Even if they know Dad," Callum reasons, "they shouldn't have access to all your information. They'd know your home address at best. But your phone number? Your boyfriend's house? The person has connections of some sort."

"Your dad is cozied up to that new mayor. Phil Draper." Willa frowns at me. "That guy seriously makes me nervous."

"Possibly," Callum says, "but I didn't get that vibe when I met him. Do you think he just unnerves you because he worked with your ex-stepdad?"

Willa's ex-stepdad and ex-stepbrother were total assholes. For the most part, they leave her alone now that she's a part of the Parks, but they still make her wary.

"Maybe," Willa admits. "Wouldn't hurt to have Sloane investigate him."

"She won't go hunting down people again," I say with a sigh. "That almost cost her her job last time, especially since she had it all wrong. She's going to want hard proof that he could be a suspect."

"I'll have Jude do a full rundown on him," Callum assures me. "We'll uncover any dirt the illegal way and then let Sloane shake down the rest the legal way."

Despite everything being so messy, I'm once again

reminded about how good my family can be. We may have our flaws, but we sure know how to band together in a crisis.

I guess my stalker is officially considered a Park family crisis now.

Family dinners at my house every Sunday are hectic, to say the least. Mom got a new, ostentatious mahogany dining room table to better fit our growing family. If we include our grandfather, his cook, and all the babies, there's something like seventeen of us. The table seats twenty-two. I don't know what Mom will do when we max out. Do they make tables any bigger than this monstrous piece?

Rex is in his highchair, already stuffing his face with macaroni and cheese, while Mom rushes around to place last-minute dishes on the table. No one pays me any attention, all of them babbling and catching up, which is good.

Two's coming to dinner.

Surprise!

Now that the cat's out of the bag, there's no reason why he can't join us. In fact, I want him to join us. Since last night and this morning went so badly, I'm aching to see him to make sure we're okay—that *he's* okay.

Of course he's late.

Naturally.

Aubrey, with her daughter Rue sitting in her lap, waves me over. As much as I want to cuddle my niece, I'd rather be ready for Two's arrival. Spencer saves me when he steals the seat beside her and then starts tickling the baby.

Dad watches me with narrowed eyes but doesn't speak to me.

Finally, the doorbell rings.

"I'll get it!" I shout, bolting for the door.

I'm grinning from ear to ear when I fling it open, ready to leap into Two's arms. Except, it's not Two. It's a man.

One of Dad's friends.

Chief of police and Sloane's boss, Hiroshi Tanaka.

The strange bird-like man bores his stare into me. Normally, I might blow off such an intense look, but something about him unnerves me.

"Hello, Gemma."

His icy cold tone makes me shiver. He waits patiently, like a friggin' vampire, for me to welcome him inside. I'm tempted to close the door in his face.

"Hiroshi," Dad greets from behind me. "So happy you could join us today."

Dad clutches my shoulder and gently moves me aside so he can usher in Tanaka. Their newly formed friendship wasn't all that surprising. Dad aligns himself with anyone and everyone of importance. Having the chief of police in your back pocket is a flex my dad no doubt wanted to have.

I want to ask Dad why this man is here, but I bite my tongue. When I catch Sloane's stare on me, she gives me a comforting smile. She's obviously trying to assure me that it's okay. Nothing to worry about.

So why do I feel edgy now that this man is here?

I could just be paranoid.

Before I can read too much into it, Two's hunk of junk roars down our road. He skids to a stop right in front of our house. Since the driveway is full, he leaves his vehicle where it stopped, blocking our road from anyone coming or going.

As soon as he steps out of the vehicle, I run out of the

house toward him. He's waiting for me and catches me when I launch myself at him. Our mouths meet for a starved kiss, each of us mauling the other with desperation.

Yeah, we're good.

Really good.

We pull apart to grin goofily at each other. He can be cantankerous and strange and obtuse, but he's also cute, sweet, and funny. I love being with him. It truly is the highlight of my day when I get to see him.

I finally pull away from him and reach for his hand. "Ready for the firing squad?"

He snorts. "Yup."

Then he pulls my hand closer to his face to inspect my nails. "I like these. It looks like real gold flecks on the matte black."

I preen at his compliment. "I did them last night after you left."

"What is that stuff?"

"It's this really fine gold foil that sort of disintegrates when you handle it, giving it a gold fleck effect. Cool, huh?"

"Very."

He kisses the back of my hand before letting our hands drop between us, though still conjoined. I lead him into my house where my family's chatter dies down to meet the newcomer.

"Two?" Tate exclaims in shock. "Holy crap!"

Tate rushes over to us and hugs Two. "This is the girl who ran you over with her car?"

I gape at Two. "You told him that?"

Two shrugs and smirks. "Yes, because you did."

"I hit you. I didn't run you over."

"Wow," Tate says breathily, eyes wide with awe. "I have so many questions. So many. We're going to talk about this tomorrow in our session." He motions for the table. "Come eat with us."

I introduce Two to everyone as my boyfriend. Some of the family doesn't know the whole drama about the canceled adoption and Mom knowing his dads, but it doesn't feel like the right time to fill them in. Especially not with Hiroshi Tanaka watching us with cool interest.

When we're finally seated to eat, Sloane leans into me and says, "Tanaka's here to meet with your dad about the stalker. See if he can offer his help. He's good people."

Is he, though?

The man continues to study me and Two.

"Yeah, sure," I mumble.

I glance past Sloane to see Dempsey frowning hard. He's never been Tanaka's biggest fan. He must be feeling my uneasy vibes through our twin bond because he's watching Tanaka like he might be about to do something stupid.

Like kidnap me?

The thought of going anywhere with Tanaka makes me shudder. Why isn't his wife along for the visit? Why doesn't he talk much? Why does he keep looking at us?

Finally, Tanaka tears his gaze away from mine to look down at his phone. He pecks away on it with one long, bony finger before he puts it away.

Seconds later, my phone buzzes in my pocket.

I freeze, terror clawing its way up my throat. It's him. Tanaka is my stalker. Swallowing down bile, I fish my phone out of my pocket and read my message.

Except it's not a message.

It's a calendar reminder to turn in an interest form for a school workshop.

Not Tanaka. Just a reminder.

Ugh.

Fear is my new normal and I hate it.

CHAPTER TWENTY-FOUR

Two

"WHAT IF IT'S MR. PEDERSON?" GEMMA WHISPERS, eyeing the papers he gave to the two of us when we came into class this morning. "He seems weirdly fixated on us as a pair."

I glance at our professor and frown. He's just some old dude who loves historical restoration, not a stalker.

"I think you're reaching," I mutter back, nudging her under the table with my foot. "You're paranoid."

She shoots me an irritated look, but it's the truth. Last night, after a loud dinner with her family, she told me all about how she thought the police chief was her stalker. I think, at this point, anyone could be the stalker according to Gemma.

Worrying about everyone without definitive proof is pointless.

Mr. Pederson continues his lecture. Rather than take notes—since I know my girlfriend will anyway—I focus on the man himself. I've been to his house before with my parents. Nothing stood out to me as creepy. He's wearing a fedora, bowtie, and suspenders, for fuck's sake.

Definitely not him.

I tear my gaze from Mr. Pederson to look down at the form he pretty much threatened me to fill out. I'd remembered seeing something about it in my school email recently but didn't bother filling out the interest form for the cultural heritage workshop. Now, as it would seem, Mr. Pederson is forcing us both to fill it out.

"My two best students."

He'd said those exact words earlier when he thrust the papers at me. Okay, so maybe she has a point about him being weirdly obsessed with us as a pair, but that doesn't make him a bad guy. He knows how much I enjoy all this historical preservation stuff and must sense Gemma's growing interest as well.

The workshop is coming up in a few weeks. Students were welcomed to apply, but there will only be a handful selected for the intimate event. Aimed for students showing a keen interest in the subject matter, the workshop is a collaborative event with local preservation societies. Mr. Pederson thinks it'll be a great way for me to get connected with the community and would look great on my résumé. Plus, there'll be dinner and I do love to eat. It sounds right up my alley and if Gemma gets to go too, it's a win-win.

Gemma must eventually give up worrying about Mr. Pederson because she studiously takes our notes. When class is over, I grab the form she's completed plus mine before turning them back in to Mr. Pederson.

"Good work, Sheridan," he says with a toothy grin. "I know your dads will be thrilled if you're accepted to attend."

I give him a nod and stride out of the classroom. Gemma hurries behind me, clasping her hand around mine as soon as we're alone. We barely make it halfway down the hallway before Dax nearly runs us over.

"I found a place," Dax exclaims, showing me his phone. "It's in a seedy part of town, but it could be ours for really cheap."

"What is it?" Gemma asks, peeking at the phone with me. "You're moving out? Why?"

"It's time," I explain with a sigh, absently searching my jacket pocket with my free hand for one of my butterscotch candies. "I haven't told my dads yet, though."

Gemma looks at the property and shakes her head. "That's in the old biker hangout. Gross. Don't get that place. Who knows what kind of bodily fluids are on every surface there."

How she knows where an old biker gang hangs out is beyond me. But after a quick glance through the pictures, I agree that it's not someplace I want to live.

"Keep looking," I tell Dax, handing him his phone back. I unwrap my candy and pop it in my mouth. "We'll find some-place better."

Dax deflates. "Mom's driving me insane, though. I'm half tempted to move into your closet, Two. Can I? Please?"

"And everyone says *I'm* the dramatic one?" I scoff. "It'll come at the right time, man."

He grunts in agreement and then heads off for his next class. I walk Gemma out of the building toward our cars that are parked side by side. As we approach hers, something yellow flutters in the wind. Gemma stops several feet from her car. I let go of her hand, striding over to it.

At least I know it's not Mr. Pederson. He was in class when we arrived and was still there when we left. I pluck the note from the wiper blade and read it.

I always have my eyes on you, pretty girl. Always. Remember that. Think before you act. Be a good girl for me.
What the fuck?

When I whirl around, Gemma is on the phone, shivering despite wearing her stylish leather jacket.

"Come on," I growl. "We're going to see the campus police."

She nods as she hurries to catch up with me. From the bits of conversation I overhear, she's on the phone with her dad. As much as this weekend sucked when our secrets were revealed, I'm thankful to be having others help with this stalker shit.

"Dad's on his way," Gemma says as she pockets her phone. "He's calling the dean, too. They're all going to meet us at the campus police office." She takes the letter from me and quickly reads it. "This guy needs to get a life."

I sling an arm over her shoulders and pull her into my side as we walk. This stalker guy is slick—too slick. It makes me nervous as fuck for her.

Soon, we're entering the campus police office and reporting our findings. The older gentleman with a thick gray mustache jovially flirts with Gemma as he fills out a report, totally not reading the room.

She's scared, dude.

Leave her the fuck alone.

Carl Vaughn.

The hairs on my arms stand on end. What if this leering old man is the creep who's been terrorizing her?

Damn, I'm getting as paranoid as she is.

Not long after, Nathan and the dean come striding in together, nearly matching in navy three-piece suits. Nathan's tie is a paler blue, whereas the dean's is red. Both men wear stern expressions.

"Miss Park," the PMU head dean, Dr. Skeller, greets. "Your dad's filled me in on what's going on. Are you okay?"

Gemma glances over at Carl and barely suppresses a shudder. The small shiver can be seen if you're really watching. Apparently, both me and her dad are because Nathan pulls her to his chest.

Gemma clings to him, letting him hug her tight. I want to do the same.

"I'm fine," she finally manages to answer. "I'm just tired of this."

"Mr. Vaughn," Dr. Skeller instructs in a firm tone, "please check any security footage we may have on the parking lot mentioned in her report. If there's anything unusual, report back. We're going to catch this guy. If he's doing this to Miss Park, he could be doing it to other students."

Carl, no longer eyeballing my girlfriend's tits, nods emphatically. "I'm on it, sir."

"I didn't think about this happening to other students," Gemma says with a grimace.

"We're going to get him," Nathan assures her. "I promise."

I hope it's one promise he can deliver on.

Rather than our usual office visit, I'm meeting Tate at Park's Peak, a trendy coffee shop in town with a magnificent view of the mountain. The report with the campus police plus the subsequent talk after with Nathan and Dr. Skeller had me missing my appointment time completely. Luckily, Tate was understanding and wants to meet up now that my classes are done for the day.

I pull into a spot next to his Jeep and climb out. He's

inside, sitting by the window, and waves. When I make my way inside, I'm happy to see he's ordered for us. In my empty spot, a coffee and a pastry await me.

"Hey, man," I say as I take my seat. "Thanks."

Tate smiles and then sips his coffee, eyes boring into me. "Do you know how hard it is for me to keep it together right now?"

A snort rips out of me. "I can only imagine."

"Seriously," he says, shaking his head in disbelief. "What are the odds that Golden was my future sister-in-law?" His features tighten. "I do want you to understand that what we talk about remains confidential. I'd never betray that and speak to her about you."

Even though I hoped that was the case, it relieves me hearing it from my new friend. Gemma knows my deep, dark secret—hell, *she's* the deep, dark secret—but I still don't like the idea of someone else telling her all there is to know about me.

"Yeah?"

Tate nods several times like a bobblehead sitting on the dash of a cruising car. "Absolutely. And now that we've cleared that up, can we please discuss everything?"

Everything.

For so long I've kept *everything* under lock and key. Now that it's out in the wide open to virtually everyone—especially those closest to me—it doesn't feel so nightmarish.

"Well, it all started when I was nine." I glance around to make sure no kids are around. "I was on a hunt to prove to my best friend Dax that Santa was real."

Tate smirks. "He totally is. I've seen him at the mall before."

I chuckle and realize I'm not dreading this as much as I thought I would. It makes me wonder if I could tell the whole story to Dax next. He certainly could use an explanation for why I can be melancholic at times.

For the next hour, I unload all of my past and all of my present onto Tate. To his credit, he listens intently, doesn't interrupt, and encourages me to keep going. Once I start talking, I can't seem to stop. We end up going for another round of coffee and pastries just so the people won't kick us out for staying so long.

"It's a lot to take in," Tate says when I finally finish. "How are you feeling now that your dads know?"

I ponder his question for a bit. "Relieved for sure. Maybe a little dumb."

"Dumb?"

"For carrying this for so long. For not talking to my dads about it sooner."

"That's not being dumb, Two. You were scared. Understandably so."

"But all of this could have been avoided if I'd spoken up."

"Hindsight is 20/20. If we all knew better, we'd never have any regrets. We're human, though, which means we fumble through life doing our best and slipping many times along the way."

I study my friend for a long beat. "You have an uncanny way of making people feel normal even though they're anything but."

"Being 'normal' is abnormal if you ask me. No one is normal. We all have our quirks and hang-ups and past experiences to haunt us. I'm glad you feel comfortable confiding in me, though."

My phone buzzes and it's Dad checking in on me. I quickly reply back to let him know I'm still with Tate. He sends an excessive amount of heart eye emojis that make me shake my head.

"Someone should take the emojis off his phone. Is it possible?" I show him the message to prove that Dad overuses the emojis more than even Dax does. "Can your hacker lover do it for me?"

"My hacker lover can do anything." Tate's grin is wide and silly. "Give your dad a break. He clearly adores you."

I let his words wash over my newly healing heart.

My dads do love me. So fucking much. In a way, I'm glad the deep, dark secret was revealed because it gave my parents the opportunity to state their case and profess how much they love their only son.

"Yeah, I guess you're right. He and Pops do love me," I say, returning his smile. "Damn, that's a really good feeling."

CHAPTER TWENTY-FIVE

Gemma
Two weeks later...

"**S**top," I say, breathless. "We're going to get caught."

Two groans, pulling his lips away from my neck where he'd been hell-bent on giving me a hickey. He also slips his hand out from under my shirt. This is the problem with us. Whenever we're alone together—which is rare these days—we collide with the fire of a thousand suns.

But we're always at risk of getting caught by someone who would frown heavily at seeing the two of us maul each other.

As much as I love our stolen moments, I want more. I want the two of us to have time to explore each other's bodies. I want to take the final step of physical intimacy with Two, but I don't want to be rushed.

His large, bony hand cradles my face as he searches my gaze. Then a devious grin curls his lips up. "I know where we can go for some privacy."

I rack my brain for what that place here at Hemingford Hall may be and land on the hidden room we found.

"I know which closet they keep their linens in," Two continues with a twinkle in his eyes. "Towels too. I could meet you in there in five." His brows knit together. "That is, if you really want to."

I'm still panting from our hot make-out session. Of course I do. Now that the possibility is finally here, though, I'm nervous.

"I want to," I squeak out.

"But?"

"I'm scared."

He presses a soft kiss to my lips. "We don't have to, Golden."

"I do want to, though." I gnaw on my bottom lip. "Will it hurt?"

"I don't think so," he answers, though he doesn't seem sure. "If it does, we'll stop. I'll do my best to make you feel good."

His sweet words chase away my unease. I nod and grin at him before I can change my mind. He gives me another quick peck on my lips before he slips out of Alexander's office on a hunt for the supplies we'll need. Meanwhile, I peek out the doorway to make sure Paula or Gregory aren't lurking.

Coast is clear.

I hurry over to the bookshelf and push inside. Now that we know how to access the room, it happens much easier than before. I turn on my flashlight on my phone and set it on the end table by the bed so that the light points up, illuminating the dark space. Then I wait awkwardly for Two to come back.

We're really going to do this.

A shiver of anticipation ripples down my spine. I always wanted my first time to be with someone special. Two is the most unique, bizarre, and completely lovable man I've ever met. Sharing this with him will be special. I just know it.

He slips in through the bookcase door and closes it behind him. I stand aside, watching him as he lays out a sheet on the old, thin mattress. He tosses a towel on the bed beside it.

Now what?

Thankfully, I don't have to make the next move. Two prowls over to me, intent on his target. Me. With his back to the light, I can't see his darkened face, but I feel his eyes roving over me nonetheless.

"I'm so fucking happy I met you, Golden."

"Likewise, buddy."

He snorts and then gently kisses my mouth. The soft, sweet kiss turns desperate quickly. Between my pants and mewls, he manages to pull off my sweatshirt and then his. Next, he removes our undershirts. I save him the trouble of figuring out the clasp of my bra and unhook it with a flick of my fingers. Once it's unfastened, he tugs it away, practically throwing it.

"So beautiful." Two cups my breasts and sweeps his thumbs over my nipples. "Perfect. Like you, Golden."

"You can't see them," I whisper, trembling at his touch.

"Everything about you is beautiful. I don't have to see them right now to know this."

His words melt my heart and then his mouth is back on mine. We each fiddle with our own jeans and awkwardly yank out of them while still managing to kiss. Somewhere in all that chaos, we kick out of our shoes, too. When his big hands cup my ass over my panties, I let out a gasp.

"Still good?" he murmurs. "We don't have to go any further."

I cup his straining cock over his boxers. "No. I want this. Now."

He yanks down my panties and then does the same with his boxers. We're naked. Completely naked. Well, aside from our socks, but neither of us seems eager to remove those. With practiced ease, he lifts me up by my ass. I wrap my legs around his waist, whimpering when his erection rubs against my pussy.

This is it.

We're going to seal the deal.

Us.

He gently lowers us to the ancient bed. It squeaks and protests under our weight but doesn't collapse. Now that we're closer to the light, I can see his handsome face.

"You're beautiful too, you know," I whisper, admiring how gorgeous he is. "I like staring at you."

He smirks. "Weirdo."

A small laugh tumbles out of me and then he's kissing it away. I expected for him to get right to business, but he doesn't. Slowly, he starts kissing down my chest, taking time to suck on each of my nipples along the way.

"W-What are you doing?" I ask, groaning with need. "I, uh, I don't know what to do."

He nips at my stomach. "Spread your legs and try to stay quiet."

His filthy words have my heart doing a summersault. I part my thighs as he makes his way lower and lower and lower and—oh God! The slick flick of his tongue along my clit has me seeing immediate stars. Before I can even recover, he's licking again and again. I can't help but thread my fingers into his hair and tug, desperately needing whatever it is he can give to me.

And oh my God does he deliver.

I've seen the man tongue his butterscotch candies wildly and his tongue on my clit is no different. He licks and sucks at it as though it's just as sweet as his beloved treat. All I can do is stifle my needy moans and hang on for the duration of this Two ride.

As he torments my clit, I feel one of his fingertips slicking over my opening. Then, gently, he eases it inside me. My mind runs wild with the sensation and wondering what it'd feel like to have more of him inside me. All of him. Satisfied that I can easily take his finger, he urges another one inside. This stings at the stretch, but I love it.

"More," I beg, tugging at his hair. "I need more."

He pulls off my clit long enough to breathe out, "Come first, Gemma. Come all over my tongue, pretty girl."

His words have me spiraling with lust and love and longing. I don't ever want to lose this feeling. Two has opened me up to a world I never knew existed. He expertly massages me inside my body while teasing me on the outside. It doesn't take long before I detonate with a strangled cry. He reaches a long arm up my torso and covers my mouth, stifling the sound while I quiver and jolt from my orgasm.

Sensing I'm past the loud part, he removes his hand off my mouth and then pulls his fingers out of me. I feel empty and boneless. When he gets off the bed completely, my heart starts to pound with panic.

"W-Where are you going?"

He returns seconds later, flashing a condom at me. "I'm still here, Golden. I'm always here."

I watch in fascination as he tears open the foil and slides the rubber down over his impressive cock. Then he uses his wet fingers to coat the outside of his sheathed cock.

"Ready?"

"More than ever."

With his cock in hand, Two prowls over my body until our mouths meet for a fiery kiss. I can taste the distinct flavor of my own juices on his tongue mixed with a faint hint of butterscotch. I decide it's not terrible and I love how it got to be there in the first place. He lines up the tip of his cock against my center but doesn't push inside.

"I fucking love you," he whispers against my mouth. "I think I have since the second I saw you."

Before I can react, he begins pushing his thickness into my tight body. I whimper, a mix of pleasure and slight pain. My eyes sting, still hung up on his profession.

He loves me.

Can he love me so soon?

Are we crazy to be in love?

I decide I don't care about timelines or what should be. I focus on the here and now. Us. The perfect beauty of the two of us coming together. He sinks all the way into my body and I hear him chanting something against my ear.

"Relax. Gemma, baby, relax. Don't cry. Should I stop?"

I come to, realizing I'm quietly sobbing. But not because I want him to stop. It's because he's perfect for me. I love him too.

"Don't stop," I croak out. "I need you to keep going. I need this."

He finds my mouth again, kissing me so reverently I start to cry harder. I feel like an idiot for crying during sex, but it's just so…powerful.

"Babe, tell me if I'm hurting you," he pleads, sounding pained. "I don't want to hurt you. I'm no expert at this. If I'm doing it wrong—"

I silence him with a desperate kiss, digging my heels into his ass cheeks and drawing him closer to me. The kiss quickly turns frantic and then he's thrusting inside me. Yes, it burns. Yes, every push inside me feels like he's wrecking my inexperienced body. Do I want to stop? Hell no.

The next few moments go by in a blur of moans, pleas, and buzzes of pleasure. Though I can't make myself come again, I'm eager for him to orgasm. Not just because I want that for him, but because I'm already feeling so sore. I imagine it's something my body will get used to with time. Finally, he grunts and then stiffens. I cry out when he nips at my lip. Then, pulsing can be felt inside me as his cock unloads.

This only goes on for a few seconds and then he collapses on me, completely spent. As we both relax, I stroke my fingers up and down his muscular back. We're both slick with sweat. My throat is dry and I'm not sure I can even speak. Luckily, we're able to just lie there for a bit. The only sound is our rapid breathing that eventually slows.

"You okay?" Two asks, breath tickling over my breast where his head rests. "I didn't hurt you, did I?"

"It was perfect," I rasp out. "Thank you."

"It was perfect for me too. Now that we've done this, I'm going to want to bang the shit out of you every time I see you."

I snort out a laugh and immediately stifle it. "That could get awkward considering we're around others most of the times we're together."

"Fuck others," he says grumpily. "When I move out, I'm going to have you every night in my bed."

That sounds like something to really look forward to.

I want to ask him about meeting his dads soon. Despite our secret being revealed, we haven't found a time that works for everyone. With me and Two knee-deep in our project and obsessed with each other, neither of us has tried very hard to make this happen. Deep down, I wonder if Two's still apprehensive about the meeting and is avoiding it. I know I'm a bit nervous.

My phone buzzes on the end table, distracting me from my uneasy thoughts. Two reaches over and grabs it for me. I turn the flashlight off to make sure I haven't missed any messages from Dad, but it's just a junk email. Two is gentle and sweet as he cleans my slick arousal up between my thighs. Then he slides off the bed to tug off the used condom.

"Hey, Two?"

"Yeah, Golden?"

"I love you too."

◎

When we leave the confines of the secret room, we're different people. Two stares at me like I'm the answer to life's most intriguing mysteries. I can't help gawking at the good-looking guy who loves me and just made love to me. If we were inseparable before, we'll be even worse now.

We actually do manage to get some work done and when it gets late, we leave Hemingford Hall hand in hand.

It's no surprise to find another note and flower. At this point, I don't even read them anymore. Two growls under his breath as I toss the flower and tuck the note away in my purse to show Dad and Sloane later.

"Fucking Phil Draper," Two mutters. "I'm going to kill him."

The mayor, and one of our newly cleared suspects, has been getting all our stalker hate. Since we don't know who it is, this gives us someone to blame. It's an inside joke between us. Poor Phil really is innocent.

Jude, the expert online digger he is, tore apart Phil from the inside out. The guy is a bit of a douchebag, but he's otherwise harmless. I know Jude really wanted someone to pin this stalker stuff on, but Phil just wasn't our guy.

"We should probably change the name to Hiroshi Tanaka," I say, glancing up at Two. "Since Phil's been cleared."

Two's features twist with pity. Not exactly a look I like seeing on him. I guess our joke's not that funny. He already thinks I'm being paranoid.

"If it turns out to be Tanaka, you owe me big," I say with a pout. "You're not always right, Tristan Sheridan."

He scoffs at the use of his full name. "Mostly, I am."

I roll my eyes. "Oh, what time is it?"

"Nine, I think."

"Shoot," I exclaim, pulling away from him to dig around in my purse. "They're supposed to send out acceptance letters for the workshop."

I flip over to my email and find the email from the dean straightaway. Approved. Within the email are all the details, including location, time, and appropriate attire to wear.

"I got in," I shriek. "Check yours!"

Two pats his pockets until he finds his phone. He goes too slow for my liking, but eventually, his face lights up. "I'm in too!"

We both laugh with excitement and hug. Tanaka, my alleged stalker, may have thought he was getting to me tonight, but nothing could ruin this perfect evening.

Nothing.

CHAPTER TWENTY-SIX

Two
A month later…

"**W**HERE ARE YOUR PARENTS?"

Gemma bursts into laughter at my question. "Why? Looking to do something naughty?"

Fuck yeah.

Ever since we had sex for the first time a month ago, we've stolen moment after moment. The secret room at Hemingford Hall has been our main haven when we want to get lost in each other, but we've fucked twice in the back of my car.

Life is good.

Really good.

I can't wait to get my own place so I can have her all the time.

The only problem is she still hasn't met my dads. They have been busy with work. We've been tirelessly chipping away on our project, too. It's all an excuse, though. I'm nervous for this meeting and the more I fall for Gemma, the more I worry about it going badly. But I'll be put out of my misery soon enough as Dad chewed me out this morning before he went to work, telling me I better bring her by this weekend or else he was going to have a fit.

"Are they here?" I ask again, gaze roving down Gemma's

front, shoving away thoughts of my dads and how their meeting with her will go. "I need to know if I'm fucking you here or on the way to the workshop."

She grabs my hand, hauling me into the house. "They'll be back soon. You have to make it quick."

Not needing to be told twice, I prowl toward my sexy girlfriend, yanking at my belt. She lifts up her black dress and shimmies her panties down her thighs before kicking them away. Then, with a coy smile, she bends over the back of the sofa.

Fuck me.

God, she's hot.

I give her bare ass a quick smack that has her yelping and then shove my slacks and boxers down my legs. Our first time we used a condom, but since she's on birth control and we're both negative for STIs, we've resorted to going bare.

And holy shit does it feel good to be bare inside her.

"Pull out when you come," she instructs, wriggling her ass at me. "I don't want cum running out of me the whole event."

I think knowing my cum is leaking out of her while we schmooze with other restoration enthusiasts sounds like a pretty fun idea. However, I'd probably never be able to get rid of my hard-on knowing that. Best we clean it up before we go. Definitely going to happen another time, though.

"Hurry," she says, tone turning bossy.

I hate how every time we're together has to be in a rush. One day, I'm going to spend hours laid up in bed with her, learning every curve and freckle.

"You don't want me to feast on this first?" I ask, running a fingertip along her slit.

She shudders and lets out a mewl. "After the event. Just fuck me, Two. We don't have time to argue."

I swat her cute ass again because she deserves it.

"Fine. If you start crying, it's not my fault. You asked for this."

She flips me off over her shoulder and I crack a grin. Despite her only crying the first time we had sex, I've been endlessly teasing her about it. That's another thing I love about this girl. I can give her shit and she gives it right back. We're fun together.

Even though she wants it quick, I take the time to massage her clit. If she can orgasm before I stick my dick in her, she'll be slicked and ready for the hard fucking she wants. Her whimpers and moans are the best sounds I've heard all day. The tip of my cock leaks with pre-cum, aching to be inside her. For all the practice we've had lately, I'm able to bring her quickly to orgasm. I don't wait for her body to stop spasming before I grab hold of my dick, line it up, and then thrust deep inside her.

"Ahh!" she cries out, arching her back.

Gripping her hips, I pummel in and out of her, marveling at how fucking wonderful she feels. I'll never get tired of this. Not ever. It doesn't take long and I'm also tipped over the edge. With the patience of a saint, I pull out at the last second and paint her pretty ass with cum.

Too bad I can't sit and stare at her marked bare ass all day.

"You look good all messy, Golden. It suits you."

Little Miss Perfect is hot as fuck when she's wrecked by me.

◎

"Tanaka came by this morning," Gemma says, staring ahead as we drive. "He skeeves me out so bad."

I glance over at her briefly before turning my attention back on the road. "He comes over a lot."

"Right? It's weird."

At one time, I'd given her crap about suspecting Tanaka, but even I'm a little unnerved that he seems to be visiting a lot lately.

"Maybe they're just working hard trying to catch the stalker," I offer with a shrug. "He's the police chief after all."

"Maybe. Turn there," Gemma says, pointing to a road quickly coming up. "This place is at one of those fancy cabins on the east side of the lake. I'm starving. They said there'd be food, right?"

I nod as I turn and then take the winding, wooded roads that'll bring us to our destination. We're about twenty minutes early. Her parents came back home not even five minutes after we cleaned up from our living room romp. We'd made a mad dash out of there to avoid any questions and awkwardness over what we'd just done in their living room.

"That's it." Gemma points through the trees toward some twinkling lights. "Wow, this place is really nice."

We pull up to a massive cabin with white string lights hung along the ceiling of the front porch that wraps around the side. There aren't any other cars here yet.

"Should we wait until more people arrive?" I ask, glancing

over at her. "I could think of a couple of things we could do to entertain ourselves."

She snorts out a laugh. "You're an insatiable horndog now, Tristan Sheridan. I created a monster."

I roll my eyes at her using my full name. "Says the monster fucker who's always ready to hop in the sack with me."

"Touché." She shakes her head. "Come on. We'll leave early if it's lame and find some dirt road to get freaky on."

Before I get the luxury of imagining what that would entail, she's already climbing out of the vehicle. I quickly stride over to her and thread our fingers together. It's nice being able to parade my girlfriend around in public without worrying about who will find out.

"Don't forget to lock it," she instructs. "I'm leaving my purse so I don't have to keep up with it."

When we reach the porch of the cabin, I skim my gaze over the chalkboard sign welcoming the guests of the workshop. Gemma knocks on the front door, sneaking a cute smile my way.

The door opens and we're greeted by the scent of savory foods. Dr. Skeller beams at us and sweeps his hand inside.

"Come in, Mr. Sheridan, Miss Park. The other guests aren't here yet, but please help yourselves to the delicious spread we had catered in for the event." Dr. Skeller closes the door behind us and shows us to a long buffet table covered in everything from cubed cheeses, olives, and pickles to trays of chicken breasts in some sort of cream sauce. "Can I offer you both something to drink?"

"Wine?" I say jokingly.

Dr. Skeller smirks. "Nice try. This is a PMU sanctioned event. How about some sweet iced tea instead?"

We both nod and he strides off to fetch our drinks.

"This isn't awkward or anything," I mutter under my breath. "The back seat of my car would have been a lot more fun."

Gemma playfully smacks my arm. "Be nice. This will be fun." She walks over to the chairs lined up in front of a make-shift podium with a microphone. "I wonder who the speakers will be."

I don't recall from the invite seeing any. Maybe it's just for Dr. Skeller to be all official and greet everyone or something.

Dr. Skeller returns with our iced teas. We thank him and accept our drinks.

"Feel free to make a plate while you're waiting for the other guests to arrive," Dr. Skeller instructs. "There should be twenty-two guests in total."

As we part from Dr. Skeller to check out the food table, Gemma nudges me with an elbow. "Don't eat like an animal."

"I never eat like an animal."

Her neatly plucked eyebrow hikes high up her forehead as she gapes at me in disbelief. "You're joking, right?"

I stare at her, unblinking.

"Oh my God. You are serious. Two, babe, you're messier than a toddler. Hate to break it to you."

Shrugging, I pile up my plate with just about everything. Gemma is more selective. By the time we eat the food and help ourselves to more iced tea, it's time for the event to begin.

Yawning, I flick my gaze down to my watch. "This is going to be boring, isn't it?"

"Hush," she admonishes, but her eyes are slightly hooded. We're both about to fall our asses asleep.

"Where is everyone?" I ask Dr. Skeller when he strides back into the room, a wide smile on his face.

"Should be here any minute," he assures me. Then, to Gemma, he gives her a tender look. "Has your stalker bothered you anymore?"

She tenses at the mention of him. "Just the usual daily reminder that he's around."

Dr. Skeller nods in sympathy with pinched eyebrows. "Your father and Police Chief Tanaka will get to the bottom of it. I have faith in them."

"Do you know Tanaka well?" Gemma asks, grimacing as she mentions his name. "Does he strike you as peculiar?"

Dr. Skeller frowns, studying her intently. "He does. Why? What are you thinking?"

"Nothing," Gemma lies and then gulps down her tea. "Just a weird guy."

"Hmm," Dr. Skeller hums. "Perhaps keep an eye on him and don't allow yourself to ever be alone with him."

She nods emphatically. "Don't worry. He creeps me out so bad."

I yawn again. "What time will everyone be here? Do you have coffee? The caffeine in this tea isn't cutting it."

Dr. Skeller beams at me.

Talk about creepy.

I blink several times and realize they've been talking, but I totally nodded off. Gemma glowers at me like I'm embarrassing her. Hell, I'm embarrassing myself.

With the heel of my palm, I rub at one eye, trying to shake the tiredness out of my bones.

What the hell?

I feel loopy and tired as fuck.

Alarm bells start ringing, but my brain can't seem to comprehend why. Gemma stands shakily and Dr. Skeller grabs her arm to keep her from falling.

"I, uh, need to use the restroom," Gemma utters. "Can you point me in the right direction?"

Dr. Skeller shows her to the restroom and then strides back over to me. The room tilts from side to side and my stomach roils.

Am I getting sick?

I think I need to call my dads.

Something's wrong.

I hear a loud thud come from the bathroom. Gemma. Without consideration, I burst to my feet. The room spins and then I stumble several steps, tripping over my feet that feel weighted down. Like an ancient tree that's been hacked through with a chainsaw, I crash to the ground, smacking my cheek hard on the wood floor.

Numbness slides through my veins and the exhaustion washes over me like a warm wave, claiming me in spotty darkness.

Don't go to sleep, Two.

Don't.

Something's really, really wrong.

Despite barely clinging to consciousness, I try to move my hand down to my pocket to retrieve my phone. I don't get very far. My fingers twitch against the hardwood and a small, defeated grunt escapes me.

I'm roused by hands patting me down and then my phone is pulled from my pocket.

Yes, I need that.

Give it to me, please.

"You won't be needing this," the deep, sinister voice croons. He also manages to find my keys and gives them a jingling shake. "Or these. Just go to sleep. Let the medicine do its job. No need to fight it. This battle is over, young man, and you have lost."

I know what this means.

I know I have to fight back.

And yet, blackness finishes cloaking me in her abysmal darkness.

Black.

Black.

Black.

Finally, nothing.

CHAPTER TWENTY-SEVEN

Gemma

I RUB AT MY ELBOW, TEARS STINGING MY EYES.

"Ow," I mutter. "What the hell?"

My body feels heavy and quickly becoming useless. What's wrong with me? First, I nearly crashed through the wall after using the toilet, my elbow taking the brunt of the fall, and now I feel like I might pass out.

I need to go home.

After fumbling through washing my hands, I unlock the bathroom door and drag my sluggish body back toward the main room to tell Two. He's no longer sitting where I left him and Dr. Skeller is gone.

Where did they go?

Outside?

I get turned around but manage to find a door that leads outside. Once I open it, I groan, realizing it's a back door that faces the lake, not the one where the car is parked. Something flutters in the wind, catching my eye, and I glance down.

Yellow flowers dance happily in their beds.

They're familiar.

I fixate on the flowers, fighting through the fog inside my head. Why are these flowers important to me?

I'm about to turn around and continue my search for

Two when a memory niggles at me. Wait. These flowers look just like the ones…

No.

A chill skitters down my spine and a shot of adrenaline sends a fleeting moment of clarity in my mind.

Oh my God.

We have to get out of here.

I spin, ready to rush back into the cabin, when I run right smack into a broad chest. Hands grip my arms to keep my swaying body from collapsing. With trepidation, I tilt my head up, finding my eyes on Dr. Skeller and not my boyfriend.

No.

Tears prickle at my eyes and a sob catches in my throat.

It's a trap.

We walked right into a trap.

My legs buckle and the room spins. I find myself blacking out and coming back to as my body bounces. I'm no longer standing, but I'm being carried. Squinting, I force myself to focus on the man carrying me.

Dr. Skeller.

Gone is his jovial smile.

Fierce determination paints his features now.

My heart hammers in my chest, but my body has become useless to me. I'm unable to move or fight. A small whimper escapes, earning his intense gaze on me.

"Hush, sweetheart," he murmurs. "You're safe. I'm going to take care of you."

For a split second, I pray I have it all wrong. That, once again, I'm overreacting and being paranoid. That this man— my dad's friend—is going to protect me, not hurt me.

Where's Two?

Where are we going?

I must doze off because I wake again in a darker space. Wine bottles line shelves on the walls. A wine cellar? My head lolls to the side and I see Two.

He's asleep on the ground, arm stretched over to a pipe. Handcuffed.

All hopeful thoughts fade as sheer terror floods in. Hot tears leak out of my eyes, but I'm unable to do anything else. My eyelids drift closed and my chaotic thoughts start to dull.

"Shh," Dr. Skeller whispers as he sets me down on something soft. "I want you to rest a bit. Don't fight the medicine, darling. Everything's been taken care of. You'll see."

I feel him gently remove my shoes and then cover me with a blanket. It's warm and feels relatively safe. I'm no longer able to fight to stay conscious. Blissful darkness steals me away.

I wake to a slight tickle on my thigh and a banging inside my skull. Nausea curdles my belly as I attempt to gain my bearings. I feel worse than the time me and Dempsey drank a whole bottle of Mom's wine when we were like ten years old. We threw up. A lot.

But this?

This is worse.

More ominous.

Why?

Cracking my eyes open, I squint to orient myself with my surroundings. I see wine bottles lining a wall.

Where am I?

When I go to rub the sleep out of my eyes, I realize my wrists are zip-tied together, resting on my belly. The rest of my body feels heavy and sluggish, but I'm quickly gaining clarity in my mind.

It all comes flooding back.

The workshop. The sweet tea. Dr. Skeller.

He drugged us.

A whimper crawls up my throat. It's then I feel the tickling again. I dart my eyes over to my right and see the wicked man himself.

"You're quite beautiful when you sleep," Dr. Skeller says with breathy awe. "Better than I imagined."

Terror prickles its way through me. "I—"

He hushes me with his thumb to my lips. "Rest, my love."

Bile burns my esophagus and I dry heave. Dr. Skeller slides off the bed I'm on to quickly grab something. The next time I heave, acidy vomit spews out of me. He positions a small bucket in front of me, catching the mess as if he's expecting it.

When I finish, he takes the bucket someplace and returns with a warm, wet washcloth. Hot tears leak from my eyes as he cleans my lips and chin.

"W-Where…" I croak out, more tears streaming.

I can't seem to make my voice work. My body sure as hell is barely responding. It's just me and my erratic, horrified thoughts running rampant.

Dr. Skeller, no longer in a suit and now donning a simple black T-shirt and jeans, strokes his fingers through my hair. I shudder at his revolting touch.

"I always thought you were cute," he says, eyes twinkling as though he's reliving a memory. "You probably don't remember this, but I saw you at the country club once. You were waiting on your father to finish talking to some of his friends.

While your brother terrorized the wait staff in the restaurant, hiding under tables and being a little shit, you stood primly right where you were told to wait."

He's right. I don't remember this. Me and Dempsey have spent a lot of time at the country club. Our parents dragged us there a lot when we were younger. Once we got old enough to stay home on our own, they'd go without us.

"The sun was beaming in through a window and found shimmering golden strands hidden in your dark hair. You wore the prettiest little smile and kept your small hands neatly clasped in front of you." He touches my bound hands. "Like this, sort of."

A full-bodied shudder ripples through me.

"My wife caught me staring," he says sadly. "We'd been trying for kids for a while at the time and couldn't have any. She mistook my longing as something fatherly."

"S-sicko," I rasp out.

He chuckles. "Oh, sweetheart. It wasn't like that. You were barely six or seven at the time." His hand finds my thigh and I realize it was what the tickling sensation was from before. "I didn't just want kids, Gemma. I wanted you. You, my perfect little girl."

"T-Two." I try to move my aching head to look for him, but I can't see past Dr. Skeller and the bed and the wine bottles.

"We'll discuss that later," he says gently, giving my thigh an affectionate squeeze. "I didn't see you much after that. It was probably for the best. Advancing my career was more important at the time. Children weren't in the cards for me and Dawn. Infertility is a bitch."

I have to get the hell out of here.

He continues with a heavy sigh. "Infertility was the death of my marriage. But it was probably for the best, though, because fate had other plans."

I'm still unable to properly move, but my mind is racing right along with my heart. In my current state, I don't think I could escape, but the second these drugs clear my system, I'm out of here.

I'll find Two and we'll run from this psychopath.

"This past summer, when your dad brought you and your brother in for a tour of PMU," he says with a wide, wistful smile, "I was reminded of that day when you'd stood so sweetly at the club. Like before, your brother was causing trouble, but not you. You were always the good little girl. Something was different this time, though. You looked at me like a woman looks at a man—with respect and admiration." He chuckles and shrugs. "To tell you the truth, it sent a thrill right through me."

"N-no," I say, barely audible, while slightly shaking my throbbing head.

"Yes," Dr. Skeller says firmly, giving my thigh a tight squeeze. "I'm not delusional. I saw it for what it was. A connection between us."

He's completely insane.

"At first, I simply wanted to admire you from afar, despite being a lonely bastard. Dawn and I had recently split at the time. She kept the house and I got our lake home. I'd spend hours down here in the cellar, making my way through our most expensive bottles, longing for another life—a better one." His palm skates up my thigh and his fingertip brushes the edge of my pussy, making me realize for the first time I'm completely naked. "And my mind always went back to you.

I'll admit, I became a bit obsessed. Thankfully, you put yourself online a lot. I'd spend hours watching your videos and scrolling through your pictures."

"Don't t-touch m-me," I stammer out, shuddering again. "W-Where are my clothes?"

"Shh," he says, not losing his smile. "You're mine now. I'll touch you as I please. Keep quiet while I finish my bedtime story, sweetheart, or I'll need to gag your pretty mouth."

Fear has a whimper rising in my chest.

"The first time I took my cock in my hand while watching you on a live feed, I came so hard I saw stars, Gemma. Fucking stars." He shakes his head in disbelief. "Of all the years with Dawn and the women I'd been with both before and after the separation, not once had I felt like that. It was otherworldly. Transcending both space and time. All because of you."

He gently slips a finger inside of my body and massages me. I gag again, feeling disgusted at his touch, but unable to do much about it. My bound hands clumsily attempt to push his hand away from me. Thankfully, he pulls it away. I watch in rapt horror as he brings his finger to his nose, closes his eyes, and inhales deeply. Then his features pinch.

"You still smell like him."

More tears stream out of the corners of my eyes. "L-Let me g-go. D-D-Dr...."

"Call me Owen, sweetheart. No need for formalities." He eyes his finger warily and sighs. "I knew I was too late. That boy got to you first. Stole what was mine."

"N-not y-yours."

He lets out a derisive snort. "I told you not to sleep with him. Over and over again I told you. Did you listen?" He closes his eyes and his jaw muscle ticks. "I'd planned to woo you the old-fashioned way, but the considerable difference in our ages, my connection with your father, and my position at the university were all roadblocks. I needed to move more quickly, especially when you started seeing that boy."

"I want t-to go home," I say through my sobs. "P-please."

Owen gives a sharp shake of his head. "That's never happening. I went through a lot of great lengths to get you here—right by my side where you belong. There's no turning back for either of us."

"The w-workshop? You f-faked that t-to get us here alone?"

"A clever ruse, indeed," he says with a delighted chuckle. "I had a lot of fun planning that. For any outsider, they'll see my receipts for the catered food, all the plans and emails via my work email, and even my speaker notes for the workshop. All of it will keep the finger from being pointed my way. No one will be the wiser that it was all a farce."

The pounding in my head intensifies. I want ibuprofen and to find Two. I want to get out of here, far, far away from this monster.

Dad will find me.

The sudden thought has my heart hammering in my chest. Yes. Dad will notice I'm missing and track me down. He's overbearing and protective, so I know he'll have tabs on me at all times.

"You w-won't get away with t-this."

Owen's lips curl into a bright grin that makes his eyes twinkle. "I already have."

"No. D-Dad will f-find me."

He smirks. "I've taken considerable steps to make sure that doesn't happen."

"How?"

"I was busy while you slept," Owen explains, once again roaming his palm up and down my thigh. "As soon as both of you were out cold, I gained access to your phones using your faces to unlock them. Then I went back and forth, texting between the two of you. To everyone else, you used the workshop as an excuse to be together but then took off for Vegas to get married."

My stomach clenches at his words. "H-How long have I been asleep?"

"Almost twenty-two hours. And that, my dear, is why you're naked. You wet the bed in your sleep, but don't worry, I took care of my girl. You're all cleaned up now."

Twenty-two hours. He undressed me and cleaned me and let me sleep for so long.

At least, by now, my parents are most definitely searching for me.

"T-Two?" I ask again, a mewl of terror following after.

"He woke up hours ago." Owen's lips thin out before he continues. "He's been gagged because he wouldn't shut his disrespectful mouth."

"They'll still find me," I rasp out. "My phone—"

"Is at the bottom of the lake. Along with that piece of shit car." He arches a brow. "Don't worry. Your parents will think you two destroyed your phones to keep them from tracking you down and they'll never find his vehicle. I tell you, it really was the ultimate plan and I executed it to perfection."

My mind reels. Without our phones and with Owen leading them in a completely different direction, they may never find us.

So what happens next?

It's clear to me Owen has plans. He speaks of us as though we're a couple finally getting to be together. I'm not sure when, but he'll eventually force himself on me. The thought of this monster on me and inside me makes me gag again.

"As soon as I get rid of that little shit," Owen states, jutting a thumb over his shoulder, "it'll be just you and me, sweetheart. Forever. Hell, I may retire early just so we can spend every waking hour together." He studies me intently. "As for your virginity, I'm going to consider it still intact. I've given it much thought. Mr. Sheridan is nothing but a boy and knows the basics at best, whereas I've had years of experience in pleasuring a woman. The moment between us will feel like heaven for you, I assure that. It'll feel like your first time when I make love to you and I'll know exactly how to make your toes curl."

"Rape," I hiss. "It's c-called rape. N-not love. Rape."

Owen ignores me as he moves to stand. My heart nearly stops beating with worry. Is this when it happens? I clench my thighs together, openly sobbing now. He leans over and grips my jaw. Then he plunges his tongue into my mouth, moaning as he kisses me. I'm glad I can still taste the puke in my mouth. I hope he gets a taste.

He pulls back, panting, eyes locking on mine. "You see how good I am with my tongue, darling? I'll show you soon. Here." He fondles me between my thighs, causing me to cry out. "After I deal with the boy."

"What are you going t-to do?" I choke out.

His grin is vicious and cruel. "End his life, sweetheart. I'll end his life so ours together can finally begin."

I find my voice and let loose a deafening scream.

CHAPTER TWENTY-EIGHT

Two

EVERY BONE IN MY BODY ACHES FROM SLEEPING FOR only God knows how long on a cold, concrete floor while handcuffed to a pipe and my bladder feels like it's going to burst at any moment. When I'd come to, Dr. Skeller wrenched my other hand to the handcuffed one and zip-tied it to it. I started cursing up a storm and making vicious threats, all of which ended with him stuffing a washcloth into my mouth and slapping thick utility tape over it from cheek to cheek.

I'd been forced to listen to his heavy breathing and then his psychotic monologue as he explained how and why we got here.

He's obsessed with Gemma.

Gemma's stalker is Dr. Skeller.

We waltzed right through his front door and right into his poisonous trap.

Unbelievable.

I wanted to believe it was only a matter of time before our parents found us, but then Dr. Skeller—or Owen as he said to Gemma—revealed his detailed plan he'd executed to lead the search elsewhere.

If we want out of here, we have to do it ourselves.

But how?

I'm handcuffed and gagged, for fuck's sake.

I attempt to shift my body to alleviate the ache in my lower back but only manage to send more pain shooting through my tressed up arms. A grunt of frustration whistles out of my nostrils.

Gemma's sudden scream has me tensing. From my position on the floor, I can't twist around to see her. Is he raping her? I yank on my bindings hard enough both metal and plastic cut into my flesh. Breaths heave in and out of my nose heavily as my eyes water.

I have to save her.

I can't.

Footsteps make their way over to me and then Owen is towering above me. He's no longer in his suit but now dons regular clothes. If I had my hands free, I'd tackle him, grip his neck, and squeeze the fucking life out of him.

If only.

He squats down in front of me and grins. "We both know you're not good enough for my Gemma." He pats the top of my head in a condescending way that makes my blood boil. "She's quite literally a gem and you're nothing but a waste of air."

If I were free, I could take this old man. There's nothing special about him. He's not big and muscular like Dax or Dempsey. He's just old and fucking crazy.

"I'm about to work on my garden," Owen says jovially. "Your rotting corpse will make for perfect compost."

He's going to kill me.

Fuck.

Tears of frustration, rage, and utter fear burn hot down

my cheeks. Owen touches my wet cheek before wiping the tear off on his jeans as though I'm diseased.

How will he kill me?

As though he can hear my thoughts, he smirks. "A gun will be too loud. I have neighbors nearby and I can't risk it."

Gemma shouts at Owen, filth flying out of her mouth, and then quickly turns on her charm to beg. She's begging for me. For my life. Trading anything he wants from her to let me live. Sex, submission, her own life. My heart aches to be with her.

"I said hush, sweetheart," Owen chides. His eyes meet mine. "It's unfortunate, but I'll need to gag her as well."

He disappears again. Then her shrieks are silenced as he does as promised. Her sobs are my undoing, breaking my heart shard by shard. I'm useless to help her—to help us.

I want my dads.

I want me and Gemma to wake up and this have all been a stupid nightmare.

"Yes, where were we?" Owen asks as he walks back over to me. "Ahh, I remember. I was explaining my kill method." He laughs as though this shit is funny. "A knife would be too messy. Again, I've contemplated this a lot. Exactly how I'd end your short life."

Groaning and grunting, I struggle against my bindings, wondering if I can swing my leg up to kick him in his face. He must sense my plan because he sidesteps me and walks up the stairs and out of the cellar without another word. Minutes later, he returns with a shovel.

"This, Mr. Sheridan," Owen says, thrusting the shovel toward me, "is how it ends. Not messy but still destructive." He cocks his head to the side. "I wonder how many bones I can break before you succumb to internal bleeding."

Gemma's sobbing grows hysterical and I ache to see her. Life is shitty. I go my entire life hurting over this girl, tormented by her existence, only to fall in love with her. Not like or smitten or whatever the fuck kids these days say. No, I love her. Deeply. I had plans for us. Long-term plans. Kids, house, dog, the whole nine yards.

Now it's being stolen from me.

Owen rests his chin on the top of the shovel, watching me with narrowed eyes. A chill skitters through me. His eyes are vacant and I sense no trepidation whatsoever. He'll kill me without a second thought.

Then what?

Then he'll spend hours, days, months, years torturing my beautiful girl. He'll rape her in captivity until she's a husk of her vibrant, beautiful self. Then he'll get bored. Probably kill her too. Maybe find a new obsession and repeat the process all over again because he never got caught.

This can't happen.

I have to stop it.

"For your sake," Owen says, straightening his spine. "I hope this goes fast for you. I can't imagine, even with the drugs still in your system, that it'll feel too good."

His features twist into something malevolent and vile— straight from a horror movie. He swings the shovel up in the air, the metal blade cracking against the ceiling before he drives it down toward me. All I can do is tense as the flat side of the shovel smacks against my ribs.

Pain explodes in my abdomen as I howl through my gag. The world in front of me blurs with my tears. Owen grunts as he swings the shovel back up above his head. This time, I manage to block with my foot. Another blast of pain assaults me, this time in my ankle. I black out, only to be awoken from another whack right smack in the gut. It knocks the breath out of me and I gasp desperately for oxygen. My bladder, unable to hold any longer through all the pain, releases.

I'm going to die on this cold floor in excruciating pain and soaked in my own piss.

I'll never see Gemma or my dads or Dax again.

This is it.

I hope I go quickly.

Owen stops, his entire body trembling, and uses the bottom of his T-shirt to swipe the sweat off his brow. He releases it and then swings the shovel up again. I brace for impact, waiting for the final, deadly blow.

Pop!

The shovel clatters to the cement, but I don't hear it because my ears are now ringing. Owen staggers away back toward Gemma, out of my line of sight. I hear her shrieking over the ringing in my ears, but there's nothing I can do about it.

Darkness clouds my vision and I fixate on a droplet of blood on the ground. My blood? His?

It's then I see a man, squatting in front of me. Not Owen. Someone else. He's speaking to me, but I can't seem to make out the words.

"Tristan Sheridan?" the man says as he fumbles with his belt. "Stay with me, buddy. I'm going to uncuff you and free your hands. Eyes on me. I'm Officer Holt. You're safe now."

I blink at him in confusion. Officer? The cops are here?

"Sit rep," a familiar female voice barks out. "Holt, how are we doing over there?"

"Vic is alive," he says back as he shoves the key into the handcuffs. "Contusions around his wrists and his ankle's sitting a funny kind of way, Detective."

More police officers flood into the cellar, guns drawn, searching for threats.

"Suspect still has a pulse," the woman hollers. "Where're the ambulances?"

"En route," another man assures her. "Ma'am, how's the girl? She alive?"

"Gemma is alive, but we're looking at a possible sexual assault," the woman says back. "They're both alive. Someone get Tanaka on the line and let him know we have them."

More people rush in, these wearing EMT uniforms. My vision grows hazy as they assess my injuries. The comforting cadence of their reassuring voices has me fading into nothingness.

We've been rescued.

"If you can't get up and use the toilet," a woman says, "we'll need to do a catheter. Come on, Mr. Sheridan. Open those eyes. Your dads are here."

The mention of my dads has me struggling to fully wake. I wince against the harsh light. It only takes a few moments to realize I'm in a hospital room and the woman is a nurse. My dads hover nearby, both of them red-faced from crying. At seeing them, a sob catches in my throat.

"Oh my God," Dad chokes out, rushing over to me. "My sweet baby boy. You're still here with us. Daddy's here."

I'm in pain from head to toe, but it's shrouded by

whatever they're pumping into my veins. The pain I'm feeling right now is in my chest.

"Gemma?" I rasp out, grimacing at the sharp stab in my ribs.

"She's okay," Pops assures me, eyes locking on mine. "Her parents are with her down the hall."

Tears flood down my cheeks but not from pain. I'm relieved to know we made it out alive. We fucking made it out.

"He was going to kill me and do awful things to her." I swallow hard and my chin wobbles. "I was scared. So fucking scared."

Dad gently squeezes my hand. Bandages cover both of my wrists. I wonder what other injuries I sustained.

"I know you all are happy to see him now that he's coherent," the nurse says, "but I'd like to get him up and over to the bathroom. I've got a crutch for him to use."

I shoot Pops a questioning look.

"Your ankle," Pops says with a frown. "They're going to have to do surgery on it once you're out of the woods from your internal injuries. It's in a bright orange cast for now."

My bladder throbs and I wonder how this nurse knew I had to pee. Grunting, I attempt to sit up, but then more pain shoots through me.

"Can you give him something?" Dad asks, terror in his voice. "He's in agony."

"I gave him something a few minutes ago through his IV. This pain is something he'll have to work through. The quicker we get him up and moving like normal, the quicker he's going to start healing."

Pops frowns and Dad rolls his eyes. My heart lurches

with happiness. They're here with me and everything's going to be okay.

We spend the next twenty minutes painfully getting me out of the bed, onto a crutch, and hobbled into the bathroom. Pops remains to help me stand as I do my business while Dad and the nurse wait outside the closed door. Once I finish, Pops kisses my head and swallows a strangled sob that makes my eyes well up all over again.

An eternity later, I make my way back to the bed and relax my hurting body.

Knock! Knock!

"Come in," Dad calls out to the visitor.

I expect Dax maybe or a doctor, but Sloane peeks her head inside. She gives me a tight smile before walking over to my bedside.

"Gemma?" I ask, still breathless from all my bathroom efforts.

"She's well. They're going to release her in the morning." Sloane crosses her arms over her chest and frowns at me. "How are you feeling?"

"Like I've been beaten nearly to death with a shovel in a maniac's wine cellar."

Sloane smirks. "I see your snark remained intact."

"He never leaves home without it," Dad chimes in with a singsong voice.

I start to laugh, but then the searing pain in my ribs stifles it. "Fuck. This hurts."

"I know," Sloane says softly. "It'll pass, though. I thought you might want to know that Skeller was treated for his gunshot wound to the shoulder and will be transported soon to jail to await sentencing. He's been arrested for kidnapping, assault, and attempted murder."

Thank fuck.

"Too bad you didn't get him center mass," I grumble. "That asshole doesn't deserve to live."

Sloane gives me a sympathetic smile. "He's going to go away for a long time. Rather than a quick death, he'll have decades to think of what he did. He'll die in prison, Two."

"How did you find us?" I rasp out. "He said he made it look like we ran away together and then got rid of the phones."

Not to mention, my car is now at the bottom of the fucking lake.

That hurts almost as much as my physical injuries.

Sloane steps closer and lowers her voice. "Let's just say we had unofficial help from an associate."

"Who?"

The nurse excuses herself and Sloane's shoulders relax.

"Jude," she says quickly. "Nathan had him looking into all of his friends for anything suspicious. Jude, no doubt illegally, hacked his way into Skeller's emails and other cloud-saved documents. In all his digging, he found pictures of Gemma. A lot of them."

I scowl, the hatred for that man boiling my blood. "Sick fuck."

"He also learned that the workshop you two supposedly bailed were the only real people he invited. The rest were newly created emails. It was obvious it was a setup and Jude picked his way through all of it."

I owe Jude a beer.

"My God," Dad hisses. "The lengths this Skeller man went through. Horrible."

"With our 'anonymous tip,'" Sloane continues, arching a blond eyebrow, "we were able to get a warrant and move quickly. It looks like we arrived just in time, too."

"If you didn't…" Dad trails off. "Thank goodness you did."

Sloane nods grimly.

"I'll get out of your hair and let you rest, but when you're up to it, we'll want to ask some questions," Sloane says, handing a business card to Pops. "Skeller was caught in the act. It's an open and closed case, but we do need Two's full statement to button everything up."

Sloane leaves and my dads relax. Exhaustion wins over and I start to drift off.

It's finally over.

That stalker is out of my girl's life.

Forever.

CHAPTER TWENTY-NINE

'M NERVOUS.

Really nervous.

I gaze up at Two's cute home through my windshield, feeling uneasy about the upcoming dinner. It's been nearly a month since the abduction and I've seen lots of Two and his fathers, but this is the first time we'll all spend some time together the four of us alone.

I hope they like me.

Shutting off my Tahoe, I exhale a deep sigh. I consider calling Willa or Tate for a quick pep talk but decide to put on my big girl panties and go inside.

My gaze travels over to Two's workshop. I know he's been itching to get back in there. He's spent a lot of time recovering from the beating he received from Owen and hasn't had the energy for much else. Our time spent together lately consists of me picking him up and driving him to and from school, to his doctor appointments, or to meet with Tate.

As I approach the front door, I can hear raised voices inside the home. It sounds like an argument. I panic for a moment, worrying if it's about me. Before I can rush back to my car to regroup, the door creaks open.

Two's dad, Grant—a burly guy with a trim beard and a

love for flannel—answers the door with a small smile. "Good to see you again, Gemma."

I officially met them the day I was released from the hospital. I'd left my room to spend much of the day at Two's bedside. His parents watched me with curiosity and were polite, but we didn't exactly spend time getting to know each other. It wasn't the right place or time.

Today, apparently, is the official meet-the-parents day.

"Hi," I say, plastering on a megawatt grin. "How's Two feeling today?"

Grant gestures for me to come inside. "Grumpy." He chuckles. "He's still upset over the loss of his car. We've been on the hunt for something vintage, but nothing compares to that Rover in his eyes. He loved that thing."

"Maybe we should try the junkyard," I offer with a laugh.

"I heard that," Two bellows from the living room.

Leo, Two's other dad, stands from the sofa and offers me a pleasant smile. "I told him we could get him a brand-new Range Rover with all the bells and whistles. He said it's a soccer mom car." Leo scoffs. "It's a freaking Range Rover. Kids these days. I swear."

We all snigger, but Two just grumpily shakes his head. I walk over to where he's camped out on the couch, bright orange cast propped up on the coffee table, with his laptop on his thighs.

"You'll find something," I say as I stand near him. "Until then, I'll drive you around. We both know I'm the better driver."

Two grunts, grabbing my hand and tugging me onto the couch beside him. "You hit me with your car, babe. You suck."

Before I can argue, he gives me a quick peck on the lips.

Leo giggles—actually giggles—which makes me start giggling too. Okay, so maybe this meeting won't be as awkward as I thought.

"Excuse our son's lack of manners," Leo says as he sits back down on Two's other side. "We found him in a barn when he was just a toddler."

I snort out a laugh.

"Don't encourage him," Two grumbles. "Dad thinks he's hilarious."

"I am hilarious," Leo argues. Then he reaches over Two to grab my hand. "Gemma, hon, these are gorgeous."

I blush at the compliment. I'd been trying to cheer my slightly depressed boyfriend up and did another design of Hemingford Hall nail art. I'd even made a copy of one of the handwritten love letters and used it as a background pattern on several of the nails. Vintage and meaningful, just like Two loves.

"She does them herself," Two says, stealing my hand from his father's to admire my art. "They're badass."

I catch Leo's gaze and he winks at me.

Grant sits in a recliner and clears his throat. "So, Gemma, how's school going for you?"

Two sniggers and I scowl at him. He thinks small talk is pointless, but I grew up learning from the best. My parents are the king and queen of small talk in our community.

"I'm enjoying my classes," I tell him, ignoring Two. "My favorite is the one with this clown."

"He says you two are nearly finished with your big project," Leo cuts in. "I've barely heard of Cedarwood anymore. It's always Hemingford Hall this and Hemingford Hall that."

Two looks over at me to share a secret smile. One thing's

for sure. What we do in the hidden room of Hemingford Hall remains a secret. It's been too long since we've had sex and I can't wait until he's well enough for us to do it again.

"Hemingford Hall is a special place," I admit with a grin. "I want to buy it."

Two's grin falls and Leo cocks his eyebrow up.

"What?" I rush out, shaking my head at Two. "I've fallen in love with it."

"Your parents really are loaded," Two mutters. I punch his arm and he yelps. "Ow. You seem to forget I'm injured."

"Keep being a butt and I'll injure you some more," I sass back.

Grant chuckles and Leo grins.

"Oh, you're going to fit right in with this family," Leo says, nodding emphatically.

I wait for Two to grimace or for some sort of awkward feeling to ruin the moment, but they all look at me expectantly, waiting for me to continue.

"Actually," I explain to my boyfriend, "I was going to offer them cash."

This has both Leo's perfectly plucked eyebrows hiking up his forehead.

"It'll wipe out my savings account," I continue, "but I've done a lot of social media collaborations that have made me quite a bit of money over the past few years."

"You think Paula and Gregory would actually sell it?" Two asks, frowning at me. "Paula seems to love it."

"But she's in over her head," I say with a shrug. "Gregory clearly resents everything Hemingford Hall represents. I think for the right price, they'd move, especially considering they know us, trust us, and can count on us to restore it to its original beauty."

"Us?" Two asks with a grin.

"I'm not doing all the work by myself," I playfully huff back. "You won't be injured forever. And last I checked, you're still great at being bossy even if you can't move around quickly."

Leo snorts out a laugh. "I think he may actually be worse because he has us at his beck and call now."

"Definitely worse," Grant agrees with a chortle.

"I'm feeling outnumbered and picked on," Two grumbles.

"He's a Four," I tell them. "They're dramatic."

Leo cackles at that. "Oh, honey, do I know that. And he's told us all about the Enneagram types. I have learned more about my son from information on Fours on the internet in the past few weeks than I have the entire time he's been our son."

The teasing banter continues until it gets close to dinner time. Leo and Grant leave us alone to start the grill and get supper going. I snuggle up against Two, careful not to agitate his sore ribs, and kiss his stubbly cheek.

"This is nice," I murmur, resting my head on his shoulder. "I was really nervous but it's actually fun hanging out with them."

Two squeezes my thigh and leans his head against mine. "It is. I thought, though, for a minute they were rethinking their choice of me over you."

"I see how they love you, dork." I tilt my head up so I can make sure he's teasing and not really feeling that way. "You can't fool me."

He dips forward and kisses me. "I'm happy you're here, Golden. My house looks good with you in it."

◎

After a dinner filled with lots of laughter and amazing food, me and Two head out to his workshop. He's pretty proficient at using his crutches, but his dads still hovered behind him the whole way across the yard. Eventually, they left us alone.

"Want to help me finish up Cedarwood Mansion?" Two asks, gesturing for the model that he tinkers on when not messing with our class project.

"Of course."

For the next several hours, we put the finishing touches on the micro-mansion. I marvel at all the tiny details he puts into the model. He may be strange and cantankerous at times, but he's extremely skilled at what he does. It makes me proud of him.

"You really want to purchase Hemingford Hall, huh?" Two asks, back hunched as he peeks in one of the stained-glass windows on his model.

"I really do. And, like Paula and Gregory, I want to move in while restoring it."

When I'd told my dad about it, he surprised me by being a hundred percent on board. In fact, he even offered to cover any additional costs outside of what I have in savings. Now all I have to do is convince the Nordstroms to sell to me.

"I was thinking," I say, running my fingers along the bones of his spine over his shirt, "that you'd want to move in with me."

He turns his head to peek over at me. "Oh yeah?"

"Yup. What do you think?"

"I like the idea of spending long, uninterrupted nights alone with you."

I smirk at him. "Besides the endless sex we'll have, I think it could be a lot of fun."

Two nods and brings his attention to a microscopic piece of glue sticking out from under one of the miniature shingles. He grabs a sharp tool and begins whittling away at it.

"What's wrong?" I ask, sensing a shift in his mood.

"Nothing." He sighs as he picks off the last of the glue and then shrugs. "I'm going to have to find a way to let Dax down easy. He was looking forward to getting out of his house and on his own."

"I thought about that too," I say with a small smile. "I think he should move in with us. Instead of rent, he can pay his way by picking up the utility bills or something. I bet we could figure something out."

Two sits up and grins at me. "Really?"

"Yeah. I like Dax. I also think he and my brother could be friends too."

"There's a lot riding on Paula letting go of her dream."

"If she really wants to see her dream come to fruition—the full restoration of Hemingford Hall—then she'll sell to me. Of all the people to do this, we're the most capable. Plus, we love that place." I hook a thumb over my shoulder, gesturing at his house. "Your dads are literally in the business of restoration, so it's not like we wouldn't get their help."

"You've thought a lot about this."

"And I've thought a lot about us," I add with a nod. "Hemingford Hall feels like a vital piece of who we are as a couple."

"I'm sure you'll get what you want," Two teases. "You always do, Golden."

"I'm a Three, remember? I achieve."

Like his parents, Two has gotten me interested in all things Enneagram. I'm learning a lot about myself and others around me.

Two finally sets his tool down and gestures at the model. "Cedarwood is finally complete. What do you think?"

I take my time inspecting all the details and offering praise over my favorite parts. He gently strokes his fingers through my hair while I prattle on about how beautiful it is. It makes me wonder if one day he'll make models with our children. The thought is such a precious one that my heart aches with happiness for what's to come.

"What do you do when you finish your models?" I ask, quirking an eyebrow.

He tugs me over to him, wrapping both arms around me, and nuzzles my neck. "I usually take a bunch of pictures to show my parents, Dax, and anyone else who'll give me the time of day. That includes you and Tate now too."

I tilt my head to the side to give him access to my neck. His hot breath tickles over my flesh, making me shiver. Then he softly kisses me there.

"I think you should take videos," I tell him with a smile. "Share it with the world. I bet there's a whole demographic of people out there who'd love to see it."

"You think?"

"Absolutely."

Two nips at my neck. "Tomorrow. But tonight, I want to do something else."

"What's that?"

"You, Golden. I want to do you."

I twist around in his arms so I'm facing him. "But you're injured."

"Guess you'll need to do all the work," he teases.

Chewing on my bottom lip, I consider his words. "Won't your parents come barging in?"

"I already warned Dad that if the workshop was a rockin' to not come a knockin'."

I giggle at his gall. "You did not."

"I totally did."

"Oh, Two…" I trail off, shaking my head.

"Hmm?"

"Don't ever change. You're perfect the way you are."

Perfectly imperfect and completely mine.

EPILOGUE

Two
Summer

I STILL CAN'T BELIEVE GEMMA BOUGHT HEMINGFORD Hall.

We've only been officially moved in for a month and it already feels like home. It took some convincing, but Gemma persuaded Paula to sell to her. Gregory didn't need to be convinced. As he put it, "It's about damn time." Paula has already come to visit three times since they closed.

"Avoiding all the chaos, man?" Dax asks as he saunters around the side of the building, ambling my way.

"Yup. Gemma's mom will put me to work if I go back inside. I don't like wedding shit."

Dax snorts out a laugh. "One day, you'll have to put up with it when you marry that girl."

I cock an eyebrow at him.

"What?" Dax says, folding his massive frame into the rickety Adirondack chair beside me. "We both know you're dying to propose to her."

"Maybe," I lie, unable to fight a smile. "I was just hoping we could elope and avoid all this." I wave a hand in the air and grunt. "This shit is exhausting."

Dax chuckles. "She's the youngest and the only girl in her family. If you think this wedding is over the top, just wait until hers comes along. Neither her parents nor yours will go for an elopement."

We sit in relative quiet. Every so often, I can hear giggles coming from inside. Gemma offered for Dempsey and Sloane to get married at Hemingford Hall as soon as she closed. Me, Dax, Gemma, and my dads all worked tirelessly this month on one of the grand rooms to make it ready for a quaint wedding. They're currently adding last-minute decorations for the wedding itself, which consisted of flowers and tulle and a lot of demanding women. I couldn't escape fast enough.

"Last week," Dax says as he fiddles with the tie hanging off his neck, "when Dempsey and Sloane came over for a few beers, Sloane answered a lot of my questions."

"About the police academy. You still thinking of joining?"

"Yeah, man. The more I think about it, the more I feel the pull to be a cop. College is fun and all, but I don't want to push papers around an office all day. We both know my grades aren't good enough to get into med school like Mom wants. I still think I can help people and make a difference. Being a cop could be the right fit for me."

I try to imagine Dax as a cop. I'm not sure they make uniforms big enough to stretch over his muscular arms, but what do I know. I've seen cops with plump bellies and their uniforms accommodated them just fine. He likes to speed, so at least he'd be good at catching reckless criminals.

"The idea of you with a gun scares the living shit out of me," I deadpan.

He kicks my dress shoe with his. "Fuck off, bro. I'd like get trained on it or whatever."

"What does your mom think?"

"I haven't told her yet. She's still miffed at me for moving in with you and Gemma."

I'd expected my dads to be upset about my decision to move out, but they'd been surprisingly agreeable to it, though a tiny bit sad. Dax's mom, though, threw a tantrum. Cried, begged, and even cursed him out at one point, none of which worked since he still moved out.

"What about you?" Dax asks. "Decided what's next for the great Tristan Sheridan besides endless sex on every surface of Hemingford Hall?"

He's griped on more than one occasion for us to keep it quiet and confine our sexual escapades to our bedroom. Unfortunately for him, we don't listen worth a damn.

"I kind of want to keep selling my miniature furniture online and shit."

Dax shakes his head. "I still can't believe people buy that stuff. It's so…weird."

Not too weird, though. Ever since Gemma created my page this past spring and got me making videos, I amassed a following twice as big as hers. There are literally millions of people who are intrigued by my models. I've had so many offers to purchase furniture and pieces that me and Gemma finally set up a website to sell them.

"Gemma thinks it's cool," I throw back with a goofy grin.

He rolls his eyes. "She thinks everything about you is cool. I'm still trying to figure out what's wrong with that girl." Dax jerks forward, rubbing the back of his head, and says, "What the fuck? You thumped me. Ow, woman."

Gemma sashays past him, looking hot as fuck in her crimson bridesmaid dress, and plops down in my lap. "You deserved it for talking crap." She turns her head to arch an eyebrow at me. "And why weren't you defending my honor?"

"I knew you could handle yourself, Golden."

She beams at me. "Good answer. Now stop hiding out here. Mom's done ranting about the height of the flower arch. Dad forced her to drink wine and she's calm again. Everything's basically done. The guests will be arriving pretty soon."

I stand up with her in my arms, only wincing slightly at the ache in my ankle. I'm not sure how long it'll take to get back to normal. Even with surgery and the cast long gone, it hurts a lot.

Ignoring the pain, I carry my girlfriend toward the front of the building, where cars are indeed starting to make their way down the long drive, and then set her down. A brand-new, deep purple Jeep pulls up and stops near us. Tate hops out of the driver's seat and waves at us.

"Nice ride," I say to my friend.

"It really is," Tate agrees, grinning. "I thought I was going to miss the old Jeep, but I really don't."

"Your loss is my gain."

Losing my car in the fucking lake of all places hurt. Bad. But after weeks and weeks of car hunting, I kept eyeing Tate's Jeep. I finally approached him about selling it to me. To my surprise, he agreed. Dad pretended to sob at my purchase, but Pops beamed at me with pride. At least he appreciates a classic.

Tate hugs me and then hooks arms with Gemma. Jude smirks at me as we follow after them inside.

As soon as we enter, I'm met with chatter and chaos. Most of Jude's family is already here and a couple of babies are crying. Dempsey's pup, Beauty, runs past us, carrying a baby bottle in her mouth. Spencer chases after her, threatening to toss her in the lake if she doesn't drop it. I'm highly amused by the entire scene.

I eventually move aside and shoot the shit with Dax until all the guests are here. Gemma is in the wedding as the maid of honor, so I sit in one of the folding chairs with Willa on one side and Dax on my other. Willa's baby, Bane, makes cute faces at me and I can't help but ruffle his hair.

A hush falls over the small group of family and friends as music begins. Gemma walks down the aisle accompanied by Sloane's nephew, Kaden, since he's the best man. The kid's face is bright red as he awkwardly escorts my stunning girl-friend. Poor dude's probably fighting a boner hard right now. I stifle an inappropriate chuckle.

Callum and Sloane's sister, Rhiannon, go next. Then, Hugo and her other sister, Nevaeh. The last ones to walk down the aisle are Jude and Sloane's niece, Lucy. My gaze finds its way over to Gemma. Her grin is wide as she waits. Dempsey starts down the aisle next, back stiff and movements rigid. I can tell he's uncomfortable being the source of everyone's attention. I feel for him. I'm definitely going to fight for an elopement for my wedding day.

Finally, the music changes and everyone stands up. Sloane, hardly recognizable with artful makeup and an el-egant updo, begins walking toward Dempsey. Tanaka, arm hooked in hers, walks her down the aisle, his birdlike features emotionless. Sloane, on the other hand, bites on her pink lip as tears well in her eyes. Dempsey gapes at her as though she's the most beautiful thing he's ever seen. The moment feels special and I'm honored to be a witness to it. Maybe eloping isn't the best idea.

Tanaka brings Sloane up to Dempsey and then leaves to sit beside his wife. Sloane and Dempsey take each other's hands and face one another, both of them grinning. The preacher's words are kind of boring and I find myself distracted once again by Bane, who's now trying to escape Willa's hold to get to me. After watching the spectacle for a moment, I take the baby from her. She mouths, "Sorry," and I wave it away.

Bane stares at me, grinning. What a cute fucking kid. I hope me and Gemma make kids even cuter if that's possible. We're definitely having kids. A lot of them.

I catch Gemma's gaze and wink at her. Her soft smile warms my heart. God, I love that damn girl.

Tate, with Beauty on a leash, walks toward the couple when the preacher asks for the rings. Everyone chuckles as Tate works on unfastening the ring box on Beauty's collar, especially when the dog starts licking his face with earnest. Finally, Tate gets the box free and tosses it to Dempsey, who catches it effortlessly.

I play with Bane some more and barely look up in time to catch the happy, now married couple, crashing together for an epic kiss. Yeah, we're definitely going to do all this shit when it's our time. Plus, Dad would lose his mind if I didn't let him plan the ultimate wedding.

Gemma is giggling, buzzing on her third glass of wine, when I steal her away from her talkative family. I whisk my beautiful girl into Alexander's office and we slip into our secret room undetected. Now that this place is ours, we have a lamp, better mattress, and everything we need to make our hideaway the perfect retreat. I stifle her laughs with my frantic kisses as we both strip down to nothing.

Despite having our own bed we now share together upstairs, we find our way into our secret room more often than not. Maybe one day, we'll have kids who run around this place, but this will always be our little secret.

It doesn't take long to get my tipsy woman primed and panting with need. I tease her needy clit even after she comes before kissing her deeply.

"I love you, Golden."

She purrs, raking her nails through my hair and messing it up. "Prove it."

I thrust hard, entering her fast and to the brim, smothering her cry with my mouth on hers. We fuck in desperation as per usual until I've come deeply inside her. After cleaning us both up, we spoon on the bed with her back to my chest and I inhale the sweet scent of her shampoo.

"I love you too, Two."

"Hey, babe," I murmur, running my nose along the curve of her shoulder.

"Hmm?"

"Let's get married." I kiss her soft skin and my heart races. "I'll find you a vintage ring and we'll make a crazy to-do list about the whole thing. What do you say?"

We're too young.

We haven't even been dating for a year.

We're complete opposites and bicker a fuckton.

But we're also stupidly in love.

"You really want to marry me?"

"Yup."

"My parents are going to freak out. All their kids are getting married the same year."

I snort. "I'm not waiting until next year, Mrs. Sheridan. Hell, I'm not sure I can wait until the end of summer."

Gemma twists around to face me. The lamplight illuminates her gorgeous face and I can't help but kiss her pert nose. "I accept, Mr. Sheridan. But only if you promise to write me gushy love letters for me to keep in our secret room."

"Gushy love letters?" I smirk at it. "I rescind my marriage proposal."

"Ugh, you're so mean."

I stroke a finger along her temple and grin. "The best I can offer is a dick pic."

"I guess I'll be a spinster my whole life," she opines.

"Fine," I concede with a mock groan. "I'll write you stupid love letters if that'll make you happy."

Hell, I'd do anything to make her happy.

"Then you, sir," she says, offering me her dainty hand, "have yourself a deal."

I grab onto her hand, not to shake it, but to pull her on top of me. All conversation is lost as we consummate our new deal with nothing but our bodies.

This girl may have been the source of my inner torment for years, but I'm quickly learning she's now a source of healing.

With Gemma, I'm better.

Together, we're perfect.

Fuckin' golden.

I hope you enjoyed Gemma and Two's story!
Want to read more small-town romance with lots of drama?
Check out *Sheriff's Secret (A Brigs Ferry Bay Novel)* next!

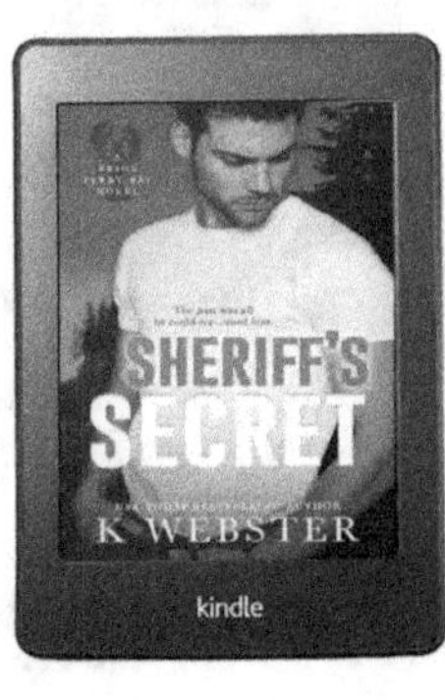

UP NEXT!

Thank you for reading!

The past was all he could
see...*until him.*

SHERIFF'S SECRET

If you're curious about Callum and Willa's story, check out The Teacher of Nothing!

Or, if you're dying to read about Spencer, Hugo, and Aubrey, check out The Tangle of Awful!

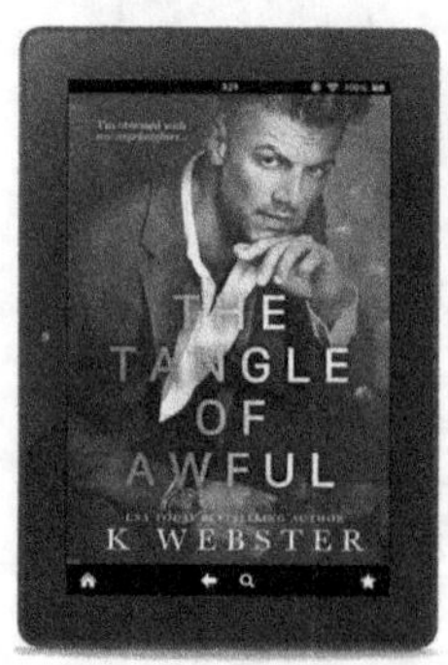

Wondering about the mysterious Jude and his therapist, Tate, check out The Heart of Smoke!

Want to read about how Dempsey and Sloane fell in love, check out The Law of Deceit!

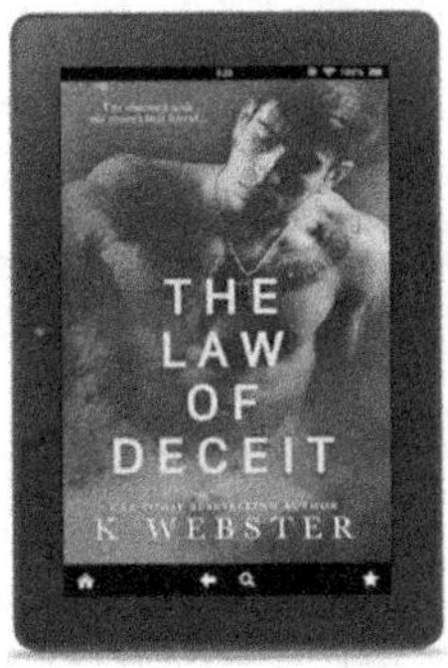

ABOUT THE AUTHOR

K Webster is a *USA Today* Bestselling author. Her titles have claimed many bestseller tags in numerous categories, are translated in multiple languages, and have been adapted into audiobooks. She lives in "Tornado Alley" with her husband, two children, and her baby dog named Blue. When she's not writing, she's reading, drinking copious amounts of coffee, and researching aliens.

Download at
books.bookfunnel.com/k_webster_short_story_bundle

JOIN MY NEWSLETTER
at authorkwebster.com/newsletter

JOIN MY PRIVATE GROUP
at reamstories.com/authorkwebster

Follow K Webster here!

Facebook: www.facebook.com/authorkwebster

Readers Group:
www.facebook.com/groups/krazyforkwebstersbooks

Patreon: patreon.com/authorkwebster

Twitter: twitter.com/KristiWebster

Goodreads:
www.goodreads.com/author/show/7741564.K_Webster

Instagram: www.instagram.com/authorkwebster

BookBub: www.bookbub.com/authors/k-webster

Wattpad: www.wattpad.com/user/kwebster-wildromance

TikTok: www.tiktok.com/@authorkwebster

Pinterest: www.pinterest.com/kwebsterwildromance

LinkedIn: www.linkedin.com/in/k-webster-396b7021

EXCERPT FROM SHERIFF'S SECRET

Dante

H E MAKES A HARSH SOUND AND SHOVES ME. THE *sheriff* of this town shoves me. I'm not some weak city boy, though, and hold my ground, stalking back up to him until my chest brushes his.

"Are you always so unprofessional?" I demand, trying not to grow drunk on the pine and salty ocean scent emanating from him.

His eyes darken. "Only with you."

"I feel so special," I tease, my lips quirking into a smirk. "Special treatment for the new guy, hmm?"

For a brief moment, his gaze falls to my lips, his entire body softening as he does it. To test my theory about my observations about him, I run my tongue across my bottom lip to wet it. He sucks in a sharp breath and nearly stumbles over his own feet to escape my nearness.

Closet gay.

If I had to guess, he hooked up with Kian, most likely in secret, and now is a jealous prick anytime anyone looks at the beautiful boy. But if my intuition serves me well like usual, I'd say Sheriff isn't ballsy enough to admit to himself, much less this town, that he's gay.

"He's been hurt enough," Jax says, his attention falling to his scuffed boots. "Don't toy with him just to get at me. I beg of you."

This guy must think I'm a real jerk.

"Don't worry, Sheriff." I give him a teasing grin. "I only toy with the ones I'm sleeping with."

He yanks his coat up from the chair and points a finger at me, his face and neck turning crimson. "Watch your back, big city man."

Read *Sheriff's Secret*, the first book in the Brigs Ferry Bay series, up next.